There *was* an Israel Potter
who wrote the story of his life.
Herman Melville read the story
and wrote a masterpiece:
ISRAEL POTTER: HIS FIFTY YEARS
OF EXILE

Israel Potter was a born loser, the Revolutionary War's "Sad Sack;" but in Melville's fictional trans-mutation of his adventures, he became the Un-known Soldier—a traveler through whom friends and foes reveal themselves. In Potter's encounters, Melville introduces the famous men of the era as heightened, exaggerated characters. Benjamin Franklin is a funny, bossy egotist dispensing wis-dom as he helps himself to all Potter's worthwhile possessions. John Paul Jones is reckless and chiv-alrous but busily making a legend of himself. And, Melville himself reveals his own feelings of alienation.

ISRAEL POTTER: HIS FIFTY YEARS OF EXILE is Alfred Kazin's choice, and his introduc-tion tells why this least-read Melville novel was the one he most wanted to share with you.

NUMBER ONE—THE REDISCOVERY SERIES

← The Rediscovery Series →

ISRAEL POTTER:

HIS FIFTY YEARS OF EXILE

by

HERMAN MELVILLE

with an introduction by
ALFRED KAZIN

WARNER
PAPERBACK
LIBRARY

A Warner Communications Company

WARNER PAPERBACK LIBRARY EDITION
First Printing: February, 1974

Copyright © 1974 by Warner Books, Inc.
All rights reserved

Cover art by Terry Karl

Cover design by The New Studio

Warner Paperback Library is a division of Warner Books, Inc.
75 Rockefeller Plaza, New York, N.Y. 10019.

Ⓦ A Warner Communications Company

Introduction to Herman Melville's
ISRAEL POTTER: His Fifty Years of Exile

Israel Potter: His Fifty Years of Exile has probably been the least read of Melville's novels up to now; it has rarely been available outside of Melville's collected works. The book has a curious history, and it is certainly a curious book. Though Melville's heroes are mostly himself under various disguises (he was complicated enough to be both Ishmael and Ahab), nowhere did he describe his psychic monomania of exile, drift, homelessness, so pointedly as he did in emphasizing Israel Potter's continual misfortunes and final beggery for almost fifty years. Yet never did he have a character less reflective, less like himself, than Israel Potter. What Israel shares with Herman Melville is "exile" seemingly perpetual, exile as a lifetime experience, exile as a feeling about life unexplained by the circumstances of exile. Fortunately, it is not Israel who dominates the book but Israel's often cliffhanger adventures. And the book has some historical actors—Benjamin Franklin, John Paul Jones, Ethan Allen—who are as powerful in their way as Melville was in his secret soul, powerful as only a great writer can be.

In 1854 Melville picked up a ragged, slatternly paperback book called *Life and Remarkable Adventures of Israel R. Potter, A Native of Cranston, R. I.* This was the hack "life and adventures" of a Revolutionary War veteran, an agile but by no means unusual man who had been captured by the British at Bunker Hill, was taken to England as a prisoner in January, 1776, escaped, was recaptured, but served under John Paul Jones in the famous battle of the *Bon Homme Richard* with the *Serapis.* Israel Potter was an unlucky fellow; even after the victory of the American cause, he was unable to get home to Rhode Island until 1823. He lived out much of his English "exile" among the poorest of the poor in London, weaving cane chairs and crying his wares.

The Life and Remarkable Adventures of Israel R. Potter is a conventionally written, stilted autobiography of a bizarre life that became so by accident. Israel was, you might say, one of history's sad sacks, and his book is not stimulating. Melville, back in 1849, visiting London, wrote in his diary that he "looked over a lot of ancient maps of London. Bought one (A.D. 1776) for 3 & 6 pence. I want to use it in case I serve up the Revolutionary narrative of the beggar." In short, when Melville was still the well-known and "successful" author of such best sellers as *Typee* and *Omoo,* and before he had injured his reputation (!) by baffling his audience with the "metaphysical nonsense" of *Moby Dick,* Melville was thinking of exploiting, for his own novelistic purposes the undistinguished, pathetic figure of Israel R. Potter. Melville had some vague plans in the back of his head—it was possible that he might yet "serve up the Revolutionary narrative of the beggar."

Something about the extraordinary adventures but miserably rootless life of Israel R. Potter fascinated Melville. The "Revolutionary" period was one of heroic individuals, like Melville's own grandfathers. But even more, the idea of using another man's actual and reported life appealed to Melville's habitual strategy as an author. This strategy was always to convert some piece of actual experience, so long as it was bizarre, exotic, unduplicated

6

by the middle-class respectable life Melville was leading as an author, husband and father into a loose, episodic, nicely spiced novel of adventure for the general public. But this genial popular adventure story also had to dramatize Melville's favorite idea of himself as a literary warrior at odds with his time. A book had to dramatize the epic struggle with the universe of Melville's own rebellious idiosyncrasy. This explains the ups and downs of his literary fortunes.

Melville, born into the best society of New York (Dutch and British), a descendant on both sides of famous (and dashing) Revolutionary War generals, had been driven, like his alter ego, Ishmael, into the "wilderness." His father, a hard-driven New York merchant, had gone bankrupt, then gone to pieces and died when his son was thirteen. Melville went to sea as a cabin boy; at twenty-two he embarked in a whaler from New Bedford on the three-and-a-half-year voyage that was to lead him to the South Seas, and into every possible scrape and adventure as a sailor. This was his making as an author. Melville began his literary career with best-selling nonfiction novels, *Typee* and *Omoo,* based on his adventures in the South Seas. Then, with *Mardi,* Melville showed that he could write a bad "visionary" novel to please himself—then turn back to more acceptable books, like *Redburn* and *White Jacket,* just to keep the pot boiling. He could also, as all the world knows now but didn't during his lifetime, write a book of headlong genius, *Moby Dick,* that would for all practical purposes sink him as a professional author.

By 1855, when Melville finally did "serve up the Revolutionary narrative of the beggar," Melville was thirty-six, had published seven books, had a wife and children, but was no longer considered a reliable literary property by publishers in New York and London. He wrote as fast as any Irving Wallace or Harold Robbins who nowadays serves up a "quick read" for the hurried man dashing to a plane. But though Melville's works usually dealt with out-of-the-way adventures in remote parts of the world, this strange philosophical streak in him, this determination to be perpetually in mutiny against a genteel American upper-crust that claimed to have the final answers to all human questions and difficulties, had made Herman Melville a most difficult and unassimilable literary property.

Here is the personal drama behind *Israel Potter*—this peculiar, fascinating, uneven, often richly comic book. We cannot overlook the (still?) surprising fact that a leading American author (admittedly of somewhat dubious reputation) took a hack book and turned it into an allegory of his own life. Melville wrote it just to make some money. But with his unstoppable creative force he turned *Israel Potter* into a satiric picaresque novel that is much more about the real Herman Melville than it is about the real Israel Potter.

Yet there *was* a real Israel Potter. And in this book he remains an historic personage even though Melville moves his birthplace from Rhode Island to the Berkshires, then puts him through adventures that are not in the original text or are jauntily expanded out of all resemblance to the humdrum original.

Most strikingly, Melville puts into his "Revolutionary narrative" one of the great satires on Benjamin Franklin, plus a brilliantly overcolored view of Ethan "Ticonderoga" Allen as an American Samson among the (British) Philistines who have captured him. There is a view of the American Navy's John Paul Jones as a restless masculine desperado who feels cooped up to the point of madness when he is not fighting. In two successive chapters, Melville gives us a marvelously old-fashioned naval battle— John Paul Jones's almost suicidal victory in the *Bon Homme Richard* over the *Serapis*—a gory killing fight to the finish that went on into the night under the light of the moon over the Cliffs of Dover, from which a crowd of spectators gaped.

Melville's *Israel Potter* is at its best as a book about American men in the old, slashing, heroic style of romantic war, escapade, incessant movement. It is a book about warriors who have the character of brigands and pirates, ferocious toughies who fight for the pleasure of fighting, and who are never so happy as when they are knocking down the enemy with everything in sight. At Bunker Hill,

8

writes Melville, "Not one American musket in twenty had a bayonet to it. So, wielding the stock right and left, the terrible farmers, with hats and coats off, fought their way among the furred grenadiers, knocking them right and left, as seal-hunters on the beach knock down with their clubs the Shetland seal."

Israel Potter is about men who are ruled less by loyalty to a specific place or country than by their own irresistible feeling for adventure, risk, deception. The portrait of Benjamin Franklin is a masterpiece of irreverence. Franklin was without doubt a genius, as he was certainly one of the most useful men who ever trod the American earth. But also an intriguer, entrepreneur, publicist, speculator, and above all a wily old hypocrite, Franklin is beautifully portrayed by Melville as a man of infinite cunning, as classical in his wiles and stratagems as Ulysses or the Biblical Jacob.

The scenes between Israel and Benjamin Franklin are straight comedy—with poor, innocent, always besought and unlucky Israel as the straight man. Franklin is shown as the gay deceiver and unctuous man of affairs in all things—above all, the canniest man with a penny in American history before Calvin Coolidge. "Every time he comes in," poor Israel soliloquizes dolefully, "he robs me; with an air all the time, too, as if he were making me presents."

John Paul Jones, who cries out when he is not on duty— "My God, why was I not born a Czar!"—is deliciously a savage. "He was a rather small, elastic, swarthy man, with an aspect of a disinherited Indian Chief in European clothes. An unvanquishable enthusiasm intensified to perfect sobriety, couched in his savage, self-possessed eye." He runs his warships right into one English harbor after another. And spiking the cannon in Whitehaven, talks to them like a Shakespearean brigand—"I'll tongue-tie the thunderers."

This emphasis on heroic, military, hell-for-leather grappling with the enemy is the really decisive element in Melville's narrative. It reflects Melville's own passionate admiration for masculine power, headlong independence at any price, a damn-the-torpedoes resistance to the hindrances that life may raise. John Paul Jones is also plainly mad; the American "Samson" in English captivity, Ethan Allen, is willfully mad, histrionically defiant, a ham acting it up. Franklin is wily to the point of being inhuman. But these are men, as we say now, in the "classic" mold—they are meant to portray the American Revolution as perhaps the last time when men could be heroes (and cutthroats) on an unlimited scale. Melville is amused by his characters, but he loves them and he loves a time when the heroic individual like Franklin, Jones, Allen, seemed to incarnate fierce strength and unquestioning self-trust. In a revolutionary period such men incarnated the energy, the new hope, of revolution.

Melville felt that to be a man of power, a true hero and rebel in behalf of "nature," you had to be somewhat touched. Like Herman Melville. Nature, the "world," are not "sane," only society tries to be. The heroic individual, striking out for a vision that exists nowhere but in his own head, does so at the expense of his "balance."

About John Paul Jones, Melville says, typically,

The career of this stubborn adventurer signally illustrates the idea that since all human affairs are subject to organic disorder, since they are created in and sustained by a sort of half-disciplined chaos, hence he who in great things seeks success must never want for smooth water, which never was and never will be, but with what straggling method he can, dash with all his derangements at his object, leaving the rest to Fortune.

Israel Potter is thus a very personal and positive novel about masculine force. The vitality is mock-heroic, lovingly satiric about American demigods like Franklin. But what of Israel Potter himself? Israel, as his Biblical name testified in Melville's time, is the perpetual victim and wanderer. He is the man things happen to—he is the dummy on whom Melville, pent up as usual in this strange, uneven book, put all the pain of his own wandering, his orphanage, his bereftness from God and society.

Poor Israel! He never really makes it. He is always out of luck. Although his creator, Herman Melville, does give him a yellow mane and once calls him a "lion," Israel is really the average man, caught up in a series of adventures and escapes. Melville was not at his best writing about the average man. But fortunately, it is not Israel himself who holds our attention in this book. It is Israel as the occasion for Melville to write about Bunker Hill, Israel as an occasion for Melville to write about Franklin, John Paul Jones, George III, various English radical sympathizers with the American Revolution, Paris during the American Revolution. Melville's versatile, comic, beautifully extreme talent came through in this book despite every possible handicap from Israel Potter himself.

Alfred Kazin

July 17, 1973

To His Highness
THE BUNKER HILL MONUMENT

Biography, in its purer form, confined to the ended lives of the true and brave, may be held the fairest meed of human virtue—one given and received in entire disinterestedness—since neither can the biographer hope for acknowledgment from the subject, nor the subject at all avail himself of the biographical distinction conferred.

Israel Potter well merits the present tribute—a private of Bunker Hill, who for his faithful services was years ago promoted to a still deeper privacy under the ground, with a posthumous pension, in default of any during life, annually paid him by the spring in ever-new mosses and sward.

I am the more encouraged to lay this performance at the feet of your Highness, because, with a change in the grammatical person, it preserves, almost as in a reprint, Israel Potter's autobiographical story. Shortly after his return in infirm old age to his native land, a little narrative of his adventures, forlornly published on sleazy gray paper, appeared among the peddlers, written, probably, not by himself, but taken down from his lips by another.

13

But like the crutch-marks of the cripple by the Beautiful Gate, this blurred record is now out of print. From a tattered copy, rescued by the merest chance from the rag-pickers, the present account has been drawn, which, with the exception of some expansions, and additions of historic and personal details, and one or two shiftings of scene, may, perhaps, be not unfitly regarded something in the light of a dilapidated old tombstone retouched.

Well aware that in your Highness' eyes the merit of the story must be in its general fidelity to the main drift of the original narrative, I forbore anywhere to mitigate the hard fortunes of my hero; and particularly towards the end, though sorely tempted, durst not substitute for the allotment of Providence any artistic recompense of poetical justice; so that no one can complain of the gloom of my closing chapters more profoundly than myself.

Such is the work, and such the man, that I have the honor to present to your Highness. That the name here noted should not have appeared in the volumes of Sparks, may or may not be a matter for astonishment; but Israel Potter seems purposely to have waited to make his popular advent under the present exalted patronage, seeing that your Highness, according to the definition above, may, in the loftiest sense, be deemed the Great Biographer: the national commemorator of such of the anonymous privates of June 17, 1775, who may never have received other requital than the solid reward of your granite.

Your Highness will pardon me, if, with the warmest ascriptions on this auspicious occasion, I take the liberty to mingle my hearty congratulations on the recurrence of the anniversary day we celebrate, wishing your Highness (though indeed your Highness be somewhat prematurely gray) many returns of the same, and that each of its summer's suns may shine as brightly on your brow as each winter snow shall lightly rest on the grave of Israel Potter.

Your Highness'
Most devoted and obsequious,
THE EDITOR

June 17, 1854

14

Contents

1

The Birthplace of Israel

The traveller who at the present day is content to travel in the good old Asiatic style, neither rushed along by a locomotive, nor dragged by a stage-coach; who is willing to enjoy hospitalities at far scattered farmhouses, instead of paying his bill at an inn; who is not to be frightened by any amount of loneliness, or to be deterred by the roughest roads or the highest hills; such a traveller in the eastern part of Berkshire, Massachusetts, will find ample food for poetic reflection in the singular scenery of a country, which, owing to the ruggedness of the soil and its lying out of the track of all public conveyances, remains almost as unknown to the general tourist as the interior of Bohemia.

Travelling northward from the township of Otis, the road leads for twenty or thirty miles towards Windsor, lengthwise upon that long broken spur of heights which the Green Mountains of Vermont send into Massachusetts. For nearly the whole of the distance, you have the continual sensation of being upon some terrace in the moon. The feeling of the plain or the valley is never yours;

scarcely the feeling of the earth. Unless by a sudden precipitation of the road you find yourself plunging into some gorge, you pass on, and on, and on, upon the crests or slopes of pastoral mountains, while far below, mapped out in its beauty, the valley of the Housatonic lies endlessly along at your feet. Often, as your horse gaining some lofty level tract, flat as a table, trots gayly over the almost deserted and sodded road, and your admiring eye sweeps the broad landscape beneath, you seem to be Boótes driving in heaven. Save a potato field here and there, at long intervals, the whole country is either in wood or pasture. Horses, cattle and sheep are the principal inhabitants of these mountains. But all through the year lazy columns of smoke, rising from the depths of the forest, proclaim the presence of that half-outlaw, the charcoal-burner; while in early spring added curls of vapor show that the maple sugar-boiler is also at work. But as for farming as a regular vocation, there is not much of it here. At any rate, no man by that means accumulates a fortune from this thin and rocky soil, all whose arable parts have long since been nearly exhausted.

Yet during the first settlement of the country, the region was not unproductive. Here it was that the original settlers came, acting upon the principle well known to have regulated their choice of site, namely, the high land in preference to the low, as less subject to the unwholesome miasmas generated by breaking into the rich valleys and alluvial bottoms of primeval regions. By degrees, however, they quitted the safety of this sterile elevation, to brave the dangers of richer though lower fields. So that, at the present day, some of those mountain townships present an aspect of singular abandonment. Though they have never known aught but peace and health, they, in one lesser aspect at least, look like countries depopulated by plague and war. Every mile or two a house is passed untenanted. The strength of the frame-work of these ancient buildings enables them long to resist the encroachments of decay. Spotted gray and green with the weather-stain, their timbers seem to have lapsed back into their woodland original, forming part now of the

18

general picturesqueness of the natural scene. They are of extraordinary size, compared with modern farmhouses. One peculiar feature is the immense chimney, of light gray stone, perforating the middle of the roof like a tower.

On all sides are seen the tokens of ancient industry. As stone abounds throughout these mountains, that material was, for fences, as ready to the hand as wood, besides being much more durable. Consequently the landscape is intersected in all directions with walls of uncommon neatness and strength.

The number and length of these walls is not more surprising than the size of some of the blocks comprising them. The very Titans seemed to have been at work. That so small an army as the first settlers must needs have been, should have taken such wonderful pains to enclose so ungrateful a soil; that they should have accomplished such herculean undertakings with so slight prospect of reward; this is a consideration which gives us a significant hint of the temper of the men of the Revolutionary era.

Nor could a fitter country be found for the birthplace of the devoted patriot, Israel Potter.

To this day the best stone-wall builders, as the best woodchoppers, come from those solitary mountain towns; a tall, athletic, and hardy race, unerring with the axe as the Indian with the tomahawk; at stone-rolling, patient as Sisyphus, powerful as Samson.

In fine clear June days, the bloom of these mountains is beyond expression delightful. Last visiting these heights ere she vanishes, Spring, like the sunset, flings her sweetest charms upon them. Each tuft of upland grass is musked like a bouquet with perfume. The balmy breeze swings to and fro like a censer. On one side the eye follows for the space of an eagle's flight, the serpentine mountain chains, southwards from the great purple dome of Taconic—the St. Peter's of these hills—northwards to the twin summits of Saddleback, which is the two-steepled natural cathedral of Berkshire; while low down to the west the Housatonic winds on in her watery labyrinth, through charming meadows basking in the reflected rays from the hill-sides. At this season the beauty of every thing around you populates the loneliness of your way. You would not have the country more settled if you could. Content to drink in such loveliness at all your senses, the heart desires no company but Nature.

With what rapture you behold, hovering over some vast hollow of the hills, or slowly drifting at an immense height over the far sunken Housatonic valley, some lordly eagle, who in unshared exaltation looks down equally upon plain and mountain. Or you behold a hawk sallying from some crag, like a Rhenish baron of old from his pinnacled castle, and darting down towards the river for his prey. Or perhaps, lazily gliding about in the zenith, this ruffian fowl is suddenly beset by a crow, who with stubborn audacity pecks at him, and, spite of all his bravery, finally persecutes him back to his stronghold. The otherwise dauntless bandit, soaring at his topmost height, must needs succumb to this sable image of death. Nor are there wanting many smaller and less famous fowl, who without contributing to the grandeur, yet greatly add to the beauty of the scene. The yellow-bird flits like a winged jonquil here and there; like knots of violets the blue-birds sport in clusters upon the grass; while hurrying from the pasture to the grove, the red robin seems an incendiary putting torch to the trees. Meanwhile the air is vocal with their hymns, and your own soul joys in the general joy. Like a stranger in an orchestra, you cannot help singing yourself when all around you raise such hosannas.

But in autumn, those gay northerners, the birds, return to their southern plantations. The mountains are left bleak and sere. Solitude settles down upon them in drizzling mists. The traveller is beset, at perilous turns, by dense masses of fog. He emerges for a moment into more penetrable air; and passing some gray, abandoned house, sees the lofty vapors plainly eddy by its desolate door; just as from the plain you may see it eddy by the pinnacles of distant and lonely heights. Or, dismounting from his frightened horse, he leads him down some scowling glen, where the road steeply dips among grim rocks, only to rise as abruptly again; and as he warily picks his way, uneasy at the menacing scene, he sees some ghost-like

20

object looming through the mist at the roadside; and wending towards it, beholds a rude white stone, uncouthly inscribed, marking the spot where, some fifty or sixty years ago, some farmer was upset in his woodsled, and perished beneath the load.

In winter this region is blocked up with snow. Inaccessible and impassable, those wild, unfrequented roads, which in August are overgrown with high grass, in December are drifted to the arm-pit with the white fleece from the sky. As if an ocean rolled between man and man, intercommunication is often suspended for weeks and weeks.

Such, at this day, is the country which gave birth to our hero: prophetically styled Israel by the good Puritans, his parents, since, for more than forty years, poor Potter wandered in the wild wilderness of the world's extremest hardships and ills.

How little he thought, when, as a boy, hunting after his father's stray cattle among these New England hills he himself like a beast should be hunted through half of Old England, as a runaway rebel. Or, how could he ever have dreamed, when involved in the autumnal vapors of these mountains, that worse bewilderments awaited him three thousand miles across the sea, wandering forlorn in the coal-fogs of London. But so it was destined to be. This little boy of the hills, born in sight of the sparkling Housatonic, was to linger out the best part of his life a prisoner or a pauper upon the grimy banks of the Thames.

2

The Youthful Adventures of Israel

Imagination will easily picture the rural day of the youth of Israel. Let us pass on to a less immature period.

It appears that he began his wanderings very early; moreover, that ere, on just principles throwing off the yoke of his king, Israel, on equally excusable grounds, emancipated himself from his sire. He continued in the enjoyment of parental love till the age of eighteen, when, having formed an attachment for a neighbor's daughter —for some reason, not deemed a suitable match by his father—he was severely reprimanded, warned to discontinue his visits, and threatened with some disgraceful punishment in case he persisted. As the girl was not only beautiful, but amiable—though, as will be seen, rather weak—and her family as respectable as any, though unfortunately but poor, Israel deemed his father's conduct unreasonable and oppressive; particularly as it turned out that he had taken secret means to thwart his son with the girl's connections, if not with the girl herself, so as to place almost insurmountable obstacles to an eventual marriage. For it had not been the purpose of Israel to marry at once, but at a future day, when prudence should approve the step. So, oppressed by his father, and bitterly disappointed in his love, the desperate boy formed the determination to quit them both, for another home and other friends.

It was on Sunday, while the family were gone to a farmhouse church near by, that he packed up as much of his clothing as might be contained in a handkerchief, which, with a small quantity of provision, he hid in a piece of woods in the rear of the house. He then returned, and continued in the house till about nine in the evening, when, pretending to go to bed, he passed out of a back door, and hastened to the woods for his bundle.

It was a sultry night in July; and that he might travel with more ease on the succeeding day, he lay down at the foot of a pine tree, reposing himself till an hour before dawn, when, upon awaking, he heard the soft, prophetic sighing of the pine, stirred by the first breath of the morning. Like the leaflets of that evergreen, all the fibres of his heart trembled within him; tears fell from his eyes. But he thought of the tyranny of his father, and what seemed to him the faithlessness of his love; and shouldering his bundle, arose, and marched on.

His intention was to reach the new countries to the northward and westward, lying between the Dutch settlements on the Hudson, and the Yankee settlements on the Housatonic. This was mainly to elude all search. For the same reason, for the first ten or twelve miles, shunning the public roads, he travelled through the woods; for he knew that he would soon be missed and pursued.

He reached his destination in safety; hired out to a farmer for a month through the harvest; then crossed from the Hudson to the Connecticut. Meeting here with an adventurer to the unknown regions lying about the head waters of the latter river, he ascended with this man in a canoe, paddling and pulling for many miles. Here again he hired himself out for three months; at the end of that time to receive for his wages, two hundred acres of land lying in New Hampshire. The cheapness of the land was not alone owing to the newness of the country, but to the perils investing it. Not only was it a wilderness abounding with wild beasts, but the widely-scattered inhabitants were in continual dread of being, at some unguarded moment, destroyed or made captive by the Canadian savages, who, ever since the French war, had improved every opportunity to make forays across the defenceless frontier.

His employer proving false to his contract in the matter of the land, and there being no law in the country to force him to fulfill it, Israel—who, however brave-hearted, and even much of a dare-devil upon a pinch, seems nevertheless to have evinced, throughout many parts of his career, a singular patience and mildness—was obliged to look round for other means of livelihood than clearing out a farm for himself in the wilderness. A party of royal surveyors were at this period surveying the unsettled regions bordering the Connecticut river to its source. At fifteen shillings per month, he engaged himself to this party as assistant chain-bearer, little thinking that the day was to come when he should clank the king's chains in a dungeon, even as now he trailed them a free ranger of the woods. It was midwinter; the land was surveyed upon snowshoes. At the close of the day, fires were kindled with dry hemlock, a hut thrown up, and the party ate and slept.

Paid off at last, Israel bought a gun and ammunition, and turned hunter. Deer, beaver, &c., were plenty. In two or three months he had many skins to show. I suppose it never entered his mind that he was thus qualifying himself for a marksman of men. But thus were tutored those wonderful shots who did such execution at Bunker's Hill; these, the hunter-soldiers, whom Putnam bade wait till the white of the enemy's eye was seen.

With the result of his hunting he purchased a hundred acres of land, further down the river, toward the more settled parts; built himself a log hut, and in two summers, with his own hands, cleared thirty acres for sowing. In the winter seasons he hunted and trapped. At the end of the two years, he sold back his land—now much improved—to the original owner, at an advance of fifty pounds. He conveyed his cash and furs to Charlestown, on the Con-

24

necticut (sometimes called No. 4), where he trafficked them away for Indian blankets, pigments, and other showy articles adapted to the business of a trader among savages. It was now winter again. Putting his goods on a hand-sled, he started towards Canada, a peddler in the wilderness, stopping at wigwams instead of cottages. One fancies that, had it been summer, Israel would have travelled with a wheelbarrow, and so trundled his wares through the primeval forests, with the same indifference as porters roll their barrows over the flagging of streets. In this way was bred that fearless self-reliance and independence which conducted our forefathers to national freedom.

This Canadian trip proved highly successful. Selling his glittering goods at a great advance, he received in exchange valuable peltries and furs at a corresponding reduction. Returning to Charlestown, he disposed of his return cargo again at a very fine profit. And now, with a light heart and a heavy purse, he resolved to visit his sweetheart and parents, of whom, for three years, he had had no tidings.

They were not less astonished than delighted at his reappearance; he had been numbered with the dead. But his love still seemed strangely coy; willing, but yet somehow mysteriously withheld. The old intrigues were still on foot. Israel soon discovered, that though rejoiced to welcome the return of the prodigal son—so some called him—his father still remained inflexibly determined against the match, and still inexplicably countermined his wooing. With a dolorous heart he mildly yielded to what seemed his fatality; and more intrepid in facing peril for himself, than in endangering others by maintaining his rights (for he was now one-and-twenty), resolved once more to retreat, and quit his blue hills for the bluer billows.

A hermitage in the forest is the refuge of the narrow-minded misanthrope; a hammock on the ocean is the asylum for the generous distressed. The ocean brims with natural griefs and tragedies; and into that watery immensity of terror, man's private grief is lost like a drop.

Travelling on foot to Providence, Rhode Island, Israel

shipped on board a sloop, bound with lime to the West Indies. On the tenth day out, the vessel caught fire, from water communicating with the lime. It was impossible to extinguish the flames. The boat was hoisted out, but owing to long exposure to the sun, it needed continual bailing to keep it afloat. They had only time to put in a firkin of butter and a ten-gallon keg of water. Eight in number, the crew entrusted themselves to the waves, in a leaky tub, many leagues from land. As the boat swept under the burning bowsprit, Israel caught at a fragment of the flying-jib, which sail had fallen down the stay, owing to the charring, nigh the deck, of the rope which hoisted it. Tanned with the smoke, and its edge blackened with the fire, this bit of canvass helped them bravely on their way. Thanks to kind Providence, on the second day they were picked up by a Dutch ship, bound from Eustatia to Holland. The castaways were humanely received, and supplied with every necessary. At the end of a week, while unsophisticated Israel was sitting in the main-top, thinking what should befall him in Holland, and wondering what sort of unsettled, wild country it was, and whether there was any deer-shooting or beaver-trapping there, lo! an American brig, bound from Piscataqua to Antigua, comes in sight. The American took them aboard, and conveyed them safely to her port. There Israel shipped for Porto Rico; from thence, sailed to Eustatia.

Other rovings ensued; until at last, entering on board a Nantucket ship, he hunted the leviathan off the Western Islands and on the coast of Africa, for sixteen months; returning at length to Nantucket with a brimming hold. From that island he sailed again on another whaling voyage, extending, this time, into the great South Sea. There, promoted to be harpooner, Israel, whose eye and arm had been so improved by practice with his gun in the wilderness, now further intensified his aim, by darting the whale-lance; still, unwittingly, preparing himself for the Bunker Hill rifle.

In this last voyage, our adventurer experienced to the extreme all the hardships and privations of the whaleman's life on a long voyage to distant and barbarous waters—

hardships and privations unknown at the present day, when science has so greatly contributed, in manifold ways, to lessen the sufferings, and add to the comforts of seafaring men. Heartily sick of the ocean, and longing once more for the bush, Israel, upon receiving his discharge at Nantucket at the end of the voyage, hied straight back for his mountain home.

But if hopes of his sweetheart winged his returning flight, such hopes were not destined to be crowned with fruition. The dear, false girl was another's.

3

Israel Goes to the Wars; and Reaching Bunker Hill in Time to Be of Service There, Soon After Is Forced to Extend His Travels Across the Sea into the Enemy's Land

Left to idle lamentations, Israel might now have planted deep furrows in his brow. But stifling his pain, he chose rather to plough, than be ploughed. Farming weans man from his sorrows. That tranquil pursuit tolerates nothing but tranquil meditations. There, too, in mother earth, you may plant and reap; not, as in other things, plant and see the planting torn up by the roots. But if wandering in the wilderness, and wandering upon the waters, if felling trees, and hunting, and shipwreck, and fighting with whales, and all his other strange adventures, had not as yet cured poor Israel of his now hopeless passion, events were at hand forever to drown it.

It was the year 1774. The difficulties long pending between the colonies and England were arriving at their crisis. Hostilities were certain. The Americans were preparing themselves. Companies were formed in most of the New England towns, whose members, receiving the name of minute-men, stood ready to march anywhere at a minute's warning. Israel, for the last eight months, sojourning as a laborer on a farm in Windsor, enrolled himself in the regiment of Colonel John Patterson of Lenox, afterwards General Patterson.

The battle of Lexington was fought on the 18th of April, 1775; news of it arrived in the county of Berkshire on the 20th about noon. The next morning at sunrise, Israel swung his knapsack, shouldered his musket, and, with Patterson's regiment, was on the march, quickstep, towards Boston.

Like Putnam, Israel received the stirring tidings at the plough. But although not less willing than Putnam to fly to battle at an instant's notice, yet—only half an acre of the field remaining to be finished—he whipped up his team and finished it. Before hastening to one duty, he would not leave a prior one undone; and ere helping to whip the British, for a little practice' sake, he applied the gad to his oxen. From the field of the farmer, he rushed to that of the soldier, mingling his blood with his sweat. While we revel in broadcloth, let us not forget what we owe to linsey-woolsey.

With other detachments from various quarters, Israel's regiment remained encamped for several days in the vicinity of Charlestown. On the 17th of June, one thousand Americans, including the regiment of Patterson, were set about fortifying Bunker's Hill. Working all through the night, by dawn of the following day, the redoubt was thrown up. But every one knows all about the battle. Suffice it, that Israel was one of those marksmen whom Putnam harangued as touching the enemy's eyes. Forbearing as he was with his oppressive father and unfaithful love, and mild as he was on the farm, Israel was not the same at Bunker Hill. Putnam had enjoined the men to aim at the officers; so Israel aimed between the golden epaulettes, as, in the wilderness, he had aimed between the branching antlers. With dogged disdain of their foes, the English grenadiers marched up the hill with sullen slowness; thus furnishing still surer aims to the muskets which bristled on the redoubt. Modest Israel was used to aver, that considering his practice in the woods, he could hardly be regarded as an inexperienced marksman; hinting, that every shot which the epauletted grenadiers received from his rifle, would, upon a different occasion, have procured him a deerskin. And like stricken deers the English, rashly brave as they were, fled from the opening fire. But the marksman's ammunition was expended; a hand-to-hand encounter ensued. Not one American musket in twenty had a bayonet to it. So, wielding the stock right and left, the terrible farmers, with hats and coats off, fought their way among the furred grenadiers, knocking them right and left, as seal-hunters on the beach, knock down with their clubs the Shetland seal. In the dense crowd and confusion, while Israel's musket got interlocked, he saw a blade horizontally menacing his feet from the ground. Thinking some fallen enemy sought to strike him at the last gasp, dropping his hold on his musket, he wrenched at the steel, but found that though a brave hand held it, that hand was powerless for ever. It was some British officer's laced sword-arm, cut from the trunk in the act of fighting, refusing to yield up its blade to the last. At that moment another sword was aimed at Israel's head by a living officer. In an instant the blow was parried by kindred steel, and the assailant fell by a brother's weapon, wielded by alien hands. But Israel did not come off unscathed. A cut on the right arm near the elbow, received in parrying the officer's blow, a long slit across the chest, a musket ball buried in his hip, and another mangling him near the ankle of the same leg, were the tokens of intrepidity which our Sicinius Dentatus carried from this memorable field. Nevertheless, with his comrades he succeeded in reaching Prospect Hill, and from thence was conveyed to the hospital at Cambridge. The bullet was extracted, his lesser wounds were dressed, and after much suffering from the fracture of the bone near the ankle, several pieces of which were extracted by the surgeon, ere long, thanks to the high health and pure blood of the farmer, Israel rejoined his regiment when they were throwing up intrenchments on Prospect Hill. Bunker Hill was now in possession of the foe, who in turn had fortified it.

On the third of July, Washington arrived from the South

to take the command. Israel witnessed his joyful reception by the huzzaing companies.

The British now quartered in Boston suffered greatly from the scarcity of provisions. Washington took every precaution to prevent their receiving a supply. Inland, all aid could easily be cut off. To guard against their receiving any by water, from tories and other disaffected persons, the General equipped three armed vessels to intercept all traitorous cruisers. Among them was the brigantine Washington, of ten guns, commanded by Captain Martindale. Seamen were hard to be had. The soldiers were called upon to volunteer for these vessels. Israel was one who so did; thinking that as an experienced sailor he should not be backward in a juncture like this, little as he fancied the new service assigned.

Three days out of Boston harbor, the brigantine was captured by the enemy's ship Foy, of twenty guns. Taken prisoner with the rest of the crew, Israel was afterwards put on board the frigate Tartar, with immediate sailing orders for England. Seventy-two were captives in this vessel. Headed by Israel, these men—half way across the sea—formed a scheme to take the ship, but were betrayed by a renegade Englishman. As ringleader, Israel was put in irons, and so remained till the frigate anchored at Portsmouth. There he was brought on deck; and would have met perhaps some terrible fate, had it not come out, during the examination, that the Englishman had been a deserter from the army of his native country ere proving a traitor to his adopted one. Relieved of his irons, Israel was placed in the marine hospital on shore, where half of the prisoners took the small-pox, which swept off a third of their number. Why talk of Jaffa?

From the hospital the survivors were conveyed to Spithead, and thrust on board a hulk. And here in the black bowels of the ship, sunk low in the sunless sea, our poor Israel lay for a month, like Jonah in the belly of the whale.

But one bright morning, Israel is hailed from the deck. A bargeman of the commander's boat is sick. Known for a sailor, Israel for the nonce is appointed to pull the absent man's oar.

The officers being landed, some of the crew propose, like merry Englishmen as they are, to hie to a neighboring ale-house, and have a cosy pot or two together. Agreed. They start, and Israel with them. As they enter the ale-house door, our prisoner is suddenly reminded of still more imperative calls. Unsuspected of any design, he is allowed to leave the party for a moment. No sooner does Israel see his companions housed, than putting speed into his feet, and letting grow all his wings, he starts like a deer. He runs four miles (so he afterwards affirmed) without halting. He sped towards London; wisely deeming that once in that crowd detection would be impossible.

Ten miles, as he computed, from where he had left the bargemen, leisurely passing a public house of a little village on the roadside, thinking himself now pretty safe—hark, what is this he hears—

"Ahoy!"

"No ship," says Israel, hurrying on.

"Stop."

"If you will attend to your business, I will endeavor to attend to mine," replies Israel coolly. And next minute he lets grow his wings again; flying, one dare say, at the rate of something less than thirty miles an hour.

"Stop thief!" is now the cry. Numbers rushed from the roadside houses. After a mile's chase, the poor panting deer is caught.

Finding it was no use now to prevaricate, Israel boldly confesses himself a prisoner-of-war. The officer, a good fellow as it turned out, had him escorted back to the inn; where, observing to the landlord that this must needs be a true-blooded Yankee, he calls for liquors to refresh Israel after his run. Two soldiers are then appointed to guard him for the present. This was towards evening; and up to a late hour at night, the inn was filled with strangers crowding to see the Yankee rebel, as they politely termed him. These honest rustics seemed to think that Yankees were a sort of wild creatures, a species of 'possum or kangaroo. But Israel is very affable with them. That liquor he drank from the hand of his foe, has perhaps warmed his heart towards all the rest of his enemies. Yet this may not be wholly so. We shall see. At any rate, still he keeps his eye on the main chance—escape. Neither the jokes nor the insults of the mob does he suffer to molest him. He is cogitating a little plot to himself.

It seems that the good officer—not more true to the king his master than indulgent towards the prisoner which that same loyalty made—had left orders that Israel should be supplied with whatever liquor he wanted that night. So, calling for the can again and again, Israel invites the two soldiers to drink and be merry. At length, a wag of the company proposes that Israel should entertain the public with a jig, he (the wag) having heard that the Yankees were extraordinary dancers. A fiddle is brought in, and poor Israel takes the floor. Not a little cut to think that these people should so unfeelingly seek to be diverted at the expense of an unfortunate prisoner, Israel, while jigging it up and down, still conspires away at his private plot, resolving ere long to give the enemy a touch of certain Yankee steps, as yet undreamed of in their simple philosophy. They would not permit any cessation of his dancing till he had danced himself into a perfect sweat, so that the drops fell from his lank and flaxen hair. But Israel, with much of the gentleness of the dove, is not wholly without the wisdom of the serpent. Pleased to see the flowing bowl, he congratulates himself that his own state of perspiration prevents it from producing any intoxicating effect upon him.

Late at night the company break up. Furnished with a pair of handcuffs, the prisoner is laid on a blanket spread upon the floor at the side of the bed in which his two keepers are to repose. Expressing much gratitude for the blanket, with apparent unconcern, Israel stretches his legs. An hour or two passes. All is quiet without.

The important moment had now arrived. Certain it was, that if this chance were suffered to pass unimproved, a second would hardly present itself. For early, doubtless, on the following morning, if not some way prevented, the two soldiers would convey Israel back to his floating prison where he would thenceforth remain confined until the close of the war; years and years, perhaps. When he thought of that horrible old hulk, his nerves were restrung for flight. But intrepid as he must be to compass it, wariness too was needed. His keepers had gone to bed pretty well under the influence of the liquor. This was favorable. But still, they were full-grown, strong men; and Israel was handcuffed. So Israel resolved upon strategy first; and if that failed, force afterwards. He eagerly listened. One of the drunken soldiers muttered in his sleep, at first lowly, then louder and louder,—"Catch 'em! Grapple 'em! Have at 'em! Ha—long cutlasses! Take that, runaway!"

"What's the matter with ye, Phil?" hiccoughed the other, who was not yet asleep. "Keep quiet, will ye? Ye ain't at Fontenoy now."

"He's a runaway prisoner, I say. Catch him, catch him!"

"Oh, stush with your drunken dreaming," again hiccoughed his comrade, violently nudging him. "This comes o' carousing."

Shortly after, the dreamer with loud snores fell back into dead sleep. But by something in the sound of the breathing of the other soldier, Israel knew that this man remained uneasily awake. He deliberated a moment what was best to do. At length he determined upon trying his old plea. Calling upon the two soldiers, he informed them that urgent necessity required his immediate presence somewhere in the rear of the house.

"Come, wake up here, Phil," roared the soldier who was awake; "the fellow here says he must step out; cuss these Yankees; no better edication than to be gettin' up on nateral necessities at this time o'night. It ain't nateral; it's unnateral. D—n ye, Yankee, don't ye know no better?"

With many more denunciations, the two now staggered to their feet, and clutching hold of Israel, escorted him down stairs, and through a long narrow, dark entry, rearward, till they came to a door. No sooner was this unbolted by the foremost guard, than, quick as a flash, manacled Israel, shaking off the grasp of the one behind him, butts him sprawling back into the entry; when, dashing in the opposite direction, he bounces the other head over heels into the garden, never using a hand; and then, leaping over the latter's head, darts blindly out into the mid-

34

night. Next moment he was at the garden wall. No outlet was discoverable in the gloom. But a fruit-tree grew close to the wall. Springing into it desperately, handcuffed as he was, Israel leaps atop of the barrier, and without pausing to see where he is, drops himself to the ground on the other side, and once more lets grow all his wings. Meantime, with loud outcries, the two baffled drunkards grope deliriously about in the garden.

After running two or three miles, and hearing no sound of pursuit, Israel reins up to rid himself of the handcuffs, which impede him. After much painful labor he succeeds in the attempt. Pressing on again with all speed, day broke, revealing a trim-looking, hedged, and beautiful country, soft, neat, and serene, all colored with the fresh early tints of the spring of 1776.

Bless me, thought Israel, all of a tremble, I shall certainly be caught now; I have broken into some nobleman's park.

But, hurrying forward again, he came to a turnpike road, and then knew that, all comely and shaven as it was, this was simply the open country of England; one bright, broad park, paled in with white foam of the sea. A copse skirting the road was just bursting out into bud. Each unrolling leaf was in very act of escaping from its prison. Israel looked at the budding leaves, and round on the budding sod, and up at the budding dawn of the day. He was so sad, and these sights were so gay, that Israel sobbed like a child, while thoughts of his mountain home rushed like a wind on his heart. But conquering this fit, he marched on, and presently passed nigh a field, where two figures were working. They had rosy cheeks, short, sturdy legs, showing the blue stocking nearly to the knee, and were clad in long, coarse, white frocks, and had on coarse, broad-brimmed straw hats. Their faces were partly averted.

"Please, ladies," half roguishly says Israel, taking off his hat, "does this road go to London?"

At this salutation, the two figures turned in a sort of stupid amazement, causing an almost corresponding expression in Israel, who now perceived that they were men, and not women. He had mistaken them, owing to their frocks, and their wearing no pantaloons, only breeches hidden by their frocks.

"Beg pardon, ladies, but I thought ye were something else," said Israel again.

Once more the two figures stared at the stranger, and with added boorishness of surprise.

"Does this road go to London, gentlemen?"

"Gentlemen—egad!" cried one of the two.

"Egad!" echoed the second.

Putting their hoes before them, the two frocked boors now took a good look at Israel, meantime scratching their heads under their plaited straw hats.

"Does it, gentlemen? Does it go to London? Be kind enough to tell a poor fellow, do."

"Yees goin' to Lunnun, are yees? Weel—all right—go along."

And without another word, having now satisfied their rustic curiosity, the two human steers, with wonderful phlegm, applied themselves to their hoes; supposing, no doubt, that they had given all requisite information.

Shortly after, Israel passed an old, dark, mossy-looking chapel, its roof all plastered with the damp yellow dead leaves of the previous autumn, showered there from a close cluster of venerable trees, with great trunks, and overstretching branches. Next moment he found himself entering a village. The silence of early morning rested upon it. But few figures were seen. Glancing through the window of a now noiseless public-house, Israel saw a table all in disorder, covered with empty flagons, and tobacco-ashes, and long pipes; some of the latter broken.

After pausing here a moment, he moved on, and observed a man over the way standing still and watching him. Instantly Israel was reminded that he had on the dress of an English sailor, and that it was this probably which had arrested the stranger's attention. Well knowing that his peculiar dress exposed him to peril, he hurried on faster to escape the village; resolving at the first opportunity to change his garments. Ere long, in a secluded place about a mile from the village, he saw an old ditcher

36

tottering beneath the weight of a pick-axe, hoe and shovel, going to his work; the very picture of poverty, toil and distress. His clothes were tatters.

Making up to this old man, Israel, after a word or two of salutation, offered to change clothes with him. As his own clothes were prince-like compared to the ditcher's, Israel thought that however much his proposition might excite the suspicion of the ditcher, yet self-interest would prevent his communicating the suspicions. To be brief, the two went behind a hedge, and presently Israel emerged, presenting the most forlorn appearance conceivable; while the old ditcher hobbled off in an opposite direction, correspondingly improved in his aspect; though it was rather ludicrous than otherwise, owing to the immense bagginess of the sailor-trowsers flapping about his lean shanks, to say nothing of the spare voluminousness of the pea-jacket. But Israel—how deplorable, how dismal his plight! Little did he ween that these wretched rags he now wore, were but suitable to that long career of destitution before him: one brief career of adventurous wanderings; and then, forty torpid years of pauperism. The coat was all patches. And no two patches were alike, and no one patch was the color of the original cloth. The stringless breeches gaped wide open at the knee; the long woollen stockings looked as if they had been set up at some time for a target. Israel looked suddenly metamorphosed from youth to old age; just like an old man of eighty he looked. But, indeed, dull, dreary adversity was now in store for him; and adversity, come it at eighteen or eighty, is the true old age of man. The dress befitted the fate.

From the friendly old ditcher, Israel learned the exact course he must steer for London; distant now between seventy and eighty miles. He was also apprised by his venerable friend, that the country was filled with soldiers on the constant look-out for deserters whether from the navy or army, for the capture of whom a stipulated reward was given, just as in Massachusetts at that time for prowling bears.

Having solemnly enjoined his old friend not to give any information, should any one he meet inquire for such a person as Israel, our adventurer walked briskly on, less heavy of heart, now that he felt comparatively safe in disguise.

Thirty miles were travelled that day. At night Israel stole into a barn, in hopes of finding straw or hay for a bed. But it was spring; all the hay and straw were gone. So after groping about in the dark, he was fain to content himself with an undressed sheep-skin. Cold, hungry, foot-sore, weary, and impatient for the morning dawn, Israel drearily dozed out the night.

By the first peep of day coming through the chinks of the barn, he was up and abroad. Ere long finding himself in the suburbs of a considerable village, the better to guard against detection he supplied himself with a rude crutch, and feigning himself a cripple, hobbled straight through the town, followed by a perverse-minded cur, which kept up a continual, spiteful, suspicious bark. Israel longed to have one good rap at him with his crutch, but thought it would hardly look in character for a poor old cripple to be vindictive.

A few miles further, and he came to a second village. While hobbling through its main street, as through the former one, he was suddenly stopped by a genuine cripple, all in tatters, too, who, with a sympathetic air, inquired after the cause of his lameness.

"White swelling," says Israel.

"That's just my ailing," wheezed the other; "but you're lamer than me," he added with a forlorn sort of self-satisfaction, critically eyeing Israel's limp as once more he stumped on his way, not liking to tarry too long.

"But halloo, what's your hurry, friend?" seeing Israel fairly departing—"where're you going?"

"To London," answered Israel, turning round, heartily wishing the old fellow any where else than present.

"Going to limp to Lunnun, eh? Well, success to ye."

"As much to you, sir," answers Israel politely.

Nigh the opposite suburbs of this village, as good fortune would have it, an empty baggage-wagon bound for the metropolis turned into the main road from a side one. Immediately Israel limps most deplorably, and begs the driver to give a poor cripple a lift. So up he climbs; but after a time, finding the gait of the elephantine draught-horses intolerably slow, Israel craves permission to dismount, when, throwing away his crutch, he takes nimbly to his legs, much to the surprise of his honest friend the driver.

The only advantage, if any, derived from his trip in the wagon, was, when passing through a third village—but a little distant from the previous one—Israel, by lying down in the wagon, had wholly avoided being seen.

The villages surprised him by their number and proximity. Nothing like this was to be seen at home. Well knowing that in these villages he ran much more risk of detection than in the open country, he henceforth did his best to avoid them, by taking a roundabout course whenever they came in sight from a distance. This mode of travelling not only lengthened his journey, but put unlooked-for obstacles in his path—walls, ditches, and streams.

Not half an hour after throwing away his crutch, he leaped a great ditch ten feet wide, and of undiscoverable muddy depth. I wonder if the old cripple would think me the lamer one now, thought Israel to himself, arriving on the hither side.

4

*Further Wanderings of the Refugee, with Some
Account of a Good Knight of Brentford Who
Befriended Him*

At nightfall, on the third day, Israel had arrived within
sixteen miles of the capital. Once more he sought refuge
in a barn. This time he found some hay, and flinging himself down procured a tolerable night's rest.

Bright and early he arose refreshed, with the pleasing
prospect of reaching his destination ere noon. Encouraged
to find himself so far from his original pursuers, Israel
relaxed in his vigilance, and about ten o'clock, while passing through the town of Staines, suddenly encountered
three soldiers. Unfortunately in exchanging clothes with
the ditcher, he could not bring himself to include his shirt
in the traffic, which shirt was a British navy shirt, a
bargeman's shirt, and though hitherto he had crumpled
the blue collar out of sight, yet, as it appeared in the
present instance, it was not thoroughly concealed. At any
rate, keenly on the lookout for deserters, and made acute
by hopes of reward for their apprehension, the soldiers
spied the fatal collar, and in an instant laid violent hands
on the refugee.

"Hey, lad!" said the foremost soldier, a corporal, "you

are one of his majesty's seamen! come along with ye."

So, unable to give any satisfactory account of himself, he was made prisoner on the spot, and soon after found himself handcuffed and locked up in the Round House of the place, a prison so called, appropriated to runaways, and those convicted of minor offences. Day passed dinnerless and supperless in this dismal durance, and night came on.

Israel had now been three days without food, except one twopenny loaf. The cravings of hunger now became sharper; his spirits, hitherto arming him with fortitude, began to forsake him. Taken captive once again upon the very brink of reaching his goal, poor Israel was on the eve of falling into helpless despair. But he rallied, and considering that grief would only add to his calamity, sought with stubborn patience to habituate himself to misery, but still hold aloof from despondency. He roused himself, and began to bethink him how to be extricated from this labyrinth.

Two hours sawing across the grating of the window, ridded him of his handcuffs. Next came the door, secured luckily with only a hasp and padlock. Thrusting the bolt of his handcuffs through a small window in the door, he succeeded in forcing the hasp and regaining his liberty about three o'clock in the morning.

Not long after sunrise, he passed nigh Brentford, some six or seven miles from the capital. So great was his hunger that downright starvation seemed before him. He chewed grass, and swallowed it. Upon first escaping from the hulk, six English pennies was all the money he had. With two of these he had bought a small loaf the day after fleeing the inn. The other four still remained in his pocket, not having met with a good opportunity to dispose of them for food.

Having torn off the collar of his shirt, and flung it into a hedge, he ventured to accost a respectable carpenter at a pale fence, about a mile this side of Brentford, to whom his deplorable situation now induced him to apply for work. The man did not wish himself to hire, but said that if he (Israel) understood farming or gardening, he might

41

perhaps procure work from Sir John Millet, whose seat, he said, was not remote. He added that the knight was in the habit of employing many men at that season of the year, so he stood a fair chance.

Revived a little by this prospect of relief, Israel starts in quest of the gentleman's seat, agreeably to the direction received. But he mistook his way, and proceeding up a gravelled and beautifully decorated walk, was terrified at catching a glimpse of a number of soldiers thronging a garden. He made an instant retreat before being espied in turn. No wild creature of the American wilderness could have been more panic-struck by a firebrand, than at this period hunted Israel was by a red coat. It afterwards appeared that this garden was the Princess Amelia's.

Taking another path, ere long he came to some laborers shovelling gravel. These proved to be men employed by Sir John. By them he was directed towards the house, when the knight was pointed out to him, walking bareheaded in the inclosure with several guests. Having heard the rich men of England charged with all sorts of domineering qualities, Israel felt no little misgiving in approaching to an audience with so imposing a stranger. But, screwing up his courage, he advanced; while seeing him coming all rags and tatters, the group of gentlemen stood in some wonder awaiting what so singular a phantom might want.

"Mr. Millet," said Israel, bowing towards the bareheaded gentleman.

"Ha,—who are you, pray?"

"A poor fellow, sir, in want of work."

"A wardrobe, too, I should say," smiled one of the guests, of a very youthful, prosperous, and dandified air.

"Where's your hoe?" said Sir John.

"I have none, sir."

"Any money to buy one?"

"Only four English pennies, sir."

"*English* pennies. What other sort would you have?"

"Why, China pennies to be sure," laughed the youthful gentleman. "See his long, yellow hair behind; he looks like a Chinaman. Some broken-down Mandarin. Pity he's no crown to his old hat; if he had, he might pass it round, and make eight pennies of his four."

"Will you hire me, Mr. Millet," said Israel.

"Ha! that's queer again," cried the knight.

"Hark ye, fellow," said a brisk servant, approaching from the porch, "this is Sir John Millet."

Seeming to take pity on his seeming ignorance, as well as on his undisputable poverty, the good knight now told Israel that if he would come the next morning he would see him supplied with a hoe, and moreover would hire him.

It would be hard to express the satisfaction of the wanderer at receiving this encouraging reply. Emboldened by it, he now returns towards a baker's he had spied, and bravely marching in, flings down all four pennies, and demands bread. Thinking he would not have any more food till next morning, Israel resolved to eat only one of the pair of twopenny loaves. But having demolished one, it so sharpened his longing, that yielding to the irresistible temptation, he bolted down the second loaf to keep the other company.

After resting under a hedge, he saw the sun far descended, and so prepared himself for another hard night. Waiting till dark, he crawled into an old carriage-house, finding nothing there but a dismantled old phaeton. Into this he climbed, and curling himself up like a carriage-dog, endeavored to sleep; but, unable to endure the constraint of such a bed, got out, and stretched himself on the bare boards of the floor.

No sooner was light in the east than he hastened to await the commands of one who, his instinct told him, was destined to prove his benefactor. On his father's farm accustomed to rise with the lark, Israel was surprised to discover, as he approached the house, that no soul was astir. It was four o'clock. For a considerable time he walked back and forth before the portal ere any one appeared. The first riser was a man servant of the household, who informed Israel that seven o'clock was the hour the people went to their work. Soon after he met an hostler of the place, who gave him permission to lie on some straw in an outhouse. There he enjoyed a sweet sleep till awakened at seven o'clock by the sounds of activity around him.

Supplied by the overseer of the men with a large iron fork and a hoe, he followed the hands into the field. He was so weak he could hardly support his tools. Unwilling to expose his debility, he yet could not succeed in concealing it. At last, to avoid worse imputations, he confessed the cause. His companions regarded him with compassion, and exempted him from the severer toil.

About noon the knight visited his workmen. Noticing that Israel made little progress, he said to him, that though he had long arms and broad shoulders, yet he was feigning himself to be a very weak man, or otherwise must in reality be so.

Hereupon one of the laborers standing by informed the gentleman how it was with Israel, when immediately the knight put a shilling into his hands and bade him go to a little roadside inn, which was nearer than the house, and buy him bread and a pot of beer. Thus refreshed he returned to the band, and toiled with them till four o'clock, when the day's work was over.

Arrived at the house he there again saw his employer, who, after attentively eyeing him without speaking, bade a meal be prepared for him, when the maid presenting a smaller supply than her kind master deemed necessary, she was ordered to return and bring out the entire dish. But aware of the danger of sudden repletion of heavy food to one in his condition, Israel, previously recruited by the frugal meal at the inn, partook but sparingly. The repast was spread on the grass, and being over, the good knight again looking inquisitively at Israel, ordered a comfortable bed to be laid in the barn, and here Israel spent a capital night.

After breakfast, next morning, he was proceeding to go with the laborers to their work, when his employer approaching him with a benevolent air, bade him return to his couch, and there remain till he had slept his fill, and was in a better state to resume his labors.

Upon coming forth again a little after noon, he found

Sir John walking alone in the grounds. Upon discovering him, Israel would have retreated, fearing that he might intrude; but beckoning him to advance, the knight, as Israel drew nigh, fixed on him such a penetrating glance, that our poor hero quaked to the core. Neither was his dread of detection relieved by the knight's now calling in a loud voice for one from the house. Israel was just on the point of fleeing, when overhearing the words of the master to the servant who now appeared, all dread departed:

"Bring hither some wine!"

It presently came; by order of the knight the salver was set down on a green bank near by, and the servant retired.

"My poor fellow," said Sir John, now pouring out a glass of wine, and handing it to Israel, "I perceive that you are an American; and, if I am not mistaken, you are an escaped prisoner of war. But no fear—drink the wine."

"Mr. Millet," exclaimed Israel aghast, the untasted wine trembling in his hand, "Mr. Millet, I——"

"*Mr.* Millet—there it is again. Why don't you say *Sir John* like the rest?"

"Why, sir—pardon me—but somehow, I can't. I've tried; but I can't. You won't betray me for that?"

"Betray—poor fellow! Hark ye, your history is doubtless a secret which you would not wish to divulge to a stranger; but whatever happens to you, I pledge you my honor I will never betray you."

"God bless you for that, Mr. Millet."

"Come, come; call me by my right name. I am not Mr. Millet. *You* have said *Sir* to me; and no doubt you have a thousand times said *John* to other people. Now can't you couple the two? Try once. Come. Only *Sir* and then *John—Sir John*—that's all."

"John—I can't—Sir, sir!—your pardon. I didn't mean that."

"My good fellow," said the knight looking sharply upon Israel, "tell me, are all your countrymen like you? If so, it's no use fighting them. To that effect, I must write to his Majesty myself. Well, I excuse you from Sir Johnning me.

But tell me the truth, are you not a seafaring man, and lately a prisoner of war?"

Israel frankly confessed it, and told his whole story. The knight listened with much interest; and at its conclusion, warned Israel to beware of the soldiers; for owing to the seats of some of the royal family being in the neighborhood, the red-coats abounded hereabout.

"I do not wish unnecessarily to speak against my own countrymen," he added, "I but plainly speak for your good. The soldiers you meet prowling on the roads, are not fair specimens of the army. They are a set of mean, dastardly banditti, who, to obtain their fee, would betray their best friends. Once more, I warn you against them. But enough; follow me now to the house, and as you tell me you have exchanged clothes before now, you can do it again. What say you? I will give you coat and breeches for your rags."

Thus generously supplied with clothes and other comforts by the good knight, and implicitly relying upon the honor of so kind-hearted a man, Israel cheered up, and in the course of two or three weeks had so fattened his flanks, that he was able completely to fill Sir John's old buckskin breeches, which at first had hung but loosely about him.

He was assigned to an occupation which removed him from the other workmen. The strawberry bed was put under his sole charge. And often, of mild, sunny afternoons, the knight, genial and gentle with dinner, would stroll bareheaded to the pleasant strawberry bed, and have nice little confidential chats with Israel; while Israel, charmed by the patriarchal demeanor of this true Abrahamic gentleman, with a smile on his lip, and tears of gratitude in his eyes, offered him, from time to time, the plumpest berries of the bed.

When the strawberry season was over, other parts of the grounds were assigned him. And so six months elapsed, when, at the recommendation of Sir John, Israel procured a good berth in the garden of the Princess Amelia.

So completely now had recent events metamorphosed him in all outward things, that few suspected him of being

46

any other than an Englishman. Not even the knight's domestics. But in the princess's garden, being obliged to work in company with many other laborers, the war was often a topic of discussion among them. And "the d——d Yankee rebels" were not seldom the object of scurrilous remark. Illy could the exile brook in silence such insults upon the country for which he had bled, and for whose honored sake he was that very instant a sufferer. More than once, his indignation came very nigh getting the better of his prudence. He longed for the war to end, that he might but speak a little bit of his mind.

Now the superintendent of the garden was a harsh, overbearing man. The workmen with tame servility endured his worst affronts. But Israel, bred among mountains, found it impossible to restrain himself when made the undeserved object of pitiless epithets. Ere two months went by, he quitted the service of the princess, and engaged himself to a farmer in a small village not far from Brentford. But hardly had he been here three weeks, when a rumor again got afloat, that he was a Yankee prisoner of war. Whence this report arose he could never discover. No sooner did it reach the ears of the soldiers, than they were on the alert. Luckily, Israel was apprised of their intentions in time. But he was hard pushed. He was hunted after with a perseverance worthy a less ignoble cause. He had many hairbreadth escapes. Most assuredly he would have been captured, had it not been for the secret good offices of a few individuals, who, perhaps, were not unfriendly to the American side of the question, though they durst not avow it.

Tracked one night by the soldiers to the house of one of these friends, in whose garret he was concealed, he was obliged to force the skuttle, and running along the roof, passed to those of adjoining houses to the number of ten or twelve, finally succeeding in making his escape.

5

Israel in the Lion's Den

Harassed day and night, hunted from food and sleep, driven from hole to hole like a fox in the woods, with no chance to earn an hour's wages, he was at last advised by one whose sincerity he could not doubt, to apply, on the good word of Sir John Millet, for a berth as laborer in the King's Gardens at Kew. There, it was said, he would be entirely safe, as no soldier durst approach those premises to molest any soul therein employed. It struck the poor exile as curious, that the very den of the British lion, the private grounds of the British King, should be commended to a refugee as his securest asylum.

His nativity carefully concealed, and being personally introduced to the chief gardener by one who well knew him; armed, too, with a line from Sir John, and recommended by his introducer as uncommonly expert at horticulture; Israel was soon installed as keeper of certain less private plants and walks of the park.

It was here, to one of his near country retreats, that, coming from perplexities of state—leaving far behind him the dingy old bricks of St. James—George the Third was wont to walk up and down beneath the long arbors formed by the interlockings of lofty trees.

More than once, raking the gravel, Israel through intervening foliage would catch peeps in some private but parallel walk, of that lonely figure, not more shadowy with overhanging leaves than with the shade of royal meditations.

Unauthorized and abhorrent thoughts will sometimes invade the best human heart. Seeing the monarch unguarded before him; remembering that the war was imputed more to the self-will of the King than to the willingness of parliament or the nation; and calling to mind all his own sufferings growing out of that war, with all the calamities of his country; dim impulses, such as those to which the regicide Ravaillac yielded, would shoot balefully across the soul of the exile. But thrusting Satan behind him, Israel vanquished all such temptations. Nor did these ever more disturb him, after his one chance conversation with the monarch.

As he was one day gravelling a little by-walk, wrapped in thought, the King turning a clump of bushes, suddenly brushed Israel's person.

Immediately Israel touched his hat—but did not remove it—bowed, and was retiring; when something in his air arrested the King's attention.

"You ain't an Englishman,—no Englishman—no, no."

Pale as death, Israel tried to answer something; but knowing not what to say, stood frozen to the ground.

"You are a Yankee—a Yankee," said the King again in his rapid and half-stammering way.

Again Israel assayed to reply, but could not. What could he say? Could he lie to a king?

"Yes, yes,—you are one of that stubborn race,—that very stubborn race. What brought you here?"

"The fate of war, sir."

"May it please your Majesty," said a low cringing voice, approaching, "this man is in the walk against orders. There is some mistake, may it please your Majesty. Quit the walk, blockhead," he hissed at Israel.

It was one of the junior gardeners who thus spoke. It

seems that Israel had mistaken his directions that morning.

"Slink, you dog," hissed the gardener again to Israel; then aloud to the King, "A mistake of the man, I assure your Majesty."

"Go you away—away with ye, and leave him with me," said the King.

Waiting a moment, till the man was out of hearing, the King again turned upon Israel.

"Were you at Bunker Hill?—that bloody Bunker Hill —eh, eh?"

"Yes, sir."

"Fought like a devil—like a very devil, I suppose?"

"Yes, sir."

"Helped flog—helped flog my soldiers?"

"Yes, sir; but very sorry to do it."

"Eh?—eh?—how's that?"

"I took it to be my sad duty, sir."

"Very much mistaken—very much mistaken, indeed. Why do ye sir me?—eh? I'm your King—your King."

"Sir," said Israel firmly, but with deep respect, "I have no king."

The King darted his eye incensedly for a moment; but without quailing, Israel, now that all was out, still stood with mute respect before him. The King, turning suddenly, walked rapidly away from Israel a moment, but presently returning with a less hasty pace, said, "You are rumored to be a spy—a spy, or something of that sort—ain't you? But I know you are not—no, no. You are a runaway prisoner of war, eh? You have sought this place to be safe from pursuit, eh? eh? Is it not so?—eh? eh? eh?

"Sir, it is."

"Well, ye're an honest rebel—rebel, yes, rebel. Hark ye, hark. Say nothing of this talk to any one. And hark again. So long as you remain here at Kew, I shall see that you are safe—safe."

"God bless your Majesty!"

"Eh?"

"God bless your noble Majesty?"

"Come—come—come," smiled the King in delight, "I thought I could conquer ye—conquer ye."

"Not the King, but the King's kindness, your Majesty."

"Join my army—army."

Sadly looking down, Israel silently shook his head.

"You won't? Well, gravel the walk then—gravel away. Very stubborn race—very stubborn race, indeed—very—very—very."

And still growling, the magnanimous lion departed.

How the monarch came by his knowledge of so humble an exile, whether through that swift insight into individual character said to form one of the miraculous qualities transmitted with a crown, or whether some of the rumors prevailing outside of the garden had come to his ear, Israel could never determine. Very probably, though, the latter was the case, inasmuch as some vague shadowy report of Israel not being an Englishman, had, a little previous to his interview with the King, been communicated to several of the inferior gardeners. Without any impeachment of Israel's fealty to his country, it must still be narrated, that from this his familiar audience with George the Third, he went away with very favorable views of that monarch. Israel now thought that it could not be the warm heart of the King, but the cold heads of his lords in council, that persuaded him so tyrannically to persecute America. Yet hitherto the precise contrary of this had been Israel's opinion, agreeably to the popular prejudice throughout New England.

Thus we see what strange and powerful magic resides in a crown, and how subtly that cheap and easy magnanimity, which in private belongs to most kings, may operate on good-natured and unfortunate souls. Indeed, had it not been for the peculiar disinterested fidelity of our adventurer's patriotism, he would have soon sported the red coat; and perhaps under the immediate patronage of his royal friend, been advanced in time to no mean rank in the army of Britain. Nor in that case would we have had to follow him, as at last we shall, through long, long years of obscure and penurious wandering.

Continuing in the service of the King's gardeners at Kew, until a season came when the work of the garden required a less number of laborers, Israel, with several

51

others, was discharged; and the day after, engaged himself for a few months to a farmer in the neighborhood where he had been last employed. But hardly a week had gone by, when the old story of his being a rebel, or a runaway prisoner, or a Yankee! or a spy, began to be revived with added malignity. Like bloodhounds, the soldiers were once more on the track. The houses where he harbored were many times searched; but thanks to the fidelity of a few earnest well-wishers, and to his own unsleeping vigilance and activity, the hunted fox still continued to elude apprehension. To such extremities of harassment, however, did this incessant pursuit subject him, that in a fit of despair he was about to surrender himself, and submit to his fate, when Providence seasonably interposed in his favor.

6

*Israel Makes the Acquaintance of Certain Secret
Friends of America, One of Them Being the Famous
Author of the "Diversions of Purley." These
Despatch Him on a Sly Errand Across the Channel*

At this period, though made the victims indeed of British oppression, yet the colonies were not totally without friends in Britain. It was but natural that when Parliament itself held patriotic and gifted men, who not only recommended conciliatory measures, but likewise denounced the war as monstrous; it was but natural that throughout the nation at large there should be many private individuals cherishing similar sentiments, and some who made no scruple clandestinely to act upon them.

Late one night while hiding in a farmer's granary, Israel saw a man with a lantern approaching. He was about to flee, when the man hailed him in a well-known voice, bidding him have no fear. It was the farmer himself. He carried a message to Israel from a gentleman of Brentford, to the effect, that the refugee was earnestly requested to repair on the following evening to that gentleman's mansion.

At first, Israel was disposed to surmise that either the farmer was playing him false, or else his honest credulity had been imposed upon by evil-minded persons. At any rate, he regarded the message as a decoy, and for half an hour refused to credit its sincerity. But at length he was induced to think a little better of it. The gentleman giving the invitation was one Squire Woodcock, of Brentford, whose loyalty to the King had been under suspicion; so at least the farmer averred. This latter information was not without its effect.

At nightfall on the following day, being disguised in strange clothes by the farmer, Israel stole from his retreat, and after a few hours' walk, arrived before the ancient brick house of the Squire; who opening the door in person, and learning who it was that stood there, at once assured Israel in the most solemn manner, that no foul play was intended. So the wanderer suffered himself to enter, and be conducted to a private chamber in the rear of the mansion, where were seated two other gentlemen, attired, in the manner of that age, in long laced coats, with smallclothes, and shoes with silver buckles.

"I am John Woodcock," said the host, "and these gentlemen are Horne Tooke and James Bridges. All three of us are friends to America. We have heard of you for some weeks past, and inferring from your conduct, that you must be a Yankee of the true blue stamp, we have resolved to employ you in a way which you cannot but gladly approve; for surely, though an exile, you are still willing to serve your country; if not as a sailor or soldier, yet as a traveller?"

"Tell me how I may do it?" demanded Israel, not completely at ease.

"At that in good time," smiled the Squire. "The point is now—do you repose confidence in my statements?"

Israel glanced inquiringly upon the Squire; then upon his companions; and meeting the expressive, enthusiastic, candid countenance of Horne Tooke—then in the first honest ardor of his political career—turned to the Squire, and said, "Sir, I believe what you have said. Tell me now what I am to do."

"Oh, there is just nothing to be done to-night," said the Squire; "nor for some days to come perhaps, but we wanted to have you prepared."

And hereupon he hinted to his guest rather vaguely of his general intention; and that over, begged him to entertain them with some account of his adventures since he first took up arms for his country. To this Israel had no objections in the world, since all men love to tell the tale of hardships endured in a righteous cause. But ere beginning his story, the Squire refreshed him with some cold beef, laid in a snowy napkin, and a glass of perry, and thrice during the narration of the adventures, pressed him with additional draughts.

But after his second glass, Israel declined to drink more, mild as the beverage was. For he noticed, that not only did the three gentlemen listen with the utmost interest to his story, but likewise interrupted him with questions and cross-questions in the most pertinacious manner. So this led him to be on his guard, not being absolutely certain yet, as to who they might really be, or what was their real design. But as it turned out, Squire Woodcock and his friends only sought to satisfy themselves thoroughly, before making their final disclosures, that the exile was one in whom implicit confidence might be placed.

And to this desirable conclusion they eventually came, for upon the ending of Israel's story, after expressing their sympathies for his hardships, and applauding his generous patriotism in so patiently enduring adversity, as well as singing the praises of his gallant fellow-soldiers of Bunker Hill, they openly revealed their scheme. They wished to know whether Israel would undertake a trip to Paris, to carry an important message—shortly to be received for transmission through them—to Doctor Franklin, then in that capital.

"All your expenses shall be paid, not to speak of a compensation besides," said the Squire; "will you go?"

"I must think of it," said Israel, not yet wholly confirmed in his mind. But once more he cast his glance on Horne Tooke, and his irresolution was gone.

The Squire now informed Israel that, to avoid suspicions, it would be necessary for him to remove to another place until the hour at which he should start for Paris. They enjoined upon him the profoundest secresy, gave him a guinea, with a letter for a gentleman in White Waltham, a town some miles from Brentford, which point they begged him to reach as soon as possible, there to tarry for further instructions.

Having informed him of thus much, Squire Woodcock asked him to hold out his right foot.

"What for?" said Israel.

"Why, would you not like to have a pair of new boots against your return?" smiled Horne Tooke.

"Oh, yes; no objection at all," said Israel.

"Well, then, let the bootmaker measure you," smiled Horne Tooke.

"Do *you* do it, Mr. Tooke," said the Squire, "you measure men's parts better than I."

"Hold out your foot, my good friend," said Horne Tooke—"there—now let's measure your heart."

"For that, measure me round the chest," said Israel.

"Just the man we want," said Mr. Bridges, triumphantly.

"Give him another glass of wine, Squire," said Horne Tooke.

Exchanging the farmer's clothes for still another disguise, Israel now set out immediately, on foot, for his destination, having received minute directions as to his road, and arriving in White Waltham on the following morning was very cordially received by the gentleman to whom he carried the letter. This person, another of the active English friends of America, possessed a particular knowledge of late events in that land. To him Israel was indebted for much entertaining information. After remaining some ten days at this place, word came from Squire Woodcock, requiring Israel's immediate return, stating the hour at which he must arrive at the house, namely, two o'clock on the following morning. So, after another night's solitary trudge across the country, the wanderer was welcomed by the same three gentlemen as before, seated in the same room.

"The time has now come," said Squire Woodcock. "You must start this morning for Paris. Take off your shoes."

56

"Am I to steal from here to Paris on my stocking-feet?" said Israel, whose late easy good living at White Waltham had not failed to bring out the good-natured and mirthful part of him, even as his prior experiences had produced, for the most part, something like a contrary result.

"Oh, no," smiled Horne Tooke, who always lived well, "we have seven-league-boots for you. Don't you remember my measuring you?"

Hereupon going to the closet, the Squire brought out a pair of new boots. They were fitted with false heels. Unscrewing these, the Squire showed Israel the papers concealed beneath. They were of a fine tissuey fibre, and contained much writing in a very small compass. The boots, it need hardly be said, had been particularly made for the occasion.

"Walk across the room with them," said the Squire, when Israel had pulled them on.

"He'll surely be discovered," smiled Horne Tooke. "Hark how he creaks."

"Come, come, it's too serious a matter for joking," said the Squire. "Now, my fine fellow, be cautious, be sober, be vigilant, and above all things be speedy."

Being furnished now with all requisite directions, and a supply of money, Israel, taking leave of Mr. Tooke and Mr. Bridges, was secretly conducted down stairs by the Squire, and in five minutes' time was on his way to Charing Cross in London, where taking the post-coach for Dover, he thence went in a packet to Calais, and in fifteen minutes after landing, was being wheeled over French soil towards Paris. He arrived there in safety, and freely declaring himself an American, the peculiarly friendly relations of the two nations at that period, procured him kindly attentions even from strangers.

7

*After a Curious Adventure upon the Pont Neuf,
Israel Enters the Presence of the Renowned Sage,
Dr. Franklin, Whom He Finds Right Learnedly and
Multifariously Employed*

Following the directions given him at the place where
the diligence stopped, Israel was crossing the Pont Neuf,
to find Doctor Franklin, when he was suddenly called to
by a man standing on one side of the bridge, just under
the equestrian statue of Henry IV.

The man had a small, shabby-looking box before him
on the ground, with a box of blacking on one side of it,
and several shoe-brushes upon the other. Holding another
brush in his hand, he politely seconded his verbal invitation by gracefully flourishing the brush in the air.

"What do you want of me, neighbor?" said Israel, pausing in somewhat uneasy astonishment.

"Ah, Monsieur," exclaimed the man, and with voluble
politeness he ran on with a long string of French, which
of course was all Greek to poor Israel. But what his
language failed to convey, his gestures now made very
plain. Pointing to the wet muddy state of the bridge,
splashed by a recent rain, and then to the feet of the way-
farer, and lastly to the brush in his hand, he appeared
to be deeply regretting that a gentleman of Israel's other-

wise imposing appearance should be seen abroad with unpolished boots, offering at the same time to remove their blemishes.

"Ah, Monsieur, Monsieur," cried the man, at last running up to Israel. And with tender violence he forced him towards the box, and lifting this unwilling customer's right foot thereon, was proceeding vigorously to work, when suddenly illuminated by a dreadful suspicion, Israel, fetching the box a terrible kick, took to his false heels and ran like mad over the bridge.

Incensed that his politeness should receive such an ungracious return, the man pursued, which but confirming Israel in his suspicions he ran all the faster, and thanks to his fleetness, soon succeeded in escaping his pursuer.

Arrived at last at the street and the house to which he had been directed, in reply to his summons, the gate very strangely of itself swung open, and much astonished at this unlooked-for sort of enchantment, Israel entered a wide vaulted passage leading to an open court within. While he was wondering that no soul appeared, suddenly he was hailed from a dark little window, where sat an old man cobbling shoes, while an old woman standing by his side was thrusting her head into the passage, intently eyeing the stranger. They proved to be the porter and portress, the latter of whom, upon hearing his summons, had invisibly thrust open the gate to Israel, by means of a spring communicating with the little apartment.

Upon hearing the name of Doctor Franklin mentioned, the old woman, all alacrity, hurried out of her den, and with much courtesy showed Israel across the court, up three flights of stairs to a door in the rear of the spacious building. There she left him while Israel knocked.

"Come in," said a voice.

And immediately Israel stood in the presence of the venerable Doctor Franklin.

Wrapped in a rich dressing-gown, a fanciful present from an admiring Marchesa, curiously embroidered with algebraic figures like a conjuror's robe, and with a skull-cap of black satin on his hive of a head, the man of gravity was seated at a huge claw-footed old table, round as the zodiac. It was covered with printed papers, files of documents, rolls of manuscripts, stray bits of strange models in wood and metal, odd-looking pamphlets in various languages, and all sorts of books, including many presentation-copies, embracing history, mechanics, diplomacy, agriculture, political economy, metaphysics, meteorology, and geometry. The walls had a necromantic look, hung round with barometers of different kinds, drawings of surprising inventions, wide maps of far countries in the New World, containing vast empty spaces in the middle, with the word DESERT diffusely printed there, so as to span five-and-twenty degrees of longitude with only two syllables,—which printed word, however, bore a vigorous pen-mark, in the Doctor's hand, drawn straight through it, as if in summary repeal of it; crowded topographical and trigonometrical charts of various parts of Europe; with geometrical diagrams, and endless other surprising hangings and upholstery of science.

The chamber itself bore evident marks of antiquity. One part of the rough-finished wall was sadly cracked, and covered with dust, looked dim and dark. But the aged inmate, though wrinkled as well, looked neat and hale. Both wall and sage were compounded of like materials,—lime and dust; both, too, were old; but while the rude earth of the wall had no painted lustre to shed off all fadings and tarnish, and still keep fresh without, though with long eld its core decayed: the living lime and dust of the sage was frescoed with defensive bloom of his soul.

The weather was warm; like some old West India hogshead on the wharf, the whole chamber buzzed with flies. But the sapient inmate sat still and cool in the midst. Absorbed in some other world of his occupations and thoughts, these insects, like daily cark and care, did not seem one whit to annoy him. It was a goodly sight to see this serene, cool and ripe old philosopher, who by sharp inquisition of man in the street, and then long meditating upon him, surrounded by all those queer old implements, charts and books, had grown at last so wondrous wise. There he sat, quite motionless among those restless flies; and, with a sound like the low noon murmur of foliage in the woods, turning over the leaves of some ancient and tattered folio, with a binding dark and shaggy as the bark of any old oak. It seemed as if supernatural lore must needs pertain to this gravely, ruddy personage; at least far foresight, pleasant wit, and working wisdom. Old age seemed in no wise to have dulled him, but to have sharpened; just as old dinner-knives—so they be of good steel— wax keen, spear-pointed, and elastic as whale-bone with long usage. Yet though he was thus lively and vigorous to behold, spite of his seventy-two years (his exact date at that time) somehow, the incredible seniority of an antediluvian seemed his. Not the years of the calendar wholly, but also the years of sapience. His white hairs and mild brow, spoke of the future as well as the past. He seemed to be seven score years old; that is, three score and ten of prescience added to three score and ten of remembrance, makes just seven score years in all.

But when Israel stepped within the chamber, he lost the complete effect of all this; for the sage's back, not his face, was turned to him.

So, intent on his errand, hurried and heated with his recent run, our courier entered the room, inadequately impressed, for the time, by either it or its occupant.

"Bon jour, bon jour, monsieur," said the man of wisdom, in a cheerful voice, but too busy to turn round just then.

"How do you do, Doctor Franklin?" said Israel.

"Ah! I smell Indian corn," said the Doctor, turning round quickly on his chair. "A countryman; sit down, my good sir. Well, what news? Special?"

"Wait a minute, sir," said Israel, stepping across the room towards a chair.

Now there was no carpet on the floor, which was of dark-colored wood, set in lozenges, and slippery with wax, after the usual French style. As Israel walked this slippery floor, his unaccustomed feet slid about very strangely as if walking on ice, so that he came very near falling.

" 'Pears to me you have rather high heels to your boots," said the grave man of utility, looking sharply down through his spectacles; "don't you know that it's both wasting leather and endangering your limbs, to wear such high heels? I have thought, at my first leisure, to write a little pamphlet against that very abuse. But pray, what are you doing now? Do your boots pinch you, my friend, that you lift one foot from the floor that way?"

At this moment, Israel having seated himself, was just putting his right foot across his left knee.

"How foolish," continued the wise man, "for a rational creature to wear tight boots. Had nature intended rational creatures should do so, she would have made the foot of solid bone, or perhaps of solid iron, instead of bone, muscle, and flesh.—But,—I see. Hold!"

And springing to his own slippered feet, the venerable sage hurried to the door and shot-to the bolt. Then drawing the curtain carefully across the window looking out across the court to various windows on the opposite side, bade Israel proceed with his operations.

"I was mistaken this time," added the Doctor, smiling, as Israel produced his documents from their curious recesses—"your high heels, instead of being idle vanities, seem to be full of meaning."

"Pretty full, Doctor," said Israel, now handing over the papers. "I had a narrow escape with them just now."

"How? How's that?" said the sage, fumbling the papers eagerly.

"Why, crossing the stone bridge there over the *Seen*—"

"*Seine*"—interrupted the Doctor, giving the French pronunciation.—"Always get a new word right in the first place, my friend, and you will never get it wrong afterwards."

"Well, I was crossing the bridge there, and who should hail me, but a suspicious-looking man, who, under pretence of seeking to polish my boots, wanted slyly to unscrew their heels, and so steal all these precious papers I've brought you."

"My good friend," said the man of gravity, glancing scrutinizingly upon his guest, "have you not in your time, undergone what they call hard times? Been set upon, and persecuted, and very illy entreated by some of your fellow-creatures?"

"That I have, Doctor; yes, indeed."

"I thought so. Sad usage has made you sadly suspicious, my honest friend. An indiscriminate distrust of human nature is the worst consequence of a miserable condition, whether brought about by innocence or guilt. And though want of suspicion more than want of sense, sometimes leads a man into harm, yet too much suspicion is as bad as too little sense. The man you met, my friend, most probably had no artful intention; he knew just nothing about you or your heels; he simply wanted to earn two sous by brushing your boots. Those blackingmen regularly station themselves on the bridge."

"How sorry I am then that I knocked over his box, and then ran away. But he didn't catch me."

"How? surely, my honest friend, you—appointed to the conveyance of important secret dispatches—did not act so imprudently as to kick over an innocent man's box in the public streets of the capital, to which you had been especially sent?"

"Yes, I did, Doctor."

"Never act so unwisely again. If the police had got hold of you, think of what might have ensued."

"Well, it was not very wise of me, that's a fact, Doctor. But, you see, I thought he meant mischief."

"And because you only thought he *meant* mischief, *you* must straightway proceed to *do* mischief. That's poor logic. But think over what I have told you now, while I look over these papers."

In half an hour's time, the Doctor, laying down the documents, again turned towards Israel, and removing his spectacles very placidly, proceeded in the kindest and most familiar manner to read him a paternal detailed lesson upon the ill-advised act he had been guilty of, upon the Pont Neuf; concluding by taking out his purse, and putting three small silver coins into Israel's hands, charging him to seek out the man that very day, and make both apology and restitution for his unlucky mistake.

"All of us, my honest friend," continued the Doctor, "are subject to making mistakes; so that the chief art of life, is to learn how best to remedy mistakes. Now one

63

remedy for mistakes is honesty. So pay the man for the damage done to his box. And now, who are you, my friend? My correspondents here mention your name—Israel Potter—and say you are an American, an escaped prisoner of war, but nothing further. I want to hear your story from your own lips."

Israel immediately began, and related to the Doctor all his adventures up to the present time.

"I suppose," said the Doctor, upon Israel's concluding, "that you desire to return to your friends across the sea?"

"That I do, Doctor," said Israel.

"Well, I think I shall be able to procure you a passage."

Israel's eyes sparkled with delight. The mild sage noticed it, and added: "But events in these times are uncertain. At the prospect of pleasure never be elated, but, without depression, respect the omens of ill. So much my life has taught me, my honest friend."

Israel felt as though a plum-pudding had been thrust under his nostrils, and then as rapidly withdrawn.

"I think it is probable that in two or three days I shall want you to return with some papers to the persons who sent you to me. In that case you will have to come here once more, and then, my good friend, we will see what can be done towards getting you safely home again."

Israel was pouring out torrents of thanks when the Doctor interrupted him.

"Gratitude, my friend, cannot be too much towards God, but towards man, it should be limited. No man can possibly so serve his fellow, as to merit unbounded gratitude. Overgratitude in the helped person, is apt to breed vanity or arrogance in the helping one. Now in assisting you to get home—if indeed I shall prove able to do so—I shall be simply doing part of my official duty as agent of our common country. So you owe me just nothing at all, but the sum of these coins I put in your hand just now. But that, instead of repaying to me hereafter, you can, when you get home, give to the first soldier's widow you meet. Don't forget it, for it is a debt, a pecuniary liability, owing to me. It will be about a quarter of a dollar, in the Yankee currency. A quarter of a dollar,

64

mind. My honest friend, in pecuniary matters always be exact as a second-hand; never mind with whom it is, father or stranger, peasant or king, be exact to a tick of your honor."

"Well, Doctor," said Israel, "since exactness in these matters is so necessary, let me pay back my debt in the very coins in which it was loaned. There will be no chance of mistake then. Thanks to my Brentford friends, I have enough to spare of my own, to settle damages with the boot-black of the bridge. I only took the money from you, because I thought it would not look well to push it back after being so kindly offered."

"My honest friend," said the Doctor, "I like your straightforward dealing. I will receive back the money."

"No interest, Doctor, I hope," said Israel.

The sage looked mildly over his spectacles upon Israel and replied: "My good friend, never permit yourself to be jocose upon pecuniary matters. Never joke at funerals, or during business transactions. The affair between us two, you perhaps deem very trivial, but trifles may involve momentous principles. But no more at present. You had better go immediately and find the boot-black. Having settled with him, return hither, and you will find a room ready for you near this, where you will stay during your sojourn in Paris."

"But I thought I would like to have a little look round the town, before I go back to England," said Israel.

"Business before pleasure, my friend. You must absolutely remain in your room, just as if you were my prisoner, until you quit Paris for Calais. Not knowing now at what instant I shall want you to start, your keeping to your room is indispensable. But when you come back from Brentford again, then, if nothing happens, you will have a chance to survey this celebrated capital ere taking ship for America. Now go directly, and pay the boot-black. Stop, have you the exact change ready? Don't be taking out all your money in the open street."

"Doctor," said Israel, "I am not so simple."

"But you knocked over the box."

"That, Doctor, was bravery."

"Bravery in a poor cause, is the height of simplicity, my friend.—Count out your change. It must be French coin, not English, that you are to pay the man with.— Ah, that will do—those three coins will be enough. Put them in a pocket separate from your other cash. Now go, and hasten to the bridge."

"Shall I stop to take a meal anywhere, Doctor, as I return? I saw several cookshops as I came hither."

"Cafés and restaurants, they are called here, my honest friend. Tell me, are you the possessor of a liberal fortune?"

"Not very liberal," said Israel.

"I thought as much. Where little wine is drunk, it is good to dine out occasionally at a friend's; but where a poor man dines out at his own charge, it is bad policy. Never dine out that way, when you can dine in. Do not stop on the way at all, my honest friend, but come directly back hither, and you shall dine at home, free of cost, with me."

"Thank you very kindly, Doctor."

And Israel departed for the Pont Neuf. Succeeding in his errand thither, he returned to Dr. Franklin, and found that worthy envoy waiting his attendance at a meal, which, according to the Doctor's custom, had been sent from a neighboring restaurant. There were two covers; and without attendance the host and guest sat down. There was only one principal dish, lamb boiled with green peas. Bread and potatoes made up the rest. A decanter-like bottle of uncolored glass, filled with some uncolored beverage, stood at the venerable envoy's elbow.

"Let me fill your glass," said the sage.

"It's white wine, ain't it?" said Israel.

"White wine of the very oldest brand; I drink your health in it, my honest friend."

"Why, it's plain water," said Israel, now tasting it.

"Plain water is a very good drink for plain men," replied the wise man.

"Yes," said Israel, "but Squire Woodcock gave me perry, and the other gentleman at White Waltham gave me port, and some other friends have given me brandy."

"Very good, my honest friend; if you like perry and

66

port and brandy, wait till you get back to Squire Woodcock, and the gentleman at White Waltham, and the other friends, and you shall drink perry and port and brandy. But while you are with me, you will drink plain water."

"So it seems, Doctor."

"What do you suppose a glass of port costs?"

"About three pence English, Doctor."

"That must be poor port. But how much good bread will three pence English purchase?"

"Three penny rolls, Doctor."

"How many glasses of port do you suppose a man may drink at a meal?"

"The gentleman at White Waltham drank a bottle at a dinner."

"A bottle contains just thirteen glasses—that's thirty-nine pence, supposing it poor wine. If something of the best, which is the only sort any sane man should drink, as being the least poisonous, it would be quadruple that sum, which is one hundred and fifty-six pence, which is seventy-eight two-penny loaves. Now, do you not think that for one man to swallow down seventy-eight two-penny rolls at one meal is rather extravagant business?"

"But he drank a bottle of wine; he did not eat seventy-eight two-penny rolls, Doctor."

"He drank the money worth of seventy-eight loaves, which is drinking the loaves themselves; for money is bread."

"But he has plenty of money to spare, Doctor."

"To have to spare, is to have to give away. Does the gentleman give much away?"

"Not that I know of, Doctor."

"Then he thinks he has nothing to spare; and thinking he has nothing to spare, and yet prodigally drinking down his money as he does every day, it seems to me that that gentleman stands self-contradicted, and therefore is no good example for plain sensible folks like you and me to follow. My honest friend, if you are poor, avoid wine as a costly luxury; if you are rich, shun it as a fatal indulgence. Stick to plain water. And now, my good friend, if you are through with your meal, we will rise. There is no pastry coming. Pastry is poisoned bread. Never eat pastry. Be a plain man, and stick to plain things. Now, my friend, I shall have to be private until nine o'clock in the evening, when I shall be again at your service. Meantime you may go to your room. I have ordered the one next to this to be prepared for you. But you must not be idle. Here is Poor Richard's Almanac, which, in view of our late conversation, I commend to your earnest perusal. And here, too, is a Guide to Paris, an English one, which you can read. Study it well, so that when you come back from England, if you should then have an opportunity to travel about Paris, to see its wonders, you will have all the chief places made historically familiar to you. In this world, men must provide knowledge before it is wanted, just as our countrymen in New England get in their winter's fuel one season, to serve them the next."

So saying, this homely sage, and household Plato, showed his humble guest to the door, and standing in the hall, pointed out to him the one which opened into his allotted apartment.

8

*Which Has Something to Say about Dr. Franklin
and the Latin Quarter*

The first, both in point of time and merit, of American
envoys was famous not less for the pastoral simplicity of
his manners than for the politic grace of his mind. Viewed
from a certain point, there was a touch of primeval ori-
entalness in Benjamin Franklin. Neither is there wanting
something like his Scriptural parallel. The history of the
patriarch Jacob is interesting not less from the unselfish
devotion which we are bound to ascribe to him, than from
the deep worldly wisdom and polished Italian tact,
gleaming under an air of Arcadian unaffectedness. The
diplomatist and the shepherd are blended; a union not
without warrant; the apostolic serpent and dove. A tanned
Machiavelli in tents.

Doubtless, too, notwithstanding his eminence as lord of
the moving manor, Jacob's raiment was of homespun;
the economic envoy's plain coat and hose, who has not
heard of?

Franklin all over is of a piece. He dressed his person
as his periods; neat, trim, nothing superfluous, nothing
deficient. In some of his works his style is only surpassed

by the unimprovable sentences of Hobbes of Malmsbury, the paragon of perspicuity. The mental habits of Hobbes and Franklin in several points, especially in one of some moment, assimilated. Indeed, making due allowance for soil and era, history presents few trios more akin, upon the whole, than Jacob, Hobbes, and Franklin; three labyrinth-minded, but plain-spoken Broadbrims, at once politicians and philosophers; keen observers of the main chance; prudent courtiers; practical magians in linsey-woolsey.

In keeping with his general habitudes, Doctor Franklin while at the French Court did not reside in the aristocratical faubourgs. He deemed his worsted hose and scientific tastes more adapted in a domestic way to the other side of the Seine, where the Latin Quarter, at once the haunt of erudition and economy, seemed peculiarly to invite the philosophical Poor Richard to its venerable retreats. Here, of gray, chilly, drizzly November mornings, in the dark-stoned quadrangle of the time-honored Sorbonne, walked the lean and slippered metaphysician,—oblivious for the moment that his sublime thoughts and tattered wardrobe were famous throughout Europe,—meditating on the theme of his next lecture; at the same time, in the well-worn chambers overhead, some clayey-visaged chemist in ragged robe-de-chambre, and with a soiled green flap over his left eye, was hard at work stooping over retorts and crucibles, discovering new antipathies in acids, again risking strange explosions similar to that whereby he had already lost the use of one optic; while in the lofty lodging-houses of the neighboring streets, indigent young students from all parts of France, were ironing their shabby cocked hats, or inking the whity seams of their small-clothes, prior to a promenade with their pink-ribboned little grisettes in the Garden of the Luxembourg.

Long ago the haunt of rank, the Latin Quarter still retains many old buildings whose imposing architecture singularly contrasts with the unassuming habits of their present occupants. In some parts its general air is dreary and dim; monastic and theurgic. In those lonely narrow ways—long-drawn prospectives of desertion—lined with huge piles of silent, vaulted, old iron-grated buildings of dark gray stone, one almost expects to encounter Paracelsus or Friar Bacon turning the next corner, with some awful vial of Black-Art elixir in his hand.

But all the lodging-houses are not so grim. Not to speak of many of comparatively modern erection, the others of the better class, however stern in exterior, evince a feminine gayety of taste, more or less, in their furnishings within. The embellishing, or softening, or screening hand of woman is to be seen all over the interiors of this metropolis. Like Augustus Cæsar with respect to Rome, the Frenchwoman leaves her obvious mark on Paris. Like the hand in nature, you know it can be none else but hers. Yet sometimes she overdoes it, as nature in the peony; or underdoes it, as nature in the bramble; or—what is still more frequent—is a little slatternly about it, as nature in the pig-weed.

In this congenial vicinity of the Latin Quarter, and in an ancient building something like those alluded to, at a point midway between the Palais des Beaux Arts and the College of the Sorbonne, the venerable American Envoy pitched his tent when not passing his time at his country retreat at Passy. The frugality of his manner of life did not lose him the good opinion even of the voluptuaries of the showiest of capitals, whose very iron railings are not free from gilt. Franklin was not less a lady's man, than a man's man, a wise man, and an old man. Not only did he enjoy the homage of the choicest Parisian literati, but at the age of seventy-two he was the caressed favorite of the highest born beauties of the Court; who through blind fashion having been originally attracted to him as a famous *savan,* were permanently retained as his admirers by his Plato-like graciousness of good humor. Having carefully weighed the world, Franklin could act any part in it. By nature turned to knowledge, his mind was often grave, but never serious. At times he had seriousness—extreme seriousness—for others, but never for himself. Tranquillity was to him instead of it. This philosophical levity of tranquillity, so to speak, is shown in his

71

easy variety of pursuits. Printer, postmaster, almanac maker, essayist, chemist, orator, tinker, statesman, humorist, philosopher, parlor man, political economist, professor of housewifery, ambassador, projector, maxim-monger, herb-doctor, wit:—Jack of all trades, master of each and mastered by none—the type and genius of his land. Franklin was everything but a poet. But since a soul with many qualities, forming of itself a sort of handy index and pocket congress of all humanity, needs the contact of just as many different men, or subjects, in order to the exhibition of its totality; hence very little indeed of the sage's multifariousness will be portrayed in a simple narrative like the present. This casual private intercourse with Israel, but served to manifest him in his far lesser lights; thrifty, domestic, dietarian, and, it may be, didactically waggish. There was much benevolent irony, innocent mischievousness, in the wise man. Seeking here to depict him in his less exalted habitudes, the narrator feels more as if he were playing with one of the sage's worsted hose, than reverentially handling the honored hat which once oracularly sat upon his brow.

So, then, in the Latin Quarter lived Doctor Franklin. And accordingly in the Latin Quarter tarried Israel for the time. And it was into a room of a house in this same Latin Quarter that Israel had been directed when the sage had requested privacy for a while.

9

*Israel Is Initiated into the Mysteries of
Lodging-Houses in the Latin Quarter*

Closing the door upon himself, Israel advanced to the middle of the chamber, and looked curiously round him.

A dark tessellated floor, but without a rug; two mahogany chairs, with embroidered seats, rather the worse for wear; one mahogany bed, with a gay but tarnished counterpane; a marble wash-stand, cracked, with a china vessel of water, minus the handle. The apartment was very large; this part of the house, which was a very extensive one, embracing the four sides of a quadrangle, having, in a former age, been the hotel of a nobleman. The magnitude of the chamber made its stinted furniture look meagre enough.

But in Israel's eyes, the marble mantel (a comparatively recent addition) and its appurtenances, not only redeemed the rest, but looked quite magnificent and hospitable in the extreme. Because, in the first place, the mantel was graced with an enormous old-fashioned square mirror, of heavy plate glass, set fast, like a tablet, into the wall. And in this mirror was genially reflected the following delicate articles:—first, two bouquets of flowers inserted in pretty vases of porcelain; second, one cake of white soap; third, one cake of rose-colored soap (both cakes very fragrant); fourth, one wax candle; fifth, one china tinder-box; sixth, one bottle of Eau de Cologne; seventh, one paper of loaf sugar, nicely broken into sugar-bowl size; eighth, one silver teaspoon; ninth, one glass tumbler; tenth, one glass decanter of cool pure water; eleventh, one sealed bottle containing a richly hued liquid, and marked "Otard."

"I wonder now what O-t-a-r-d is?" soliloquised Israel, slowly spelling the word. "I have a good mind to step in and ask Dr. Franklin. He knows everything. Let me smell it. No, it's sealed; smell is locked in. Those are pretty flowers. Let's smell them: no smell again. Ah, I see—sort of flowers in women's bonnets—sort of calico flowers. Beautiful soap. This smells anyhow—regular soap-roses —a white rose and a red one. That long-necked bottle there looks like a crane. I wonder what's in that? Hallo! E-a-u—d-e—C-o-l-o-g-n-e. I wonder if Dr. Franklin understands that? It looks like his white wine. This is nice sugar. Let's taste. Yes, this is very nice sugar, sweet as— yes, it's sweet as sugar; better than maple sugar, such as they make at home. But I'm crunching it too loud, the Doctor will hear me. But here's a teaspoon. What's this for? There's no tea, nor tea-cup; but here's a tumbler, and here's drinking water. Let me see. Seems to me, putting this and that and the other thing together, it's a sort of alphabet that spells something. Spoon, tumbler, water, sugar,—— brandy—that's it. O-t-a-r-d is brandy. Who put these things here? What does it all mean? Don't put sugar here for show, don't put a spoon here for ornament, nor a jug of water. There is only one meaning to it, and that is a very polite invitation from some invisible person to help myself, if I like, to a glass of brandy and sugar, and if I don't like, let it alone. That's my reading. I have a good mind to ask Dr. Franklin about it, though, for there's just a chance I may be mistaken, and these things here be some other person's private property, not at all meant for me to help myself from. Co-logne, what's that— never mind. Soap: soap's to wash with. I want to use

74

soap, anyway. Let me see—no, there's no soap on the wash-stand. I see, soap is not given gratis here in Paris, to boarders. But if you want it, take it from the marble, and it will be charged in the bill. If you don't want it let it alone, and no charge. Well, that's fair, anyway. But then to a man who could not afford to use soap, such beautiful cakes as these lying before his eyes all the time, would be a strong temptation. And now that I think of it, the O-t-a-r-d looks rather tempting too. But if I don't like it now, I can let it alone. I've a good mind to try it. But it's sealed. I wonder now if I am right in my understanding of this alphabet? Who knows? I'll venture one little sip, anyhow. Come, cork. Hark!"

There was a rapid knock at the door.

Clapping down the bottle, Israel said, "Come in."

It was the man of wisdom.

"My honest friend," said the Doctor, stepping with venerable briskness into the room, "I was so busy during your visit to the Pont Neuf, that I did not have time to see that your room was all right. I merely gave the order, and heard that it had been fulfilled. But it just occurred to me, that as the landladies of Paris have some curious customs which might puzzle an entire stranger, my presence here for a moment might explain any little obscurity. Yes, it is as I thought," glancing towards the mantel.

"Oh, Doctor, that reminds me; what is O-t-a-r-d, pray?"

"Otard is poison."

"Shocking."

"Yes, and I think I had best remove it from the room forthwith," replied the sage, in a business-like manner putting the bottle under his arm; "I hope you never use Cologne, do you?"

"What—what is that, Doctor?"

"I see. You never heard of the senseless luxury—a wise ignorance. You smelt flowers upon your mountains. You won't want this, either;" and the Cologne bottle was put under the other arm. "Candle—you'll want that. Soap—you want soap. Use the white cake."

"Is that cheaper, Doctor?"

"Yes, but just as good as the other. You don't ever

munch sugar, do you? It's bad for the teeth. I'll take the sugar." So the paper of sugar was likewise dropped into one of the capacious coat pockets.

"Oh, you better take the whole furniture, Doctor Franklin. Here, I'll help you drag out the bedstead."

"My honest friend," said the wise man, pausing solemnly, with the two bottles, like swimmer's bladders, under his arm-pits; "my honest friend, the bedstead you will want; what I propose to remove you will not want."

"Oh, I was only joking, Doctor."

"I knew that. It's a bad habit, except at the proper time, and with the proper person. The things left on the mantel were there placed by the landlady to be used if wanted; if not, to be left untouched. To-morrow morning, upon the chambermaid's coming in to make your bed, all such articles as remained obviously untouched would have been removed, the rest would have been charged in the bill, whether you used them up completely or not."

"Just as I thought. Then why not let the bottles stay, Doctor, and save yourself all this trouble?"

"Ah! Why indeed. My honest friend, are you not my guest? It were unhandsome in me to permit a third person superfluously to entertain you under what, for the time being, is my own roof."

These words came from the wise man in the most graciously bland and flowing tones. As he ended, he made a sort of conciliatory half bow towards Israel.

Charmed with his condescending affability, Israel, without another word, suffered him to march from the room, bottles and all. Not till the first impression of the venerable envoy's suavity had left him, did Israel begin to surmise the mild superiority of successful strategy which lurked beneath this highly ingratiating air.

"Ah," pondered Israel, sitting gloomily before the rifled mantel, with the empty tumbler and teaspoon in his hand, "it's sad business to have a Doctor Franklin lodging in the next room. I wonder if he sees to all the boarders this way. How the O-t-a-r-d merchants must hate him, and the pastry-cooks too. I wish I had a good pie to pass the time. I wonder if they ever make pumpkin pies in

Paris? So I've got to stay in this room all the time. Somehow I'm bound to be a prisoner, one way or another. Never mind, I'm an ambassador; that's satisfaction. Hark! The Doctor again.—Come in."

No venerable doctor, but in tripped a young French lass, bloom on her cheek, pink ribbons in her cap, liveliness in all her air, grace in the very tips of her elbows. The most bewitching little chambermaid in Paris. All art, but the picture of artlessness.

"Monsieur! pardon!"

"Oh, I pardong ye freely," said Israel. "Come to call on the Ambassador?"

"Monsieur, is de—de—" but, breaking down at the very threshold in her English, she poured out a long ribbon of sparkling French, the purpose of which was to convey a profusion of fine compliments to the stranger, with many tender inquiries as to whether he was comfortably roomed, and whether there might not be something, however trifling, wanting to his complete accommodation. But Israel understood nothing, at the time, but the exceeding grace, and trim, bewitching figure of the girl.

She stood eyeing him for a few moments more, with a look of pretty theatrical despair, and, after vaguely lingering a while, with another shower of incomprehensible compliments and apologies, tripped like a fairy from the chamber. Directly she was gone Israel pondered upon a singular glance of the girl. It seemed to him that he had, by his reception, in some way, unaccountably disappointed his beautiful visitor. It struck him very strangely that she had entered all sweetness and friendliness, but had retired as if slighted, with a sort of disdainful and sarcastic levity, all the more stinging from its apparent politeness.

Not long had she disappeared, when a noise in the passage apprised him that, in her hurried retreat, the girl must have stumbled against something. The next moment he heard a chair scraping in the adjacent apartment, and there was another knock at the door.

It was the man of wisdom this time.

"My honest friend, did you not have a visitor, just now?"

77

"Yes, Doctor, a very pretty girl called upon me."

"Well, I just stopped in to tell you of another strange custom of Paris. That girl is the chambermaid, but she does not confine herself altogether to one vocation. You must beware of the chambermaids of Paris, my honest friend. Shall I tell the girl, from you, that, unwilling to give her the fatigue of going up and down so many flights of stairs, you will for the future waive her visits of ceremony?"

"Why, Doctor Franklin, she is a very sweet little girl."

"I know it, my honest friend; the sweeter the more dangerous. Arsenic is sweeter than sugar. I know you are a very sensible young man, not to be taken in by an artful Ammonite, and so I think I had better convey your message to the girl forthwith."

So saying, the sage withdrew, leaving Israel once more gloomily seated before the rifled mantel, whose mirror was not again to reflect the form of the charming chambermaid.

"Every time he comes in he robs me," soliloquised Israel, dolefully; "with an air all the time, too, as if he were making me presents. If he thinks me such a very sensible young man, why not let me take care of myself?"

It was growing dusk, and Israel, lighting the wax candle, proceeded to read in his Guide-book.

"This is poor sight-seeing," muttered he at last, "sitting here all by myself, with no company but an empty tumbler, reading about the fine things in Paris, and I myself a prisoner in Paris. I wish something extraordinary would turn up now; for instance, a man come in and give me ten thousand pounds. But here's 'Poor Richard'; I am a poor fellow myself; so let's see what comfort he has for a comrade."

Opening the little pamphlet, at random, Israel's eyes fell on the following passages: he read them aloud—

" *'So what signifies waiting and hoping for better times? We may make these times better, if we bestir ourselves. Industry need not wish, and he that lives upon hope will die fasting, as Poor Richard says. There are no gains, without pains. Then help hands, for I have no lands, as Poor Richard says.'* Oh, confound all this wisdom! It's a sort of insulting to talk wisdom to a man like me. It's wisdom that's cheap, and it's fortune that's dear. That ain't in Poor Richard; but it ought to be," concluded Israel, suddenly slamming down the pamphlet.

He walked across the room, looked at the artificial flowers, and the rose-colored soap, and again went to the table and took up the two books.

"So here is the 'Way to Wealth,' and here is the 'Guide to Paris.' Wonder now whether Paris lies on the Way to Wealth? if so, I am on the road. More likely though, it's a parting-of-the-ways. I shouldn't be surprised if the Doctor meant something sly by putting these two books in my hand. Somehow, the old gentleman has an amazing sly look—a sort of wild slyness—about him, seems to me. His wisdom seems a sort of sly, too. But all in honor, though. I rather think he's one of those old gentlemen who say a vast deal of sense, but hint a world more. Depend upon it, he's sly, sly, sly. Ah, what's this Poor Richard says: 'God helps them that help themselves.' Let's consider that. Poor Richard ain't a Dunker, that's certain, though he has lived in Pennsylvania. 'God helps them that help themselves.' I'll just mark that saw, and leave the pamphlet open to refer to it again—Ah!"

At this point, the Doctor knocked, summoning Israel to his own apartment. Here, after a cup of weak tea, and a little toast, the two had a long, familiar talk together; during which, Israel was delighted with the unpretending talkativeness, serene insight, and benign amiability of the sage. But, for all this, he could hardly forgive him for the Cologne and Otard depredations.

Discovering that, in early life, Israel had been employed on a farm, the man of wisdom at length turned the conversation in that direction; among other things, mentioning to his guest a plan of his (the Doctor's) for yoking oxen, with a yoke to go by a spring instead of a bolt; thus greatly facilitating the operation of hitching on the team to the cart. Israel was very much struck with the improvement; and thought that, if he were home, upon his mountains, he would immediately introduce it among the farmers.

10

*Another Adventurer
Appears upon the Scene*

About half-past ten o'clock, as they were thus conversing, Israel's acquaintance, the pretty chambermaid, rapped at the door, saying, with a titter, that a very rude gentleman in the passage of the court, desired to see Doctor Franklin.

"A very rude gentleman?" repeated the wise man in French, narrowly looking at the girl; "that means, a very fine gentleman who has just paid you some energetic compliment. But let him come up, my girl," he added patriarchially.

In a few moments, a swift coquettish step was heard, followed, as if in chase, by a sharp and manly one. The door opened. Israel was sitting so that, accidentally, his eye pierced the crevice made by the opening of the door, which, like a theatrical screen, stood for a moment between Doctor Franklin and the just entering visitor. And behind that screen, through the crack, Israel caught one momentary glimpse of a little bit of by-play between the pretty chambermaid and the stranger. The vivacious nymph appeared to have affectedly run from him on the stairs—doubtless in freakish return for some liberal advances—

but had suffered herself to be overtaken at last ere too late; and on the instant Israel caught sight of her, was with an insincere air of rosy resentment, receiving a roguish pinch on the arm, and a still more roguish salute on the cheek.

The next instant both disappeared from the range of the crevice; the girl departing whence she had come; the stranger—transiently invisible as he advanced behind the door—entering the room. When Israel now perceived him again, he seemed, while momentarily hidden, to have undergone a complete transformation.

He was a rather small, elastic, swarthy man, with an aspect as of a disinherited Indian Chief in European clothes. An unvanquishable enthusiasm, intensified to perfect sobriety, couched in his savage, self-possessed eye. He was elegantly and somewhat extravagantly dressed as a civilian; he carried himself with a rustic, barbaric jauntiness, strangely dashed with a superinduced touch of the Parisian *salon*. His tawny cheek, like a date, spoke of the tropic. A wonderful atmosphere of proud friendlessness and scornful isolation invested him. Yet there was a bit of the poet as well as the outlaw in him, too. A cool solemnity of intrepidity sat on his lip. He looked like one who of purpose sought out harm's way. He looked like one who never had been, and never would be, a subordinate.

Israel thought to himself that seldom before had he seen such a being. Though dressed à-la-mode, he did not seem to be altogether civilized.

So absorbed was our adventurer by the person of the stranger, that a few moments passed ere he began to be aware of the circumstance, that Dr. Franklin and this new visitor having saluted as old acquaintances, were now sitting in earnest conversation together.

"Do as you please; but I will not bide a suitor much longer," said the stranger in bitterness. "Congress gave me to understand that, upon my arrival here, I should be given immediate command of the *Indien;* and now, for no earthly reason that I can see, you Commissioners have presented her, fresh from the stocks at Amsterdam, to the King of France, and not to me. What does the King of

France with such a frigate? And what can I *not* do with her? Give me back the *Indien,* and in less than one month, you shall hear glorious or fatal news of Paul Jones."

"Come, come, Captain," said Doctor Franklin, soothingly, "tell me now, what would you do with her, if you had her?"

"I would teach the British that Paul Jones, though born in Britain, is no subject to the British King, but an untrammelled citizen and sailor of the universe; and I would teach them, too, that if they ruthlessly ravage the American coasts, their own coasts are vulnerable as New Holland's. Give me the *Indien,* and I will rain down on wicked England like fire on Sodom."

These words of bravado were not spoken in the tone of a bravo, but a prophet. Erect upon his chair, like an Iroquois, the speaker's look was like that of an unflickering torch.

His air seemed slightly to disturb the old sage's philosophic repose, who, while not seeking to disguise his admiration of the unmistakable spirit of the man, seemed but illy to relish his apparent measureless boasting.

As if both to change the subject a little, as well as put his visitor in better mood—though indeed it might have been but covertly to play with his enthusiasm—the man of wisdom now drew his chair confidentially nearer to the stranger's, and putting one hand in a very friendly, conciliatory way upon his visitor's knee, and rubbing it gentle to and fro there, much as a lion-tamer might soothingly manipulate the aggravated king of beasts, said in a winning manner:—"Never mind at present, Captain, about the *Indien* affair. Let that sleep a moment. See now, the Jersey privateers do us a great deal of mischief by intercepting our supplies. It has been mentioned to me, that if you had a small vessel—say, even your present ship, the Amphitrite,—then, by your singular bravery, you might render great service, by following those privateers where larger ships durst not venture their bottoms; or, if but supported by some frigates from Brest at a proper distance, might draw them out, so that the larger vessels could capture them."

"Decoy-duck to French frigates!—Very dignified office, truly!" hissed Paul in a fiery rage. "Doctor Franklin, whatever Paul Jones does for the cause of America, it must be done through unlimited orders: a separate, supreme command; no leader and no counsellor but himself. Have I not already by my services on the American coast shown that I am well worthy all this? Why then do you seek to degrade me below my previous level? I will mount, not sink. I live but for honor and glory. Give me, then, something honorable and glorious to do, and something famous to do it with. Give me the *Indien*."

The man of wisdom slowly shook his head. "Everything is lost through this shillyshallying timidity, called prudence," cried Paul Jones, starting to his feet; "to be effectual, war should be carried on like a monsoon, one changeless determination of every particle towards the one unalterable aim. But in vacillating councils, statesmen idle about like the cats'-paws in calms. My God, why was I not born a Czar!"

"A Nor'wester, rather. Come, come, Captain," added the sage, "sit down, we have a third person present, you see," pointing towards Israel, who sat rapt at the volcanic spirit of the stranger.

Paul slightly started, and turned inquiringly upon Israel, who, equally owing to Paul's own earnestness of discourse and Israel's motionless bearing, had thus far remained undiscovered.

"Never fear, Captain," said the sage, "this man is true blue, a secret courier, and an American born. He is an escaped prisoner of war."

"Ah, captured in a ship?" asked Paul eagerly; "what ship? None of mine! Paul Jones never was captured."

"No, sir, in the brigantine Washington, out of Boston," replied Israel; "we were cruising to cut off supplies to the English."

"Did your shipmates talk much of me?" demanded Paul, with a look as of a parading Sioux demanding homage to his gewgaws; "what did they say of Paul Jones?"

"I never heard the name before this evening," said Israel.

"What? Ah—brigantine Washington—let me see; that

was before I had outwitted the Soleby frigate, fought the Milford, and captured the Mellish and the rest off Louisbergh. You were long before the news, my lad," he added, with a sort of compassionate air.

"Our friend here gave you a rather blunt answer," said the wise man, sagely mischievous, and addressing Paul.

"Yes. And I like him for it. My man, will you go a cruise with Paul Jones? You fellows so blunt with the tongue, are apt to be sharp with the steel. Come, my lad, return with me to Brest. I go in a few days."

Fired by the contagious spirit of Paul, Israel, forgetting all about his previous desire to reach home, sparkled with response to the summons. But Doctor Franklin interrupted him.

"Our friend here," said he to the Captain, "is at present engaged for very different duty."

Much other conversation followed, during which Paul Jones again and again expressed his impatience at being unemployed, and his resolution to accept of no employ unless it gave him supreme authority; while in answer to all this Dr. Franklin, not uninfluenced by the uncompromising spirit of his guest, and well knowing that however unpleasant a trait in conversation, or in the transaction of civil affairs, yet in war this very quality was invaluable, as projectiles and combustibles, finally assured Paul, after many complimentary remarks, that he would immediately exert himself to the utmost to procure for him some enterprise which should come up to his merits.

"Thank you for your frankness," said Paul; "frank myself, I love to deal with a frank man. You, Doctor Franklin, are true and deep, and so you are frank."

The sage sedately smiled, a queer incredulity just lurking in the corner of his mouth.

"But how about our little scheme for new modelling ships-of-war?" said the Doctor, shifting the subject; "it will be a great thing for our infant navy, if we succeed. Since our last conversation on that subject, Captain, at odds and ends of time, I have thought over the matter, and have begun a little skeleton of the thing here, which I will show you. Whenever one has a new idea of any thing mechanical, it is best to clothe it with a body as soon as possible. For you can't improve so well on ideas as you can on bodies."

With that, going to a little drawer, he produced a small basket, filled with a curious looking unfinished frame-work of wood, and several bits of wood unattached. It looked like a nursery basket containing broken odds and ends of playthings.

"Now look here, Captain, though the thing is but begun at present, yet there is enough to show that *one* idea at least of yours is not feasible."

Paul was all attention, as if having unbounded confidence in whatever the sage might suggest, while Israel looked on quite as interested as either, his heart swelling with the thought of being privy to the consultations of two such men; consultations, too, having ultimate reference to such momentous affairs as the freeing of nations.

"If," continued the Doctor, taking up some of the loose bits and piling them along on one side of the top of the frame, "if the better to shelter your crew in an engagement, you construct your rail in the manner proposed—as thus—then, by the excessive weight of the timber, you will too much interfere with the ship's centre of gravity. You will have that too high."

"Ballast in the hold in proportion," said Paul.

"Then you will sink the whole hull too low. But here, to have less smoke in time of battle, especially on the lower decks, you proposed a new sort of hatchway. But that won't do. See here now, I have invented certain ventilating pipes, they are to traverse the vessel thus"— laying some toilette pins along—"the current of air to enter here and be discharged there. What do you think of that? But now about the main things—fast sailing driving little to leeward, and drawing little water. Look now at this keel. I whittled it only night before last, just before going to bed. Do you see now how"—

At this crisis, a knock was heard at the door, and the chambermaid reappeared, announcing that two gentlemen were that moment crossing the court below to see Doctor Franklin.

85

"The Duke de Chartres, and Count D'Estang," said the Doctor; "they appointed for last night, but did not come. Captain, this has something indirectly to do with your affair. Through the Duke, Count D'Estang has spoken to the King about the secret expedition, the design of which you first threw out. Call early to-morrow, and I will inform you of the result."

With his tawny hand Paul pulled out his watch, a small, richly-jeweled lady's watch.

"It is so late, I will stay here to-night," he said; "is there a convenient room?"

"Quick," said the Doctor, "it might be ill-advised of you to be seen with me just now. Our friend here will let you share his chamber. Quick, Israel, and show the Captain thither."

As the door closed upon them in Israel's apartment, Doctor Franklin's door closed upon the Duke and the Count. Leaving the latter to their discussion of profound plans for the timely befriending of the American cause, and the crippling of the power of England on the seas, let us pass the night with Paul Jones and Israel in the neighboring room.

11

Paul Jones in a Reverie

" 'God helps them that help themselves.' That's a clincher. That's been my experience. But I never saw it in words before. What pamphlet is this? 'Poor Richard,' hey!"

Upon entering Israel's room, Captain Paul, stepping towards the table and spying the open pamphlet there, had taken it up, his eye being immediately attracted to the passage previously marked by our adventurer.

"A rare old gentleman is 'Poor Richard,' " said Israel in response to Paul's observations.

"So he seems, so he seems," answered Paul, his eye still running over the pamphlet again; "why, 'Poor Richard' reads very much as Doctor Franklin speaks."

"He wrote it," said Israel.

"Aye? Good. So it is, so it is; it's the wise man all over. I must get me a copy of this and wear it around my neck for a charm. And now about our quarters for the night. I am not going to deprive you of your bed, my man. Do you go to bed and I will doze in the chair here. It's good dozing in the crosstrees."

"Why not sleep together?" said Israel; "see, it is a big

bed. Or perhaps you don't fancy your bed-fellow, Captain?"

"When, before the mast, I first sailed out of Whitehaven to Norway," said Paul, coolly, "I had for hammockmate a full-blooded Congo. We had a white blanket spread in our hammock. Every time I turned in I found the Congo's black wool worked in with the white worsted. By the end of the voyage the blanket was of a pepper-and-salt look, like an old man's turning head. So it's not because I am notional at all, but because I don't care to, my lad. Turn in and go to sleep. Let the lamp burn. I'll see to it. There, go to sleep."

Complying with what seemed as much a command as a request, Israel, though in bed, could not fall into slumber for thinking of the little circumstance that this strange swarthy man, flaming with wild enterprises, sat in full suit in the chair. He felt an uneasy misgiving sensation, as if he had retired, not only without covering up the fire, but leaving it fiercely burning with spitting fagots of hemlock.

But his natural complaisance induced him at least to feign himself asleep; whereupon Paul, laying down "Poor Richard," rose from his chair, and, withdrawing his boots, began walking rapidly but noiselessly to and fro, in his stockings, in the spacious room, wrapped in Indian meditations. Israel furtively eyed him from beneath the coverlid, and was anew struck by his aspect, now that Paul thought himself unwatched. Stern relentless purposes, to be pursued to the points of adverse bayonets and the muzzles of hostile cannon, were expressed in the now rigid lines of his brow. His ruffled right hand was clutched by his side, as if grasping a cutlass. He paced the room as if advancing upon a fortification. Meantime a confused buzz of discussion came from the neighboring chamber. All else was profound midnight tranquillity. Presently, passing the large mirror over the mantel, Paul caught a glimpse of his person. He paused, grimly regarding it, while a dash of pleased coxcombry seemed to mingle with the otherwise savage satisfaction expressed in his face. But the latter predominated. Soon, rolling up his sleeve, with a queer wild smile, Paul lifted his right arm, and stood thus for an interval, eyeing its image in the glass. From where he lay, Israel could not see that side of the arm presented to the mirror, but he saw its reflection, and started at perceiving there, framed in the carved and gilded wood, certain large intertwisted ciphers covering the whole inside of the arm, so far as exposed, with mysterious tattooings. The design was wholly unlike the fanciful figures of anchors, hearts, and cables, sometimes decorating small portions of seamen's bodies. It was a sort of tattooing such as is seen only on thorough-bred savages—deep blue, elaborate, labyrinthine, cabalistic. Israel remembered having beheld, on one of his early voyages, something similar on the arm of a New Zealand warrior, once met, fresh from battle, in his native village. He concluded that on some similar early voyage Paul must have undergone the manipulations of some pagan artist.

Covering his arm again with his laced coat-sleeve, Paul glanced ironically at the hand of the same arm, now again half muffled in ruffles, and ornamented with several Parisian rings. He then resumed his walking with a prowling air, like one haunting an ambuscade; while a gleam of the consciousness of possessing a character as yet unfathomed, and hidden power to back unsuspected projects, irradiated his cold white brow, which, owing to the shade of his hat in equatorial climates, had been left surmounting his swarthy face, like the snow topping the Andes.

So at midnight, the heart of the metropolis of modern civilization was secretly trod by this jaunty barbarian in broadcloth; a sort of prophetical ghost, glimmering in anticipation upon the advent of those tragic scenes of the French Revolution which levelled the exquisite refinement of Paris with the bloodthirsty ferocity of Borneo; showing that broaches and finger-rings, not less than nose-rings and tattooing, are tokens of the primeval savageness which ever slumbers in human kind, civilized or uncivilized.

Israel slept not a wink that night. The troubled spirit of Paul paced the chamber till morning; when, copiously bathing himself at the wash-stand, Paul looked care-free and fresh as a day-break hawk. After a closeted consultation with Doctor Franklin, he left the place with a light and dandified air, switching his gold-headed cane, and throwing a passing arm round all the pretty chambermaids he encountered, kissing them resoundingly, as if saluting a frigate. All barbarians are rakes.

12

*Recrossing the Channel, Israel Returns to the
Squire's Abode—His Adventures There*

On the third day, as Israel was walking to and fro in
his room, having removed his courier's boots, for fear of
disturbing the Doctor, a quick sharp rap at the door
announced the American envoy. The man of wisdom
entered, with two small wads of paper in one hand, and
several crackers and a bit of cheese in the other. There
was such an eloquent air of instantaneous dispatch about
him, that Israel involuntarily sprang to his boots, and,
with two vigorous jerks, hauled them on, and then seizing
his hat, like any bird, stood poised for his flight across
the channel.

"Well done, my honest friend," said the Doctor; "you
have the papers in your heel, I suppose."

"Ah," exclaimed Israel, perceiving the mild irony; and
in an instant his boots were off again; when, without
another word, the Doctor took one boot, and Israel the
other, and forthwith both parties proceeded to secrete
the documents.

"I think I could improve the design," said the sage,
as, notwithstanding his haste, he critically eyed the screw-

ing apparatus of the boot. "The vacancy should have been in the standing part of the heel, not in the lid. It should go with a spring, too, for better dispatch. I'll draw up a paper on false heels one of these days, and send it to a private reading at the Institute. But no time for it now. My honest friend, it is now half-past ten o'clock. At half-past eleven the diligence starts from the Place-du-Carrousel for Calais. Make all haste till you arrive at Brentford. I have a little provender here for you to eat in the diligence, as you will not have time for a regular meal. A day-and-night courier should never be without a cracker in his pocket. You will probably leave Brentford in a day or two after your arrival there. Be wary, now, my good friend; heed well, that, if you are caught with these papers on British ground, you will involve both yourself and our Brentford friends in fatal calamities. Kick no man's box, never mind whose, in the way. Mind your own box. You can't be too cautious, but don't be too suspicious. God bless you, my honest friend. Go!"

And, flinging the door open for his exit, the Doctor saw Israel dart into the entry, vigorously spring down the stairs, and disappear with all celerity across the court into the vaulted way.

The man of wisdom stood mildly motionless a moment, with a look of sagacious, humane meditation on his face, as if pondering upon the chances of the important enterprise: one which, perhaps, might in the sequel affect the weal or woe of nations yet to come. Then suddenly clapping his hand to his capacious coat-pocket, dragged out a bit of cork with some hen's feathers, and hurrying to his room, took out his knife, and proceeded to whittle away at a shuttlecock of an original scientific construction, which at some prior time he had promised to send to the young Duchess D'Abrantes that very afternoon.

Safely reaching Calais, at night, Israel stepped almost from the diligence into the packet, and, in a few moments, was cutting the water. As on the diligence he took an outside and plebian seat, so, with the same secret motive of preserving unsuspected the character assumed, he took a deck passage in the packet. It coming on to rain violently, he stole down into the forecastle, dimly lit by a solitary swinging lamp, where were two men industriously smoking, and filling the narrow hole with soporific vapors. These induced strange drowsiness in Israel, and he pondered how best he might indulge it, for a time, without imperilling the precious documents in his custody.

But this pondering in such soporific vapors had the effect of those mathematical devices whereby restless people cipher themselves to sleep. His languid head fell to his breast. In another moment, he drooped half-lengthwise upon a chest, his legs outstretched before him.

Presently he was awakened by some intermeddlement with his feet. Starting to his elbow, he saw one of the two men in the act of slyly slipping off his right boot, while the left one, already removed, lay on the floor, all ready against the rascal's retreat. Had it not been for the lesson learned on the Pont Neuf, Israel would instantly have inferred that his secret mission was known, and the operator some designed diplomatic knave or other, hired by the British Cabinet, thus to lie in wait for him, fume him into slumber with tobacco, and then rifle him of his momentous dispatches. But as it was, he recalled Doctor Franklin's prudent admonitions against the indulgence of premature suspicions.

"Sir," said Israel very civilly, "I will thank you for that boot which lies on the floor, and, if you please, you can let the other stay where it is."

"Excuse me," said the rascal, an accomplished, self-possessed practitioner in his thievish art; "I thought your boots might be pinching you, and only wished to ease you a little."

"Much obliged to ye for your kindness, sir," said Israel; "but they don't pinch me at all. I suppose, though, you think they wouldn't pinch *you* either; your foot looks rather small. Were you going to try 'em on, just to see how they fitted?"

"No," said the fellow, with sanctimonious seriousness; "but with your permission I should like to try them on, when we get to Dover. I couldn't try them well walking on this tipsy craft's deck, you know."

"No," answered Israel, "and the beach at Dover ain't very smooth either. I guess, upon second thought, you had better not try 'em on at all. Besides, I am a simple sort of a soul—eccentric they call me—and don't like my boots to go out of my sight. Ha! ha!"

"What are you laughing at?" said the fellow testily.

"Odd idea! I was just looking at those sad old patched boots there on your feet, and thinking to myself what leaky fire-buckets they would be to pass up a ladder on a burning building. It would hardly be fair now to swap my new boots for those old fire-buckets, would it?"

"By plunko!" cried the fellow, willing now by a bold stroke to change the subject, which was growing slightly annoying; "by plunko, I believe we are getting nigh Dover. Let's see."

And so saying, he sprang up the ladder to the deck. Upon Israel following, he found the little craft half becalmed, rolling on short swells almost in the exact middle of the channel. It was just before break of the morning; the air clear and fine; the heavens spangled with moistly twinkling stars. The French and English coasts lay distinctly visible in the strange starlight, the white cliffs of Dover resembling a long gabled block of marble houses. Both shores showed a long straight row of lamps. Israel seemed standing in the middle of the crossing of some wide stately street in London. Presently a breeze sprang up, and ere long our adventurer disembarked at his destined port, and directly posted on for Brentford.

The following afternoon, having gained unobserved admittance into the house, according to preconcerted signals, he was sitting in Squire Woodcock's closet, pulling off his boots and delivering his dispatches.

Having looked over the compressed tissuey sheets, and read a line particularly addressed to himself, the Squire, turning round upon Israel, congratulated him upon his successful mission, placed some refreshment before him, and apprised him that, owing to certain suspicious symptoms in the neighborhood, he (Israel) must now remain concealed in the house for a day or two, till an answer should be ready for Paris.

94

It was a venerable mansion, as was somewhere previously stated, of a wide and rambling disorderly spaciousness, built, for the most part, of weather-stained old bricks, in the goodly style called Elizabethan. As without, it was all dark russet bricks, so within, it was nothing but tawny oak panels.

"Now, my good fellow," said the Squire, "my wife has a number of guests, who wander from room to room, having the freedom of the house. So I shall have to put you very snugly away, to guard against any chance of discovery."

So saying, first locking the door, he touched a spring nigh the open fire-place, whereupon one of the black sooty stone jambs of the chimney started ajar, just like the marble gate of a tomb. Inserting one leg of the heavy tongs in the crack, the Squire pried this cavernous gate wide open.

"Why, Squire Woodcock, what is the matter with your chimney?" said Israel.

"Quick, go in."

"Am I to sweep the chimney?" demanded Israel; "I didn't engage for that."

"Pooh, pooh, this is your hiding-place. Come, move in."

"But where does it go to, Squire Woodcock? I don't like the looks of it."

"Follow me. I'll show you."

Pushing his florid corpulence into the mysterious aperture, the elderly Squire led the way up steep stairs of stone, hardly two feet in width, till they reached a little closet, or rather cell, built into the massive main wall of the mansion, and ventilated and dimly lit by two little sloping slits, ingeniously concealed without, by their forming the sculptured mouths of two griffins cut in a great stone tablet decorating that external part of the dwelling. A mattress lay rolled up in one corner, with a jug of water, a flask of wine, and a wooden trencher containing cold roast beef and bread.

"And I am to be buried alive here?" said Israel, ruefully looking round.

"But your resurrection will soon be at hand," smiled the Squire; "two days at the furthest."

"Though to be sure I was a sort of prisoner in Paris, just as I seem about to be made here," said Israel, "yet Doctor Franklin put me in a better jug than this, Squire Woodcock. It was set out with bouquets and a mirror, and other fine things. Besides, I could step out into the entry whenever I wanted."

"Ah, but, my hero, that was in France, and this is in England. There you were in a friendly country: here you are in the enemy's. If you should be discovered in my house, and your connection with me became known, do you know that it would go very hard with me; very hard indeed?"

"Then, for your sake, I am willing to stay wherever you think best to put me," replied Israel.

"Well, then, you say you want bouquets and a mirror. If those articles will at all help to solace your seclusion, I will bring them to you."

"They really would be company; the sight of my own face particularly."

"Stay here, then. I will be back in ten minutes."

In less than that time, the good old Squire returned, puffing and panting, with a great bunch of flowers, and a small shaving-glass.

"There," said he, putting them down; "now keep perfectly quiet; avoid making any undue noise, and on no account descend the stairs, till I come for you again."

"But when will that be?" asked Israel.

"I will try to come twice each day while you are here. But there is no knowing what may happen. If I should not visit you till I come to liberate you—on the evening of the second day, or the morning of the third—you must not be at all surprised, my good fellow. There is plenty of food and water to last you. But mind, on no account descend the stone-stairs till I come for you."

With that, bidding his guest adieu, he left him.

Israel stood glancing pensively around for a time. By and by, moving the rolled mattress under the two air-slits, he mounted, to try if aught were visible beyond. But nothing was to be seen but a very thin slice of blue sky peeping through the lofty foliage of a great tree planted near the side-portal of the mansion; an ancient tree, coeval with the ancient dwelling it guarded.

Sitting down on the mattress, Israel fell into a reverie.

"Poverty and liberty, or plenty and a prison, seem to be the two horns of the constant dilemma of my life," thought he. "Let's look at the prisoner."

And taking up the shaving-glass, he surveyed his lineaments.

"What a pity I didn't think to ask for razors and soap. I want shaving very badly. I shaved last in France. How it would pass the time here. Had I a comb now and a razor, I might shave and curl my hair, and keep making a continual toilet all through the two days, and look spruce as a robin when I get out. I'll ask the Squire for the things this very night when he drops in. Hark! ain't that a sort of rumbling in the wall? I hope there ain't any oven next door; if so, I shall be scorched out. Here I am, just like a rat in the wainscot. I wish there was a low window to look out of. I wonder what Doctor Franklin is doing now, and Paul Jones? Hark! there's a bird singing in the leaves. Bell for dinner, that."

And for pastime, he applied himself to the beef and bread, and took a draught of the wine and water.

At last night fell. He was left in utter darkness. No Squire.

After an anxious, sleepless night, he saw two long flecks of pale gray light slanting into the cell from the slits, like two long spears. He rose, rolled up his mattress, got upon the roll, and put his mouth to one of the griffins' mouths. He gave a low, just audible whistle, directing it towards the foliage of the tree. Presently there was a slight rustling among the leaves, then one solitary chirrup, and in three minutes a whole chorus of melody burst upon his ear.

"I've waked the first bird," said he to himself, with a smile, "and he's waked all the rest. Now then for breakfast. That over, I dare say the Squire will drop in."

But the breakfast was over, and the two flecks of pale light had changed to golden beams, and the golden beams grew less and less slanting, till they straightened themselves up out of sight altogether. It was noon, and no Squire.

"He's gone a-hunting before breakfast, and got belated," thought Israel.

The afternoon shadows lengthened. It was sunset; no Squire.

"He must be very busy trying some sheep-stealer in the hall," mused Israel. "I hope he won't forget all about me till to-morrow."

He waited and listened; and listened and waited.

Another restless night; no sleep; morning came. The second day passed like the first, and the night. On the third morning the flowers lay shrunken by his side. Drops of wet oozing through the air-slits, fell dully on the stone floor. He heard the dreary beatings of the tree's leaves against the mouths of the griffins, bedashing them with the spray of the rain-storm without. At intervals a burst of thunder rolled over his head, and lightning flashing down through the slits, lit up the cell with a greenish glare, followed by sharp splashings and rattlings of the redoubled rain-storm.

"This is the morning of the third day," murmured Israel to himself; "he said he would at the furthest come to me on the morning of the third day. This is it. Patience, he will be here yet. Morning lasts till noon."

But, owing to the murkiness of the day, it was very hard to tell when noon came. Israel refused to credit that noon had come and gone, till dusk set plainly in. Dreading he knew not what, he found himself buried in the darkness of still another night. However patient and hopeful hitherto, fortitude now presently left him. Suddenly, as if some contagious fever had seized him, he was afflicted with strange enchantments of misery, undreamed of till now.

He had eaten all the beef, but there was bread and water sufficient to last, by economy, for two or three days to come. It was not the pang of hunger then, but a nightmare originating in his mysterious incarceration, which appalled him. All through the long hours of this particular night, the sense of being masoned up in the wall, grew, and grew, and grew upon him, till again and again he lifted himself convulsively from the floor, as if vast blocks of stone had been laid on him; as if he had been digging a deep well, and the stonework with all the excavated earth had caved in upon him, where he burrowed ninety feet beneath the clover. In the blind tomb of the midnight he stretched his two arms sideways, and felt as if coffined at not being able to extend them straight out, on opposite sides, for the narrowness of the cell. He seated himself against one side of the wall, crosswise with the cell, and pushed with his feet at the opposite wall. But still mindful of his promise in this extremity, he uttered no cry. He mutely raved in the darkness. The delirious sense of the absence of light was soon added to his other delirium as to the contraction of space. The lids of his eyes burst with impotent distension. Then he thought the air itself was getting unbearable. He stood up at the griffin slits, pressing his lips far into them till he moulded his lips there, to suck the utmost of the open air possible.

And continually, to heighten his frenzy, there recurred to him again and again what the Squire had told him as to the origin of the cell. It seemed that this part of the old house, or rather this wall of it, was extremely ancient, dating far beyond the era of Elizabeth, having once formed portion of a religious retreat belonging to the Templars. The domestic discipline of this order was rigid and merciless in the extreme. In a side wall of their second-story chapel, horizontal and on a level with the floor, they had an internal vacancy left, exactly of the shape and average size of a coffin. In this place, from time to time, inmates convicted of contumacy were confined; but, strange to say, not till they were penitent. A small hole, of the girth of one's wrist, sunk like a telescope three feet through the masonry into the cell, served at once for ventilation, and to push through food to the prisoner. This hole opening into the chapel also enabled the poor solitaire, as intended, to overhear the religious services at the altar; and, without being present, take part in the same. It was deemed a good sign of the state of the sufferer's soul, if from the gloomy recesses of the wall was heard the agonized groan of his dismal response. This was regarded in the light of a penitent wail from the dead, because the customs of the order ordained that when any inmate should be first incarcerated in the wall, he should be committed to it in the presence of all the brethren, the chief reading the burial service as the live body was sepulchred. Sometimes several weeks elapsed ere the disentombment, the penitent being then usually found numb and congealed in all his extremities, like one newly stricken with paralysis.

This coffin-cell of the Templars had been suffered to remain in the demolition of the general edifice, to make way for the erection of the new, in the reign of Queen Elizabeth. It was enlarged somewhat, and altered, and additionally ventilated, to adapt it for a place of concealment in times of civil dissension.

With this history ringing in his solitary brain, it may readily be conceived what Israel's feelings must have been. Here, in this very darkness, centuries ago, hearts, human as his, had mildewed in despair; limbs, robust as his own, had stiffened in immovable torpor.

At length, after what seemed all the prophetic days and years of Daniel, morning broke. The benevolent light entered the cell, soothing his frenzy, as if it had been some smiling human face—nay, the Squire himself, come at last to redeem him from thrall. Soon his dumb ravings entirely left him, and gradually, with a sane, calm mind, he revolved all the circumstances of his condition.

He could not be mistaken; something fatal must have befallen his friend. Israel remembered the Squire's hinting that in case of the discovery of his clandestine proceedings it would fare extremely hard with him. Israel was forced to conclude that this same unhappy discovery had been made; that owing to some untoward misadventure his good friend had been carried off a State-prisoner to London; that prior to his going the Squire had not apprised any member of his household that he was about to leave behind him a prisoner in the wall; this seemed evident from the circumstance that, thus far, no soul had visited that prisoner. It could not be otherwise. Doubtless the

100

Squire, having no opportunity to converse in private with his relatives or friends at the moment of his sudden arrest, had been forced to keep his secret, for the present, for fear of involving Israel in still worse calamities. But would he leave him to perish piecemeal in the wall? All surmise was baffled in the unconjecturable possibilities of the case. But some sort of action must speedily be determined upon. Israel would not additionally endanger the Squire, but he could not in such uncertainty consent to perish where he was. He resolved at all hazards to escape, by stealth and noiselessly, if possible; by violence and outcry, if indispensable.

Gliding out of the cell, he descended the stone stairs, and stood before the interior of the jamb. He felt an immovable iron knob, but no more. He groped about gently for some bolt or spring. When before he had passed through the passage with his guide, he had omitted to notice by what precise mechanism the jamb was to be opened from within, or whether, indeed, it could at all be opened except from without.

He was about giving up the search in despair, after sweeping with his two hands every spot of the wall-surface around him, when chancing to turn his whole body a little to one side, he heard a creak, and saw a thin lance of light. His foot had unconsciously pressed some spring laid in the floor. The jamb was ajar. Pushing it open, he stood at liberty in the Squire's closet.

13

His Escape from the House,
with Various Adventures Following

He started at the funereal aspect of the room, into which, since he last stood there, undertakers seemed to have stolen. The curtains of the window were festooned with long weepers of crape. The four corners of the red cloth on the round table were knotted with crape.

Knowing nothing of these mournful customs of the country, nevertheless, Israel's instinct whispered him that Squire Woodcock lived no more on this earth. At once the whole three days' mystery was made clear. But what was now to be done? His friend must have died very suddenly; most probably struck down in a fit, from which he never more rose. With him had perished all knowledge of the fact that a stranger was immured in the mansion. If discovered then, prowling here in the inmost privacies of a gentleman's abode, what would befall the wanderer, already not unsuspected in the neighborhood of some underhand guilt as a fugitive? If he adhered to the strict truth, what could he offer in his own defence without convicting himself of acts which, by English tribunals, would be accounted flagitious crimes? Unless, indeed, by involving the memory of the deceased Squire Woodcock in his own self-acknowledged proceedings, so ungenerous a charge should result in an abhorrent refusal to credit his extraordinary tale, whether as referring to himself or another, and so throw him open to still more grievous suspicions?

While wrapped in these dispiriting reveries, he heard a step not very far off in the passage. It seemed approaching. Instantly he flew to the jamb, which remained unclosed, and disappearing within, drew the stone after him by the iron knob. Owing to his hurried violence the jamb closed with a dull, dismal and singular noise. A shriek followed from within the room. In a panic, Israel fled up the dark stairs, and near the top, in his eagerness, stumbled and fell back to the last step with a rolling din, which, reverberated by the arch overhead, smote through and through the wall, dying away at last indistinctly, like low muffled thunder among the clefts of deep hills. When raising himself instantly, not seriously bruised by his fall, Israel instantly listened, the echoing sounds of his descent were mingled with added shrieks from within the room. They seemed some nervous female's, alarmed by what must have appeared to her supernatural, or at least unaccountable, noises in the wall. Directly he heard other voices of alarm undistinguishably commingled, and then they retreated together, and all again was still.

Recovering from his first amazement, Israel revolved these occurrences. "No creature now in the house knows of the cell," thought he. "Some woman, the housekeeper, perhaps, first entered the room alone. Just as she entered the jamb closed. The sudden report made her shriek; then, afterwards, the noise of my fall prolonging itself, added to her fright, while her repeated shrieks brought every soul in the house to her, who aghast at seeing her lying in a pale faint, it may be, like a corpse, in a room hung with crape for a man just dead, they also shrieked out, and then with blended lamentations they bore the fainting person away. Now this will follow; no doubt it *has* followed ere now:—they believe that the woman saw or heard the spirit of Squire Woodcock. Since I seem then to understand how all these strange events have occurred, since I seem to know that they have plain common causes, I begin to feel cool and calm again. Let me see. Yes. I have it. By means of the idea of the ghost prevailing among the frightened household, by that means I will this very night make good my escape. If I can but lay hands on some of the late Squire's clothing, if but a coat and hat of his, I shall be certain to succeed. It is not too early to begin now. They will hardly come back to the room in a hurry. I will return to it and see what I can find to serve my purpose. It is the Squire's private closet, hence it is not unlikely that here some at least of his clothing will be found."

With these thoughts, he cautiously sprung the iron under foot, peeped in, and, seeing all clear, boldly reentered the apartment. He went straight to a high, narrow door in the opposite wall. The key was in the lock. Opening the door, there hung several coats, small-clothes, pairs of silk stockings, and hats of the deceased. With little difficulty Israel selected from these the complete suit in which he had last seen his once jovial friend. Carefully closing the door, and carrying the suit with him, he was returning towards the chimney, when he saw the Squire's silver-headed cane leaning against a corner of the wainscot. Taking this also, he stole back to his cell.

Slipping off his own clothing, he deliberately arrayed himself in the borrowed raiment, silk small-clothes and all, then put on the cocked hat, grasped the silver-headed cane in his right hand, and moving his small shaving-glass slowly up and down before him, so as by piecemeal to take in his whole figure, felt convinced that he would well pass for Squire Woodcock's genuine phantom. But after the first feeling of self-satisfaction with his anticipated success had left him, it was not without some superstitious embarrassment that Israel felt himself encased in a dead man's broadcloth; nay, in the very coat in which the deceased had no doubt fallen down in his fit. By degrees he began to feel almost as unreal and shadowy as the shade whose part he intended to enact.

Waiting long and anxiously till darkness came, and then till he thought it was fairly midnight, he stole back into the closet, and standing for a moment uneasily in the middle of the floor, thinking over all the risks he might run, he lingered till he felt himself resolute and calm. Then groping for the door leading into the hall, put his hand on the knob and turned it. But the door refused to budge. Was it locked? The key was not in. Turning the knob once more, and holding it so, he pressed firmly against the door. It did not move. More firmly still, when suddenly it burst open with a loud crackling report. Being cramped, it had stuck in the sill. Less than three seconds passed when, as Israel was groping his way down the long wide hall towards the large staircase at its opposite end, he heard confused hurrying noises from the neighboring rooms, and in another instant several persons, mostly in night-dresses, appeared at their chamber-doors, thrusting out alarmed faces, lit by a lamp held by one of the number, a rather elderly lady in widow's weeds, who by her appearance seemed to have just risen from a sleepless chair, instead of an oblivious couch. Israel's heart beat like a hammer; his face turned like a sheet. But bracing himself, pulling his hat lower down over his eyes, settling his head in the collar of his coat, he advanced along the defile of wildly staring faces. He advanced with a slow and stately step, looked neither to the right nor the left, but went solemnly forward on his now faintly illuminated way, sounding his cane on the floor as he passed. The faces in the doorways curdled his blood by their rooted looks. Glued to the spot, they seemed incapable of motion. Each one was silent as he advanced towards him or her, but as he left each individual, one after another, behind, each in a frenzy shrieked out, "The Squire, the Squire!" As he passed the lady in the widow's weeds, she fell senseless and crosswise before him. But forced to be immutable in his purpose, Israel, solemnly stepping over her prostrate form, marched deliberately on.

In a few minutes more he had reached the main door of the mansion, and withdrawing the chain and bolt, stood in the open air. It was a bright moonlight night. He struck slowly across the open grounds towards the sunken fields beyond. When midway across the grounds, he turned towards the mansion, and saw three of the front windows filled with white faces, gazing in terror at the wonderful spectre. Soon descending a slope, he disappeared from their view.

Presently he came to hilly land in meadow, whose grass having been lately cut, now lay dotting the slope in cocks; a sinuous line of creamy vapor meandered through the lowlands at the base of the hill; while beyond was a dense grove of dwarfish trees, with here and there a tall tapering dead trunk, peeled of the bark, and overpeering the rest. The vapor wore the semblance of a deep stream of water, imperfectly described; the grove looked like some closely-clustering town on its banks, lorded over by spires of churches.

The whole scene magically reproduced to our adventurer the aspect of Bunker Hill, Charles River, and Boston town, on the well-remembered night of the 16th of June. The same season; the same moon; the same new-mown hay on the shaven sward; hay which was scraped together during the night to help pack into the redoubt so hurriedly thrown up.

Acted on as if by enchantment, Israel sat down on one of the cocks, and gave himself up to reverie. But, worn out by long loss of sleep, his reveries would have soon merged into slumber's still wilder dreams, had he not rallied himself, and departed on his way, fearful of forgetting himself in an emergency like the present. It now occurred to him that, well as his disguise had served him in escaping from the mansion of Squire Woodcock, that disguise might fatally endanger him if he should be discovered in it abroad. He might pass for a ghost at night, and among the relations and immediate friends of the gentleman deceased; but by day, and among indifferent persons, he ran no small risk of being apprehended for an entry-thief. He bitterly lamented his omission in not pulling on the Squire's clothes over his own, so that he might now have reappeared in his former guise.

As meditating over this difficulty, he was passing along, suddenly he saw a man in black standing right in his path, about fifty yards distant, in a field of some growing barley

106

or wheat. The gloomy stranger was standing stock-still; one outstretched arm, with weird intimation pointing towards the deceased Squire's abode. To the brooding soul of the now desolate Israel, so strange a sight roused a supernatural suspicion. His conscience morbidly reproaching him for the terrors he had bred in making his escape from the house, he seemed to see in the fixed gesture of the stranger something more than humanly significant. But somewhat of his intrepidity returned; he resolved to test the apparition. Composing itself to the same deliberate stateliness with which it had paced the hall, the phantom of Squire Woodcock firmly advanced its cane, and marched straight forward towards the mysterious stranger.

As he neared him, Israel shrunk. The dark coat-sleeve flapped on the bony skeleton of the unknown arm. The face was lost in a sort of ghastly blank. It was no living man.

But mechanically continuing his course, Israel drew still nearer and saw a scarecrow.

AN ENCOUNTER OF GHOSTS

Not a little relieved by the discovery, our adventurer paused, more particularly to survey so deceptive an object, which seemed to have been constructed on the most efficient principles; probably by some broken-down wax-figure costumer. It comprised the complete wardrobe of a scarecrow, namely: a cocked hat, bunged; tattered coat; old velveteen breeches; and long worsted stockings, full of holes; all stuffed very nicely with straw, and skeletoned by a framework of poles. There was a great flapped pocket to the coat—which seemed to have been some laborer's—standing invitingly opened. Putting his hands in, Israel drew out the lid of an old tobacco-box, the broken bowl of a pipe, two rusty nails, and a few kernels of wheat. This reminded him of the Squire's pockets. Trying them, he produced a handsome handkerchief, a spectacle-case, with a purse containing some silver and gold, amounting to a little more than five pounds. Such is the difference between the contents of the pockets of scarecrows and the pockets of well-to-do squires. Ere donning his present habiliments, Israel had not omitted to withdraw his own money from his own coat, and put it in the pocket of his own waistcoat, which he had not exchanged.

Looking upon the scarecrow more attentively, it struck him that, miserable as its wardrobe was, nevertheless here was a chance for getting rid of the unsuitable and perilous clothes of the Squire. No other available opportunity might present itself for a time. Before he encountered any living creature by daylight, another suit must somehow be had. His exchange with the old ditcher, after his escape from the inn near Portsmouth, had familiarized him with the most deplorable of wardrobes. Well, too, he knew, and had experienced it, that for a man desirous of avoiding notice, the more wretched the clothes, the better. For who does not shun the scurvy wretch, Poverty, advancing in battered hat and lamentable coat?

Without more ado, slipping off the Squire's raiment, he donned the scarecrow's, after carefully shaking out the hay, which, from many alternate soakings and bakings in rain and sun, had become quite broken up, and would have been almost dust, were it not for the mildew which damped it. But sufficient of this wretched old hay remained adhesive to the inside of the breeches and coat-sleeves, to produce the most irritating torment.

The grand moral question now came up, what to do with the purse. Would it be dishonest under the circumstances to appropriate that purse? Considering the whole matter, and not forgetting that he had not received from the gentleman deceased the promised reward for his services as courier, Israel concluded that he might justly use the money for his own. To which opinion surely no charitable judge will demur. Besides, what should he do with the purse, if not use it for his own? It would have been insane to have returned it to the relations. Such mysterious honesty would have but resulted in his arrest as a rebel, or rascal. As for the Squire's clothes, handkerchief, and spectacle-case, they must be put out of sight with all dispatch. So, going to a morass not remote, Israel sunk them deep down, and heaped tufts of the rank sod upon them. Then returning to the field of corn, sat down under the lee of a rock, about a hundred yards from where the scarecrow had stood, thinking which way he now had best direct his steps. But his late ramble coming after so long a deprivation of rest, soon produced effects not so easy to be shaken off, as when reposing upon the haycock. He felt less anxious too, since changing his apparel. So before he was aware, he fell into deep sleep.

When he awoke, the sun was well up in the sky. Looking around he saw a farm-laborer with a pitchfork coming at a distance into view, whose steps seemed bent in a direction not far from the spot where he lay. Immediately it struck our adventurer that this man must be familiar with the scarecrow; perhaps had himself fashioned it. Should he miss it then, he might make immediate search, and so discover the thief so imprudently loitering upon the very field of his operations.

Waiting until the man momentarily disappeared in a little hollow, Israel ran briskly to the identical spot where the scarecrow had stood, where, standing stiffly erect, pulling the hat well over his face, and thrusting out his arm, pointed steadfastly towards the Squire's abode, he awaited the event. Soon the man reappeared in sight, and marching right on, paused not far from Israel, and gave him an one earnest look, as if it were his daily wont to satisfy that all was right with the scarecrow. No sooner was the man departed to a reasonable distance, than, quitting his post, Israel struck across the fields towards London. But he had not yet quite quitted the field when it occurred to him to turn round and see if the man was completely out of sight, when, to his consternation, he saw the man returning towards him, evidently by his pace and gesture in unmixed amazement. The man must have turned round to look before Israel had done so. Frozen to the ground, Israel knew not what to do; but next moment it struck him that this very motionlessness was the least hazardous plan in such a strait. Thrusting out his arm again towards the house, once more he stood stock still, and again awaited the event.

It so happened that this time, in pointing towards the house, Israel unavoidably pointed towards the advancing man. Hoping that the strangeness of this coincidence might, by operating on the man's superstition, incline him to beat an immediate retreat, Israel kept cool as he might. But the man proved to be of a braver metal than anticipated. In passing the spot where the scarecrow had stood, and perceiving, beyond the possibility of mistake, that by some unaccountable agency it had suddenly removed itself to a distance, instead of being terrified at this verification of his worst apprehensions, the man pushed on for Israel, apparently resolved to sift this mystery to the bottom.

Seeing him now determinately coming, with pitchfork valiantly presented, Israel, as a last means of practising on the fellow's fears of the supernatural, suddenly doubled up both fists, presenting them savagely towards him at a distance of about twenty paces, at the same time showing his teeth like a skull's, and demoniacally rolling his eyes. The man paused bewildered, looked all round him, looked at the springing grain, then across at some trees, then up at the sky, and satisfied at last by those observations that the world at large had not undergone a miracle in the last fifteen minutes, resolutely resumed his advance; the pitchfork, like a boarding-pike, now aimed full at the breast of the object. Seeing all his stratagems vain, Israel now threw himself into the original attitude of the scarecrow, and once again stood immovable. Abating his pace by degrees almost to a mere creep, the man at last came within three feet of him, and, pausing, gazed amazed into Israel's eyes. With a stern and terrible expression Israel resolutely returned the glance, but otherwise remained like a statue, hoping thus to stare his pursuer out of countenance. At last the man slowly presented one prong of his fork towards Israel's left eye. Nearer and nearer the sharp point came, till no longer capable of enduring such a test, Israel took to his heels with all speed, his tattered coat-tails streaming behind him. With inveterate purpose the man pursued. Darting blindly on, Israel, leaping a gate, suddenly found himself in a field where some dozen laborers were at work, who recognizing the scarecrow—an old acquaintance of theirs, as it would seem—lifted all their hands as the astounding apparition swept by, followed by the man with the pitchfork. Soon all joined in the chase, but Israel proved to have better wind and bottom than any. Outstripping the whole pack he finally shot out of their sight in an extensive park, heavily timbered in one quarter. He never saw more of these people.

Loitering in the wood till nightfall, he then stole out and made the best of his way towards the house of that good-natured farmer in whose corn-loft he had received his first message from Squire Woodcock. Rousing this man up a little before midnight, he informed him somewhat of his recent adventures, but carefully concealed his having been employed as a secret courier, together with his escape from Squire Woodcock's. All he craved at present was a meal. The meal being over, Israel offered to buy from the farmer his best suit of clothes, and displayed the money on the spot.

"Where did you get so much money?" said his entertainer in a tone of surprise; "your clothes here don't look as if you had seen prosperous times since you left me. Why, you look like a scarecrow."

"That may well be," replied Israel, very soberly. "But what do you say? will you sell me your suit?—here's the cash."

"I don't know about it," said the farmer, in doubt; "let me look at the money. Ha!—a silk purse come out of a beggar's pocket!—Quit the house, rascal, you've turned thief."

Thinking that he could not swear to his having come by his money with absolute honesty—since indeed the case was one for the most subtle casuist—Israel knew not what to reply. This honest confusion confirmed the farmer, who with many abusive epithets drove him into the road, telling him that he might thank himself that he did not arrest him on the spot.

In great dolor at this unhappy repulse, Israel trudged

111

on in the moonlight some three miles to the house of another friend, who also had once succored him in extremity. This man proved a very sound sleeper. Instead of succeeding in rousing him by his knocking, Israel but succeeded in rousing his wife, a person not of the greatest amiability. Raising the sash, and seeing so shocking a pauper before her, the woman upbraided him with shameless impropriety in asking charity at dead of night, in a dress so improper too. Looking down at his deplorable velveteens, Israel discovered that his extensive travels had produced a great rent in one loin of the rotten old breeches, through which a whitish fragment protruded.

Remedying this oversight as well as he might, he again implored the woman to wake her husband.

"That I sha'n't!" said the woman, morosely. "Quit the premises, or I'll throw something on ye."

With that she brought some earthenware to the window, and would have fulfilled her threat, had not Israel prudently retreated some paces. Here he entreated the woman to take mercy on his plight, and since she would not waken her husband, at least throw to him (Israel) her husband's breeches, and he would leave the price of them, with his own breeches to boot, on the sill of the door.

"You behold how sadly I need them," said he; "for heaven's sake befriend me."

"Quit the premises!" reiterated the woman.

"The breeches, the breeches! here is the money," cried Israel, half furious with anxiety.

"Saucy cur," cried the woman, somehow misunderstanding him; "do you cunningly taunt me with *wearing* the breeches? begone!"

Once more poor Israel decamped, and made for another friend. But here a monstrous bull-dog, indignant that the peace of a quiet family should be disturbed by so outrageous a tatterdemalion, flew at Israel's unfortunate coat, whose rotten skirts the brute tore completely off, leaving the coat razeed to a spencer, which barely came down to the wearer's waist. In attempting to drive the monster away, Israel's hat fell off, upon which the dog pounced with the utmost fierceness, and thrusting both paws into it, rammed out the crown and went snuffling the wreck before him. Recovering the wretched hat, Israel again beat a retreat, his wardrobe sorely the worse for his visits. Not only was his coat a mere rag, but his breeches, clawed by the dog, were slashed into yawning gaps, while his yellow hair waved over the top of the crownless beaver, like a lonely tuft of heather on the highlands.

In this plight the morning discovered him dubiously skirmishing on the outskirts of a village.

"Ah! what a true patriot gets for serving his country!" murmured Israel. But soon thinking a little better of his case, and seeing yet another house which had once furnished him with an asylum, he made bold to advance to the door. Luckily he this time met the man himself, just emerging from bed. At first the farmer did not recognize the fugitive, but upon another look, seconded by Israel's plaintive appeal, beckoned him into the barn, where directly our adventurer told him all he thought prudent to disclose of his story, ending by once more offering to negotiate for breeches and coat. Having ere this emptied and thrown away the purse which had played him so scurvy a trick with the first farmer, he now produced three crown-pieces.

"Three crown-pieces in your pocket, and no crown to your hat!" said the farmer.

"But I assure you, my friend," rejoined Israel, "that a finer hat was never worn, until that confounded bull-dog ruined it."

"True," said the farmer, "I forgot that part of your story. Well, I have a tolerable coat and breeches which I will sell you for your money."

In ten minutes more Israel was equipped in a gray coat of coarse cloth, not much improved by wear, and breeches to match. For half-a-crown more he procured a highly respectable looking hat.

"Now, my kind friend," said Israel, "can you tell me where Horne Tooke and John Bridges live?"

Our adventurer thought it his best plan to seek out one or other of those gentlemen, both to report proceedings and learn confirmatory tidings concerning Squire Wood-

113

cock, touching whose fate he did not like to inquire of others.

"Horne Tooke? What do you want with Horne Tooke?" said the farmer. "He was Squire Woodcock's friend, wasn't he? The poor Squire! Who would have thought he'd have gone off so suddenly. But apoplexy comes like a bullet."

"I was right," thought Israel to himself. "But where does Horne Tooke live?" he demanded again.

"He once lived in Brentford, and wore a cassock there. But I hear he's sold out his living, and gone in his surplice to study law in Lunnon."

This was all news to Israel, who, from various amiable remarks he had heard from Horne Tooke at the Squire's, little dreamed he was an ordained clergyman. Yet a good-natured English clergyman translated Lucian; another, equally good-natured, wrote Tristram Shandy; and a third, an ill-natured appreciator of good-natured Rabelais, died a dean; not to speak of others. Thus ingenious and ingenuous are some of the English clergy.

"You can't tell me, then, where to find Horne Tooke?" said Israel, in perplexity.

"You'll find him, I suppose, in Lunnon."

"What street and number?"

"Don't know. Needle in a haystack."

"Where does Mr. Bridges live?"

"Never heard of any Bridges, except Lunnon bridges, and one Molly Bridges in Bridewell."

So Israel departed; better clothed, but no wiser than before.

What to do next? He reckoned up his money, and concluded he had plenty to carry him back to Doctor Franklin in Paris. Accordingly, taking a turn to avoid the two nearest villages, he directed his steps towards London, where, again taking the post-coach for Dover, he arrived on the channel shore just in time to learn that the very coach in which he rode brought the news to the authorities there that all intercourse between the two nations was indefinitely suspended. The characteristic taciturnity and formal stolidity of his fellow-travellers—all Englishmen, mutually unacquainted with each other, and occupying different positions in life—having prevented his sooner hearing the tidings.

Here was another accumulation of misfortunes. All visions but those of eventual imprisonment or starvation vanished from before the present realities of poor Israel Potter. The Brentford gentleman had flattered him with the prospect of receiving something very handsome for his services as courier. That hope was no more. Doctor Franklin had promised him his good offices in procuring him a passage home to America. Quite out of the question now. The sage had likewise intimated that he might possibly see him some way remunerated for his sufferings in his country's cause. An idea no longer to be harbored. Then Israel recalled the mild man of wisdom's words— "At the prospect of pleasure never be elated; but without depression respect the omens of ill." But he found it as difficult now to comply, in all respects, with the last section of the maxim, as before he had with the first.

While standing wrapped in afflictive reflections on the shore, gazing towards the unattainable coast of France, a pleasant-looking cousinly stranger, in seamen's dress, accosted him, and, after some pleasant conversation, very civilly invited him up a lane into a house of rather secret entertainment. Pleased to be befriended in this his strait, Israel yet looked inquisitively upon the man, not completely satisfied with his good intentions. But the other, with good-humored violence, hurried him up the lane into the inn, when, calling for some spirits, he and Israel very affectionately drank to each other's better health and prosperity.

"Take another glass," said the stranger, affably.

Israel, to drown his heavy-heartedness, complied. The liquor began to take effect.

"Ever at sea?" said the stranger, lightly.

"Oh, yes; been a whaling."

"Ah!" said the other, "happy to hear that, I assure you. Jim! Bill!" And beckoning very quietly to two brawny fellows, in a trice Israel found himself kidnapped into the naval service of the magnanimous old gentleman of Kew Gardens—his Royal Majesty, George III.

"Hands off!" said Israel, fiercely, as the two men pinioned him.

"Regular game-cock," said the cousinly-looking man. "I must get three guineas for cribbing him. Pleasant voyage to ye, my friend," and, leaving Israel a prisoner, the crimp, buttoning his coat, sauntered leisurely out of the inn.

"I'm no Englishman," roared Israel, in a foam.

"Oh! that's the old story," grinned his jailers. "Come along. There's no Englishman in the English fleet. All foreigners. You may take their own word for it."

To be short, in less than a week Israel found himself at Portsmouth, and, ere long, a foretopman in his Majesty's ship of the line, Unprincipled, scudding before the wind down channel, in company with the Undaunted, and the Unconquerable; all three haughty Dons bound to the East Indian waters as reinforcements to the fleet of Sir Edward Hughs.

And now, we might shortly have to record our adventurer's part in the famous engagement off the coast of Coromandel, between Admiral Suffren's fleet and the English squadron, were it not that fate snatched him on the threshold of events, and, turning him short round whither he had come, sent him back congenially to war against England, instead of on her behalf. Thus repeatedly and rapidly were the fortunes of our wanderer planted, torn up, transplanted, and dropped again, hither and thither, according as the Supreme Disposer of sailors and soldiers saw fit to appoint.

14

*In Which Israel Is Sailor under Two Flags,
and in Three Ships, and All in One Night*

As running down channel at evening, Israel walked the crowded main-deck of the seventy-four, continually brushed by a thousand hurrying wayfarers, as if he were in some great street in London, jammed with artisans, just returning from their day's labor, novel and painful emotions were his. He found himself dropped into the naval mob without one friend; nay, among enemies, since his country's enemies were his own, and against the kith and kin of these very beings around him, he himself had once lifted a fatal hand. The martial bustle of a great man-of-war, on her first day out of port, was indescribably jarring to his present mood. Those sounds of the human multitude disturbing the solemn natural solitudes of the sea, mysteriously afflicted him. He murmured against that untowardness which, after condemning him to long sorrows on the land, now pursued him with added griefs on the deep. Why should a patriot, leaping for the chance again to attack the oppressor, as at Bunker Hill, now be kidnapped to fight that oppressor's battles on the endless drifts of the Bunker Hills of the billows? But like many other repiners, Israel was perhaps a little premature with upbraidings like these.

Plying on between Scilly and Cape Clear, the Unprincipled—which vessel somewhat outsailed her consorts—fell in, just before dusk, with a large revenue cutter close to, and showing signals of distress. At the moment, no other sail was in sight.

Cursing the necessity of pausing with a strong fair wind at a juncture like this, the officer-of-the-deck shortened sail, and hove to; hailing the cutter, to know what was the matter. As he hailed the small craft from the lofty poop of the bristling seventy-four, this lieutenant seemed standing on the top of Gibraltar, talking to some lowland peasant in a hut. The reply was, that in a sudden flaw of wind, which came nigh capsizing them, not an hour since, the cutter had lost all four foremast men by the violent jibing of a boom. She wanted help to get back to port.

"You shall have one man," said the officer-of-the-deck, morosely.

"Let him be a good one then, for heaven's sake," said he in the cutter; "I ought to have at least two."

During this talk, Israel's curiosity had prompted him to dart up the ladder from the main-deck, and stand right in the gangway above, looking out on the strange craft. Meantime the order had been given to drop a boat. Thinking this a favorable chance, he stationed himself so that he should be the foremost to spring into the boat; though crowds of English sailors, eager as himself for the same opportunity to escape from foreign service, clung to the chains of the as yet imperfectly disciplined man-of-war. As the two men who had been lowered in the boat hooked her, when afloat, along to the gangway, Israel dropped like a comet into the stern-sheets, stumbled forward, and seized an oar. In a moment more, all the oarsmen were in their places, and with a few strokes the boat lay alongside the cutter.

"Take which of them you please," said the lieutenant in command, addressing the officer in the revenue-cutter and motioning with his hand to his boat's crew, as if they were a parcel of carcasses of mutton, of which the first

118

pick was offered to some customer. "Quick and choose. Sit down, men"—to the sailors. "Oh, you are in a great hurry to get rid of the king's service, ain't you? Brave chaps indeed!—Have you chosen your man?"

All this while the ten faces of the anxious oarsmen looked with mute longings and appealings towards the officer of the cutter; every face turned at the same angle, as if managed by one machine. And so they were. One motive.

"I take the freckled chap with the yellow hair—him," pointing to Israel.

Nine of the upturned faces fell in sullen despair, and ere Israel could spring to his feet, he felt a violent thrust in his rear from the toes of one of the disappointed behind him.

"Jump, dobbin!" cried the officer of the boat.

But Israel was already on board. Another moment, and the boat and cutter parted. Ere long, night fell, and the man-of-war and her consorts were out of sight.

The revenue vessel resumed her course towards the nighest port, worked by but four men: the captain, Israel, and two officers. The cabin-boy was kept at the helm. As the only foremast man, Israel was put to it pretty hard. Where there is but one man to three masters, woe betide that lonely slave. Besides, it was of itself severe work enough to manage the vessel thus short of hands. But to make matters still worse, the captain and his officers were ugly-tempered fellows. The one kicked, and the others cuffed Israel. Whereupon, not sugared with his recent experiences, and maddened by his present hap, Israel seeing himself alone at sea, with only three men, instead of a thousand, to contend against, plucked up a heart, knocked the captain into the lee scuppers, and in his fury was about tumbling the first-officer, a small wash of a fellow, plump overboard, when the captain, jumping to his feet, seized him by his long yellow hair, vowing he would slaughter him. Meanwhile the cutter flew foaming through the channel, as if in demoniac glee at this uproar on her imperilled deck. While the consternation was at its height, a dark body suddenly loomed at a moderate distance into view, shooting right athwart the stern of the cutter. The next moment a shot struck the water within a boat's length.

"Heave to, and send a boat on board!" roared a voice almost as loud as the cannon.

"That's a war-ship," cried the captain of the revenue vessel, in alarm; "but she ain't a countryman."

Meantime the officers and Israel stopped the cutter's way.

"Send a boat on board, or I'll sink you," again came roaring from the stranger, followed by another shot, striking the water still nearer the cutter.

"For God's sake, don't cannonade us. I haven't got the crew to man a boat," replied the captain of the cutter. "Who are you?"

"Wait till I send a boat to you for that," replied the stranger.

"She's an enemy of some sort, that's plain," said the Englishman now to his officers; "we ain't at open war with France; she's some bloodthirsty pirate or other. What d'ye say, men?" turning to his officers; "let's outsail her, or be shot to chips. We can beat her at sailing, I know."

With that, nothing doubting that his counsel would be heartily responded to, he ran to the braces to get the cutter before the wind, followed by one officer, while the other, for a useless bravado, hoisted the colors at the stern.

But Israel stood indifferent, or rather all in a fever of conflicting emotions. He thought he recognized the voice from the strange vessel.

"Come, what do ye standing there, fool? Spring to the ropes here!" cried the furious captain.

But Israel did not stir.

Meantime the confusion on board the stranger, owing to the hurried lowering of her boat, with the cloudiness of the sky darkening the misty sea, united to conceal the bold manœuvre of the cutter. She had almost gained full headway ere an oblique shot, directed by mere chance, struck her stern, tearing the upcurved head of the tiller in the hands of the cabin-boy, and killing him with the splinters. Running to the stump, the captain huzzaed, and

120

steered the reeling ship on. Forced now to hoist back the boat ere giving chase, the stranger was dropped rapidly astern.

All this while storms of maledictions were hurled on Israel. But their exertions at the ropes prevented his shipmates for the time from using personal violence. While observing their efforts, Israel could not but say to himself, "These fellows are as brave as they are brutal."

Soon the stranger was seen dimly wallowing along astern, crowding all sail in chase, while now and then her bow-gun, showing its red tongue, bellowed after them like a mad bull. Two more shots struck the cutter, but without materially damaging her sails, or the ropes immediately upholding them. Several of her less important stays were sundered, however, whose loose tarry ends lashed the air like scorpions. It seemed not improbable that, owing to her superior sailing, the keen cutter would yet get clear.

At this juncture Israel, running towards the captain, who still held the splintered stump of the tiller, stood full before him, saying, "I am an enemy, a Yankee, look to yourself."

"Help here, lads, help," roared the captain, "a traitor, a traitor!"

The words were hardly out of his mouth when his voice was silenced for ever. With one prodigious heave of his whole physical force, Israel smote him over the taffrail into the sea, as if the man had fallen backwards over a teetering chair. By this time the two officers were hurrying aft. Ere meeting them midway, Israel, quick as lightning, cast off the two principal halyards, thus letting the large sails all in a tumble of canvas to the deck. Next moment one of the officers was at the helm, to prevent the cutter from capsizing by being without a steersman in such an emergency. The other officer and Israel interlocked. The battle was in the midst of the chaos of blowing canvas. Caught in a rent of the sail, the officer slipped and fell near the sharp iron edge of the hatchway. As he fell he caught Israel by the most terrible part in which mortality can be grappled. Insane with pain, Israel dashed

121

his adversary's skull against the sharp iron. The officer's hold relaxed, but himself stiffened. Israel made for the helmsman, who as yet knew not the issue of the late tussle. He caught him round the loins, bedding his fingers like grisly claws into his flesh, and hugging him to his heart. The man's ghost, caught like a broken cork in a gurgling bottle's neck, gasped with the embrace. Loosening him suddenly, Israel hurled him from him against the bulwarks. That instant another report was heard, followed by the savage hail—"You down sail at last, do ye? I'm a good mind to sink ye for your scurvy trick. Pull down that dirty rag there, astern!"

With a loud huzza, Israel hauled down the flag with one hand, while with the other he helped the now slowly gliding craft from falling off before the wind.

In a few moments a boat was alongside. As its commander stepped to the deck he stumbled against the body of the first officer, which, owing to the sudden slant of the cutter in coming to the wind, had rolled against the side near the gangway. As he came aft he heard the moan of the other officer, where he lay under the mizzen shrouds.

"What is all this?" demanded the stranger of Israel.

"It means that I am a Yankee impressed into the king's service, and for their pains I have taken the cutter."

Giving vent to his surprise, the officer looked narrowly at the body by the shrouds, and said, "This man is as good as dead, but we will take him to Captain Paul as a witness in your behalf."

"Captain Paul?—Paul Jones?" cried Israel.

"The same."

"I thought so. I thought that was his voice hailing. It was Captain Paul's voice that somehow put me up to this deed."

"Captain Paul is the devil for putting men up to be tigers. But where are the rest of the crew?"

"Overboard."

"What?" cried the officer; "come on board the Ranger. Captain Paul will use you for a broadside."

Taking the moaning man along with them, and leaving the cutter untenanted by any living soul, the boat now

122

left her for the enemy's ship. But ere they reached it the man had expired.

Standing foremost on the deck, crowded with three hundred men, as Israel climbed the side, he saw, by the light of battle-lanterns, a small, smart, brigandish-looking man, wearing a Scotch bonnet, with a gold band to it.

"You rascal," said this person, "why did your paltry smack give me this chase? Where's the rest of your gang?"

"Captain Paul," said Israel, "I believe I remember you. I believe I offered you my bed in Paris some months ago. How is Poor Richard?"

"God! Is this the courier? The Yankee courier? But how now? in an English revenue cutter?"

"Impressed, sir; that's the way."

"But where's the rest of them?" demanded Paul, turning to the officer.

Thereupon the officer very briefly told Paul what Israel told him.

"Are we to sink the cutter, sir?" said the gunner, now advancing towards Captain Paul. "If it is to be done, now is the time. She is close under us, astern; a few guns pointed downwards will settle her like a shotted corpse."

"No. Let her drift into Penzance, an anonymous earnest of what the whitesquall in Paul Jones intends for the future."

Then giving directions as to the course of the ship, with an order for himself to be called at the first glimpse of a sail, Paul took Israel down with him into his cabin.

"Tell me your story now, my yellow lion. How was it all? Don't stand, sit right down there on the transom. I'm a democratic sort of sea-king. Plump on the woolsack, I say, and spin the yarn. But hold; you want some grog first."

As Paul handed the flagon, Israel's eye fell upon his hand.

"You don't wear any rings now, Captain, I see. Left them in Paris for safety."

"Aye, with a certain marchioness there," replied Paul, with a dandyish look of sentimental conceit, which sat strangely enough on his otherwise grim and Feejee air.

123

"I should think rings would be somewhat inconvenient at sea," resumed Israel. "On my first voyage to the West Indies, I wore a girl's ring on my middle finger here, and it wasn't long before, what with hauling wet ropes, and what not, it got a kind of grown down into the flesh, and pained me very bad, let me tell you, it hugged the finger so."

"And did the girl grow as close to your heart, lad?"

"Ah, Captain, girls grow themselves off quicker than we grow them on."

"Some experience with the countesses as well as myself, eh? But the story; wave your yellow mane, my lion—the story."

So Israel went on and told the story in all particulars.

At its conclusion Captain Paul eyed him very earnestly. His wild, lonely heart, incapable of sympathizing with cuddled natures made humdrum by long exemption from pain, was yet drawn towards a being, who in desperation of friendlessness, something like his own, had so fiercely waged battle against tyrannical odds.

"Did you go to sea young, lad?"

"Yes, pretty young."

"I went at twelve, from Whitehaven. Only so high," raising his hand some four feet from the deck. "I was so small, and looked so queer in my little blue jacket, that they called me the monkey. They'll call me something else before long. Did you ever sail out of Whitehaven?"

"No, Captain."

"If you had, you'd have heard sad stories about me. To this hour they say there that I—bloodthirsty, coward dog that I am—flogged a sailor, one Mungo Maxwell, to death. It's a lie, by Heaven! I flogged him, for he was a mutinous scamp. But he died naturally, some time afterwards, and on board another ship. But why talk? They didn't believe the affidavits of others taken before London courts, triumphantly acquitting me; how then will they credit *my* interested words? If slander, however much a lie, once gets hold of a man, it will stick closer than fair fame, as black pitch sticks closer than white cream. But let 'em slander. I will give the slanderers matter for curses.

124

When last I left Whitehaven, I swore never again to set foot on her pier, except, like Cæsar, at Sandwich, as a foreign invader. Spring under me, good ship; on you I bound to my vengeance!"

Men with poignant feelings, buried under an air of carefree self-command, are never proof to the sudden incitements of passion. Though in the main they may control themselves, yet if they but once permit the smallest vent, then they may bid adieu to all self-restraint, at least for that time. Thus with Paul on the present occasion. His sympathy with Israel had prompted this momentary ebullition. When it was gone by, he seemed not a little to regret it. But he passed it over lightly, saying, "You see, my fine fellow, what sort of a bloody cannibal I am. Will you be a sailor of mine? A sailor of the Captain who flogged poor Mungo Maxwell to death?"

"I will be very happy, Captain Paul, to be sailor under the man who will yet, I dare say, help flog the British nation to death."

"You hate 'em, do ye?"

"Like snakes. For months they've hunted me as a dog," half howled and half wailed Israel, at the memory of all he had suffered.

"Give me your hand, my lion; wave your wild flax again. By Heaven, you hate so well, I love ye. You shall be my confidential man; stand sentry at my cabin door; sleep in the cabin; steer my boat; keep by my side whenever I land. What do you say?"

"I say I'm glad to hear you."

"You are a good, brave soul. You are the first among the millions of mankind that I ever naturally took to. Come, you are tired. There, go into that state-room for to-night—it's mine. You offered me your bed in Paris."

"But you begged off, Captain, and so must I. Where do you sleep?"

"Lad, I don't sleep half a night out of three. My clothes have not been off now for five days."

"Ah, Captain, you sleep so little and scheme so much, you will die young."

"I know it: I want to: I mean to. Who would live a

125

doddered old stump? What do you think of my Scotch bonnet?"

"It looks well on you, Captain."

"Do you think so? A Scotch bonnet, though, ought to look well on a Scotchman. I'm such by birth. Is the gold band too much?"

"I like the gold band, Captain. It looks something as I should think a crown might on a king."

"Aye?"

"You would make a better-looking king than George III."

"Did you ever see that old granny? Waddles about in farthingales, and carries a peacock fan, don't he? Did you ever see him?"

"Was as close to him as I am to you now, Captain. In Kew Gardens it was, where I worked gravelling the walks. I was all alone with him, talking for some ten minutes."

"By Jove, what a chance! Had I but been there! What an opportunity for kidnapping a British king, and carrying him off in a fast sailing smack to Boston, a hostage for American freedom. But what did you? Didn't you try to do something to him?"

"I had a wicked thought or two, Captain; but I got the better of it. Besides, the King behaved handsomely towards me; yes, like a true man. God bless him for it. But it was before that, that I got the better of the wicked thought."

"Ah, meant to stick him, I suppose. Glad you didn't. It would have been very shabby. Never kill a king, but make him captive. He looks better as a led horse, than a dead carcass. I propose now, this trip, falling on the grounds of the Earl of Selkirk, a privy counsellor and particular private friend of George III. But I won't hurt a hair of his head. When I get him on board here, he shall lodge in my best state-room, which I mean to hang with damask for him. I shall drink wine with him, and be very friendly; take him to America, and introduce his lordship into the best circles there; only I shall have him accompanied on his calls by a sentry of two disguised as valets. For the Earl's to be on sale, mind; so much ransom; that is, the nobleman, Lord Selkirk, shall have a bodily price pinned on his coat-tail, like any slave up at auction in Charleston. But, my lad with the yellow mane, you very strangely draw out my secrets. And yet you don't talk. Your honesty is a magnet which attracts my sincerity. But I rely on your fidelity."

"I shall be a vice to your plans, Captain Paul. I will receive, but I won't let go, unless you alone loose the screw."

"Well said. To bed now; you ought to. I go on deck. Good night, ace-of-hearts."

"That is fitter for yourself, Captain Paul, lonely leader of the suit."

"Lonely? Aye, but number one cannot but be lonely, my trump."

"Again I give it back. Ace-of-trumps may it prove to you, Captain Paul; may it be impossible for you ever to be taken. But for me—poor deuce, a trey, that comes in your wake—any king or knave may take me, as before now the knaves have."

"Tut, tut, lad; never be more cheery for another than for yourself. But a fagged body fags the soul. To hammock, to hammock! while I go on deck to clap on more sail to your cradle."

And they separated for that night.

15

They Sail as Far as the Crag of Ailsa

Next morning Israel was appointed quartermaster—a subaltern selected from the common seamen, and whose duty mostly stations him in the stern of the ship, where the captain walks. His business is to carry the glass on the look-out for sails; hoist or lower the colors; and keep an eye on the helmsman. Picked out from the crew for their superior respectability and intelligence, as well as for their excellent seamanship, it is not unusual to find the quartermasters of an armed ship on peculiarly easy terms with the commissioned officers and captain. This berth, therefore, placed Israel in official contiguity to Paul, and without subjecting either to animadversion, made their public intercourse on deck almost as familiar as their unrestrained converse in the cabin.

It was a fine cool day in the beginning of April. They were now off the coast of Wales, whose lofty mountains, crested with snow, presented a Norwegian aspect. The wind was fair, and blew with a strange, bestirring power. The ship—running between Ireland and England, northwards, towards the Irish Sea, the inmost heart of the

British waters—seemed, as she snortingly shook the spray from her bow, to be conscious of the dare-devil defiance of the soul which conducted her on this anomalous cruise. Sailing alone from out a naval port of France, crowded with ships-of-the-line, Paul Jones, in his small craft, went forth in single-armed championship against the English host. Armed with but the sling-stones in his one shot-locker, like young David of old, Paul bearded the British giant of Gath. It is not easy, at the present day, to conceive the hardihood of this enterprise. It was a marching up to the muzzle; the act of one who made no compromise with the cannonadings of danger or death; such a scheme as only could have inspired a heart which held at nothing all the prescribed prudence of war, and every obligation of peace; combining in one breast the vengeful indignation and bitter ambition of an outraged hero, with the uncompunctious desperation of a renegade. In one view, the Coriolanus of the sea; in another, a cross between the gentleman and the wolf.

As Paul stood on the elevated part of the quarterdeck, with none but his confidential quartermaster near him, he yielded to Israel's natural curiosity to learn something concerning the sailing of the expedition. Paul stood lightly, swaying his body over the sea, by holding on to the mizzen-shrouds, an attitude not inexpressive of his easy audacity; while near by, pacing a few steps to and fro, his long spy-glass now under his arm, and now presented at his eye, Israel, looking the very image of vigilant prudence, listened to the warrior's story. It appeared that on the night of the visit of the Duke de Chartres and Count D'Estang to Doctor Franklin in Paris—the same night that Captain Paul and Israel were joint occupants of the neighboring chamber—the final sanction of the French king to the sailing of an American armament against England, under the direction of the Colonial Commissioner, was made known to the latter functionary. It was a very ticklish affair. Though swaying on the brink of avowed hostilities with England, no verbal declaration had as yet been made by France. Undoubtedly, this enigmatic position of things was highly advantageous to such an enterprise as Paul's.

Without detailing all the steps taken through the united efforts of Captain Paul and Doctor Franklin, suffice it that the determined rover had now attained his wish— the unfettered command of an armed ship in the British waters; a ship legitimately authorized to hoist the American colors, her commander having in his cabin-locker a regular commission as an officer of the American navy. He sailed without any instructions. With that rare insight into rare natures which so largely distinguished the sagacious Franklin, the sage well knew that a prowling *brave*, like Paul Jones, was, like the prowling lion, by nature a solitary warrior. "Let him alone," was the wise man's answer to some statesman who sought to hamper Paul with a letter of instructions.

Much subtle casuistry has been expended upon the point, whether Paul Jones was a knave or a hero, or a union of both. But war and warriors, like politics and politicians, like religion and religionists, admit of no metaphysics.

On the second day after Israel's arrival on board the Ranger, as he and Paul were conversing on the deck, Israel suddenly levelling his glass towards the Irish coast, announced a large sail bound in. The Ranger gave chase, and soon, almost within sight of her destination—the port of Dublin—the stranger was taken, manned, and turned round for Brest.

The Ranger then stood over, passed the Isle of Man towards the Cumberland shore, arriving within remote sight of Whitehaven about sunset. At dark she was hovering off the harbor, with a party of volunteers all ready to descend. But the wind shifted and blew fresh with a violent sea.

"I won't call on old friends in foul weather," said Captain Paul to Israel. "We'll saunter about a little, and leave our cards in a day or two."

Next morning, in Glentinebay, on the south shore of Scotland, they fell in with a revenue wherry. It was the practice of such craft to board merchant vessels. The

130

Ranger was disguised as a merchantman, presenting a broad drab-colored belt all round her hull; under the coat of a Quaker, concealing the intent of a Turk. It was expected that the chartered rover would come alongside the unchartered one. But the former took to flight, her two lug sails staggering under a heavy wind, which the pursuing guns of the Ranger pelted with a hail-storm of shot. The wherry escaped, spite the severe cannonade.

Off the Mull of Galoway, the day following, Paul found himself so nigh a large barley-freighted Scotch coaster, that, to prevent her carrying tidings of him to land, he dispatched her with the news, stern foremost, to Hades; sinking her, and sowing her barley in the sea broadcast by a broadside. From her crew he learned that there was a fleet of twenty or thirty sail at anchor in Lochryan, with an armed brigantine. He pointed his prow thither; but at the mouth of the lock, the wind turned against him again in hard squalls. He abandoned the project. Shortly after, he encountered a sloop from Dublin. He sunk her to prevent intelligence.

Thus, seeming as much to bear the elemental commission of Nature, as the military warrant of Congress, swarthy Paul darted hither and thither; hovering like a thunder-cloud off the crowded harbors; then, beaten off by an adverse wind, discharging his lightnings on uncompanioned vessels, whose solitude made them a more conspicuous and easier mark, like lonely trees on the heath. Yet all this while the land was full of garrisons, the embayed waters full of fleets. With the impunity of a Levanter, Paul skimmed his craft in the land-locked heart of the supreme naval power of earth; a torpedo-eel, unknowingly swallowed by Britain in a draught of old ocean, and making sad havoc with her vitals.

Seeing next a large vessel steering for the Clyde, he gave chase, hoping to cut her off. The stranger proving a fast sailer, the pursuit was urged on with vehemence, Paul standing, plank-proud, on the quarter-deck, calling for pulls upon every rope, to stretch each already half-burst sail to the uttermost.

While thus engaged, suddenly a shadow, like that

131

thrown by an eclipse, was seen rapidly gaining along the deck, with a sharp defined line, plain as a seam of the planks. It involved all before it. It was the domineering shadow of the Juan Ferandez-like crag of Ailsa. The Ranger was in the deep water which makes all round and close up to this great summit of the submarine Grampians.

The crag, more than a mile in circuit, is over a thousand feet high, eight miles from the Ayrshire shore. There stands the cove, lonely as a foundling, proud as Cheops. But, like the battered brains surmounting the Giant of Gath, its haughty summit is crowned by a desolate castle, in and out of whose arches the aerial mists eddy like purposeless phantoms, thronging the soul of some ruinous genius, who, even in overthrow, harbors none but lofty conceptions.

As the Ranger shot nigher under the crag, its height and bulk dwarfed both pursuer and pursued into nut-shells. The main-truck of the Ranger was nine hundred feet below the foundations of the ruin on the crag's top.

While the ship was yet under the shadow, and each seaman's face shared in the general eclipse, a sudden change came over Paul. He issued no more sultanical orders. He did not look so elate as before. At length he gave the command to discontinue the chase. Turning about, they sailed southward.

"Captain Paul," said Israel, shortly afterwards, "you changed your mind rather queerly about catching that craft. But you thought she was drawing us too far up into the land, I suppose."

"Sink the craft," cried Paul; "it was not any fear of her, nor of King George, which made me turn on my heel; it was yon cock of the walk."

"Cock of the walk?"

"Aye, cock of the walk of the sea; look—yon Crag of Ailsa."

16

They Look in at Carrickfergus,
and Descend on Whitehaven

Next day, off Carrickfergus, on the Irish coast, a fishing
boat, allured by the Quaker-like look of the incognito
craft, came off in full confidence. Her men were seized,
their vessel sunk. From them Paul learned that the large
ship at anchor in the road, was the ship-of-war Drake,
of twenty guns. Upon this he steered away, resolving to
return secretly, and attack her that night.

"Surely, Captain Paul," said Israel to his commander,
as about sunset they backed and stood in again for the
land, "surely, sir, you are not going right in among them
this way? Why not wait till she comes out?"

"Because, Yellow-hair, my boy, I am engaged to marry
her to-night. The bride's friends won't like the match; and
so, this very night, the bride must be carried away. She
has a nice tapering waist, hasn't she, through the glass?
Ah! I will clasp her to my heart."

He steered straight in like a friend; under easy sail,
lounging towards the Drake, with anchor ready to drop,
and grapnels to hug. But the wind was high; the anchor
was not dropped at the ordered time. The ranger came

to a stand three biscuits' toss off the unmisgiving enemy's quarter, like a peaceful merchantman from the Canadas, laden with harmless lumber.

"I sha'n't marry her just yet," whispered Paul, seeing his plans for the time frustrated. Gazing in audacious tranquillity upon the decks of the enemy, and amicably answering her hail, with complete self-possession, he commanded the cable to be slipped, and then, as if he had accidentally parted his anchor, turned his prow on the seaward tack, meaning to return again immediately with the same prospect of advantage possessed at first—his plan being to crash suddenly athwart the Drake's bow, so as to have all her decks exposed point-blank to his musketry. But once more the winds interposed. It came on with a storm of snow; he was obliged to give up his project.

Thus, without any warlike appearance, and giving no alarm, Paul, like an invisible ghost, glided by night close to land, actually came to anchor, for an instant, within speaking-distance of an English ship-of-war; and yet came, anchored, answered hail, reconnoitered, debated, decided, and retired, without exciting the least suspicion. His purpose was chain-shot destruction. So easily may the deadliest foe—so he be but dexterous—slide, undreamed of, into human harbors or hearts. And not awakened conscience, but mere prudence, restrain such, if they vanish again without doing harm. At daybreak no soul in Carrickfergus knew that the devil, in a Scotch bonnet, had passed close that way overnight.

Seldom has regicidal daring been more strangely coupled with octogenarian prudence, than in many of the predatory enterprises of Paul. It is this combination of apparent incompatibilities which ranks him among extraordinary warriors.

Ere daylight, the storm of the night blew over. The sun saw the Ranger lying midway over channel at the head of the Irish Sea; England, Scotland, and Ireland, with all their lofty cliffs, being as simultaneously as plainly in sight beyond the grass-green waters, as the City Hall, St. Paul's, and the Astor House, from the triangular Park in

New York. The three kingdoms lay covered with snow, far as the eye could reach.

"Ah, Yellow-hair," said Paul, with a smile, "they show the white flag, the cravens. And, while the white flag stays blanketing yonder heights, we'll make for Whitehaven, my boy. I promised to drop in there a moment ere quitting the country for good. Israel, lad, I mean to step ashore in person, and have a personal hand in the thing. Did you ever drive spikes?"

"I've driven the spike-teeth into harrows before now," replied Israel; "but that was before I was a sailor."

"Well, then, driving spikes into harrows is a good introduction to driving spikes into cannon. You are just the man. Put down your glass; go to the carpenter, get a hundred spikes, put them in a bucket with a hammer, and bring all to me."

As evening fell, the great promontory of St. Bee's Head, with its lighthouse, not far from Whitehaven, was in distant sight. But the wind became so light that Paul could not work his ship in close enough at an hour as early as intended. His purpose had been to make the descent and retire ere break of day. But though this intention was frustrated, he did not renounce his plan, for the present would be his last opportunity.

As the night wore on, and the ship, with a very light wind, glided nigher and nigher the mark, Paul called upon Israel to produce his bucket for final inspection. Thinking some of the spikes too large, he had them filed down a little. He saw to the lanterns and combustibles. Like Peter the Great, he went into the smallest details, while still possessing a genius competent to plan the aggregate. But oversee as one may, it is impossible to guard against carelessness in subordinates. One's sharp eyes can't see behind one's back. It will yet be noted that an important omission was made in the preparations for Whitehaven.

The town contained, at that period, a population of some six or seven thousand inhabitants, defended by forts.

At midnight, Paul Jones, Israel Potter, and twenty-nine others, rowed in two boats to attack the six or seven thousand inhabitants of Whitehaven. There was a long way to pull. This was done in perfect silence. Not a sound was heard except the oars turning in the rowlocks. Nothing was seen except the two lighthouses of the harbor. Through the stillness and darkness, the two deep-laden boats swam into the haven, like two mysterious whales from the Arctic Sea. As they reached the outer pier, the men saw each other's faces. The day was dawning. The riggers and other artisans of the shipping would before very long be astir. No matter.

The great staple exported from Whitehaven was then, and still is, coal. The town is surrounded by mines; the town is built on mines; the ships moor over mines. The mines honeycomb the land in all directions, and extend in galleries of grottoes for two miles under the sea. By the falling in of the more ancient collieries numerous houses have been swallowed, as if by an earthquake, and a consternation spread, like that of Lisbon, in 1755. So insecure and treacherous was the site of the place now about to be assailed by a desperado, nursed, like the coal, in its vitals.

Now, sailing on the Thames, nigh its mouth, of fair days, when the wind is favorable for inward-bound craft, the stranger will sometimes see processions of vessels, all of similar size and rig, stretching for miles and miles, like a long string of horses tied two and two to a rope and driven to market. These are colliers going to London with coal.

About three hundred of these vessels now lay, all crowded together, in one dense mob, at Whitehaven. The tide was out. They lay completely helpless, clear of water, and grounded. They were sooty in hue. Their black yards were deeply canted, like spears, to avoid collision. The three hundred grimy hulls lay wallowing in the mud, like a herd of hippopotami asleep in the alluvium of the Nile. Their sailless, raking masts, and canted yards, resembled a forest of fish-spears thrust into those same hippopotamus hides. Partly flanking one side of the grounded fleet was a fort, whose batteries were raised from the beach. On a little strip of this beach, at the base of the fort, lay a number of small rusty guns, dismounted, heaped together in disorder, as a litter of dogs. Above them projected the mounted cannon.

Paul landed in his own boat at the foot of this fort. He dispatched the other boat to the north side of the haven, with orders to fire the shipping there. Leaving two men at the beach, he then proceeded to get possession of the fort.

"Hold on to the bucket, and give me your shoulder," said he to Israel.

Using Israel for a ladder, in a trice he scaled the wall. The bucket and the men followed. He led the way softly to the guard-house, burst in, and bound the sentinels in their sleep. Then arranging his force, ordered four men to spike the cannon there.

"Now, Israel, your bucket, and follow me to the other fort."

The two went alone about a quarter of a mile.

"Captain Paul," said Israel, on the way, "can we two manage the sentinels?"

"There are none in the fort we go to."

"You know all about the place, Captain?"

"Pretty well informed on that subject, I believe. Come along. Yes, lad, I am tolerably well acquainted with Whitehaven. And this morning intend that Whitehaven shall have a slight inkling of *me*. Come on. Here we are."

Scaling the walls, the two involuntarily stood for an instant gazing upon the scene. The gray light of the dawn showed the crowded houses and thronged ships with a haggard distinctness.

"Spike and hammer, lad;—so,—now follow me along, as I go, and give me a spike for every cannon. I'll tongue-tie the thunderers. Speak no more!" and he spiked the first gun. "Be a mute," and he spiked the second. "Dumb-founder thee," and he spiked the third. And so, on, and on, and on, Israel following him with the bucket, like a footman, or some charitable gentleman with a basket of alms.

"There, it is done. D'ye see the fire yet, lad, from the south? I don't."

137

"Not a spark, Captain. But day-sparks come on in the east."

"Forked flames into the hounds! What are they about? Quick, let us back to the first fort; perhaps something has happened, and they are there."

Sure enough, on their return from spiking the cannon, Paul and Israel found the other boat back, the crew in confusion, their lantern having burnt out at the very instant they wanted it. By a singular fatality the other lantern, belonging to Paul's boat, was likewise extinguished. No tinder-box had been brought. They had no matches but sulphur matches. Locofocos were not then known.

The day came on apace.

"Captain Paul," said the lieutenant of the second boat, "it is madness to stay longer. See!" and he pointed to the town, now plainly discernible in the gray light.

"Traitor, or coward!" howled Paul, "how came the lanterns out? Israel, my lion, now prove your blood. Get me a light—but one spark!"

"Has any man here a bit of pipe and tobacco in his pocket?" said Israel.

A sailor quickly produced an old stump of a pipe, with tobacco.

"That will do," and Israel hurried away towards the town.

"What will the loon do with the pipe?" said one. "And where goes he?" cried another.

"Let him alone," said Paul.

The invader now disposed his whole force so as to retreat at an instant's warning. Meantime the hardy Israel, long experienced in all sorts of shifts and emergencies, boldly ventured to procure, from some inhabitant of Whitehaven, a spark to kindle all Whitehaven's habitations in flames.

There was a lonely house standing somewhat disjointed from the town, some poor laborer's abode. Rapping at the door, Israel, pipe in mouth, begged the inmates for a light for his tobacco.

"What the devil," roared a voice from within, "knock up a man this time of night to light your pipe? Begone!"

"You are lazy this morning, my friend," replied Israel, "it is daylight. Quick, give me a light. Don't you know your old friend? Shame! open the door."

In a moment a sleepy fellow appeared, let down the bar, and Israel, stalking into the dim room, piloted himself straight to the fire-place, raked away the cinders, lighted his tobacco, and vanished.

All was done in a flash. The man, stupid with sleep, had looked on bewildered. He reeled to the door, but, dodging behind a pile of bricks, Israel had already hurried himself out of sight.

"Well done, my lion," was the hail he received from Paul, who, during his absence, had mustered as many pipes as possible, in order to communicate and multiply the fire.

Both boats now pulled to a favorable point of the principal pier of the harbor, crowded close up to a part of which lay one wing of the colliers.

The men began to murmur at persisting in an attempt impossible to be concealed much longer. They were afraid to venture on board the grim colliers, and go groping down into their hulls to fire them. It seemed like a voluntary entrance into dungeons and death.

"Follow me, all of you but ten by the boats," said Paul, without noticing their murmurs. "And now, to put an end to all future burnings in America, by one mighty conflagration of shipping in England. Come on, lads! Pipes and matches in the van!"

He would have distributed the men so simultaneously to different ships at different points, were it not that the lateness of the hour rendered such a course insanely hazardous. Stationing his party in front of one of the windward colliers, Paul and Israel sprang on board.

In a twinkling they had broken open a boatswain's locker, and, with great bunches of oakum, fine and dry as tinder, had leaped into the steerage. Here, while Paul made a blaze, Israel ran to collect the tar-pots, which being presently poured on the burning matches, oakum and wood, soon increased the flame.

"It is not a sure thing yet," said Paul, "we must have a barrel of tar."

They searched about until they found one, knocked out the head and bottom, and stood it like a martyr in the midst of the flames. They then retreated up the forward hatchway, while volumes of smoke were belched from the after one. Not till this moment did Paul hear the cries of his men, warning him that the inhabitants were not only actually astir, but crowds were on their way to the pier.

As he sprang out of the smoke towards the rail of the collier, he saw the sun risen, with thousands of the people. Individuals hurried close to the burning vessel. Leaping to the ground, Paul, bidding his men stand fast, ran to their front, and, advancing about thirty feet, presented his own pistol at now tumultuous Whitehaven.

Those who had rushed to extinguish what they had deemed but an accidental fire, were now paralyzed into idiotic inaction at the defiance of the incendiary, thinking him some sudden pirate or fiend dropped down from the moon.

While Paul thus stood guarding the incipient conflagration, Israel, without a weapon, dashed crazily towards the mob on the shore.

"Come back, come back," cried Paul.

"Not till I start these sheep, as their own wolves many a time started me!"

As he rushed bare-headed like a madman, towards the crowd, the panic spread. They fled from unarmed Israel, further than they had from the pistol of Paul.

The flames now catching the rigging and spiralling around the masts, the whole ship burned at one end of the harbor, while the sun, an hour high, burned at the other. Alarm and amazement, not sleep, now ruled the world. It was time to retreat.

They re-embarked without opposition, first releasing a few prisoners, as the boats could not carry them.

Just as Israel was leaping into the boat, he saw the man at whose house he had procured the fire, staring like a simpleton at him.

"That was good seed you gave me"; said Israel, "see what a yield," pointing to the flames. He then dropped into the boat, leaving only Paul on the pier.

The men cried to their commander, conjuring him not to linger.

But Paul remained for several moments, confronting in silence the clamors of the mob beyond, and waving his solitary hand, like a disdainful tomahawk, towards the surrounding eminences, also covered with the affrighted inhabitants.

When the assailants had rowed pretty well off, the English rushed in great numbers to their forts, but only to find their cannon no better than so much iron in the ore. At length, however, they began to fire, having either brought down some ship's guns, or else mounted the rusty old dogs lying at the foot of the first fort.

In their eagerness they fired with no discretion. The shot fell short; they did not the slightest damage.

Paul's men laughed aloud, and fired their pistols in the air.

Not a splinter was made, not a drop of blood spilled throughout the affair. The intentional harmlessness of the result, as to human life, was only equalled by the desperate courage of the deed. It formed, doubtless, one feature of the compassionate contempt of Paul towards the town, that he took such paternal care of their lives and limbs.

Had it been possible to have landed a few hours earlier not a ship nor a house could have escaped. But it was the lesson, not the loss, that told. As it was, enough damage had been done to demonstrate—as Paul had declared to the wise man of Paris—that the disasters caused by the wanton fires and assaults on the American coasts, could be easily brought home to the enemy's doors. Though, indeed, if the retaliators were headed by Paul Jones, the satisfaction would not be equal to the insult, being abated by the magnanimity of a chivalrous, however unprincipled foe.

17

*They Call at the Earl of Selkirk's, and Afterwards
Fight the Ship-of-War Drake*

The Ranger now stood over the Solway Frith for the
Scottish shore, and at noon on the same day, Paul, with
twelve men, including two officers and Israel, landed
on St. Mary's Isle, one of the seats of the Earl of Selkirk.

In three consecutive days this elemental warrior either
entered the harbors or landed on the shores of each of
the Three Kingdoms.

The morning was fair and clear. St. Mary's Isle lay
shimmering in the sun. The light crust of snow had melted,
revealing the tender grass and sweet buds of spring man-
tling the sides of the cliffs.

At once, upon advancing with his party towards the
house, Paul augured ill for his project from the loneliness
of the spot. No being was seen. But cocking his bonnet
at a jaunty angle, he continued his way. Stationing the
men silently round about the house, followed by Israel,
he announced his presence at the porch.

A gray-headed domestic at length responded.

"Is the Earl within?"

"He is in Edinburgh, sir."

"Ah—sure?—Is your lady within?"

"Yes, sir—who shall I say it is?"

"A gentleman who calls to pay his respects. Here, take my card."

And he handed the man his name, as a private gentleman, superbly engraved at Paris, on gilded paper.

Israel tarried in the hall while the old servant led Paul into a parlor.

Presently the lady appeared.

"Charming Madame, I wish you a very good morning."

"Who may it be, sir, that I have the happiness to see?" said the lady, censoriously drawing herself up at the too frank gallantry of the stranger.

"Madame, I sent you my card."

"Which leaves me equally ignorant, sir," said the lady, coldly, twirling the gilded pasteboard.

"A courier dispatched to Whitehaven, charming Madame, might bring you more particular tidings as to who has the honor of being your visitor."

Not comprehending what this meant, and deeply displeased, if not vaguely alarmed, at the characteristic manner of Paul, the lady, not entirely unembarrassed, replied, that if the gentleman came to view the isle, he was at liberty so to do. She would retire and send him a guide.

"Countess of Selkirk," said Paul, advancing a step, "I call to see the Earl. On business of urgent importance, I call."

"The Earl is in Edinburgh," uneasily responded the lady, again about to retire.

"Do you give me your honor as a lady that it is as you say?"

The lady looked at him in dubious resentment.

"Pardon, Madame, I would not lightly impugn a lady's lightest word, but I surmised that, possibly, you might suspect the object of my call, in which case it would be the most excusable thing in the world for you to seek to shelter from my knowledge the presence of the Earl on the isle."

"I do not dream what you mean by all this," said the lady with a decided alarm, yet even in her panic courageously maintaining her dignity, as she retired, rather than retreated, nearer the door.

"Madame," said Paul, hereupon waving his hand imploringly, and then tenderly playing with his bonnet with the golden band, while an expression poetically sad and sentimental stole over his tawny face; "it cannot be too poignantly lamented that, in the profession of arms, the officer of fine feelings and genuine sensibility should be sometimes necessitated to public actions which his own private heart cannot approve. This hard case is mine. The Earl, Madame, you say is absent. I believe those words. Far be it from my soul, enchantress, to ascribe a fault to syllables which have proceeded from so faultless a source."

This probably he said in reference to the lady's mouth, which was beautiful in the extreme.

He bowed very lowly, while the lady eyed him with conflicting and troubled emotions, but as yet all in darkness as to his ultimate meaning. But her more immediate alarm had subsided, seeing now that the sailor-like extravagance of Paul's homage was entirely unaccompanied with any touch of intentional disrespect. Indeed, hyperbolical as were his phrases, his gestures and whole carriage were most heedfully deferential.

Paul continued: "The Earl, Madame, being absent, and he being the sole object of my call, you cannot labor under the least apprehension, when I now inform you, that I have the honor of being an officer in the American Navy, who, having stopped at this isle to secure the person of the Earl of Selkirk as a hostage for the American cause, am, by your assurances, turned away from that intent; pleased, even in disappointment, since that disappointment has served to prolong my interview with the noble lady before me, as well as to leave her domestic tranquillity unimpaired."

"Can you really speak true?" said the lady in undismayed wonderment.

"Madame, through your window you will catch a little peep of the American colonial ship-of-war, Ranger, which I have the honor to command. With my best respects to your lord, and sincere regrets at not finding him at home, permit me to salute your ladyship's hand and withdraw."

But feigning not to notice this Parisian proposition, and artfully entrenching her hand, without seeming to do so, the lady, in a conciliatory tone, begged her visitor to partake of some refreshment ere he departed, at the same time thanking him for his great civility. But declining these hospitalities, Paul bowed thrice and quitted the room.

In the hall he encountered Israel, standing all agape before a Highland target of steel, with a claymore and foil crossed on top.

"Looks like a pewter platter and knife and fork, Captain Paul."

"So they do, my lion; but come, curse it, the old cock has flown; fine hen, though, left in the nest; no use; we must away empty-handed."

"Why, ain't Mr. Selkirk in?" demanded Israel in roguish concern.

"Mr. Selkirk? Alexander Selkirk, you mean. No, lad, he's not on the Isle of St. Mary's; he's away off, a hermit, on the Isle of Juan Fernandez—the more's the pity; come."

In the porch they encountered the two officers. Paul briefly informed them of the circumstances, saying, nothing remained but to depart forthwith.

"With nothing at all for our pains?" murmured the two officers.

"What, pray, would you have?"

"Some pillage, to be sure—plate."

"Shame. I thought we were three gentlemen."

"So are the English officers in America; but they help themselves to plate whenever they can get it from the private houses of the enemy."

"Come, now, don't be slanderous," said Paul; "these officers you speak of are but one or two out of twenty, mere burglars and light-fingered gentry, using the King's livery but as a disguise to their nefarious trade. The rest are men of honor."

"Captain Paul Jones," responded the two, "we have not come on this expedition in much expectation of regular pay; but we *did* rely upon honorable plunder."

"Honorable plunder! That's something new."

But the officers were not to be turned aside. They were

the most efficient in the ship. Seeing them resolute, Paul, for fear of incensing them, was at last, as a matter of policy, obliged to comply. For himself, however, he resolved to have nothing to do with the affair. Charging the officers not to allow the men to enter the house on any pretence, and that no search must be made, and nothing must be taken away, except what the lady should offer them upon making known their demand, he beckoned to Israel and retired indignantly towards the beach. Upon second thoughts, he dispatched Israel back, to enter the house with the officers, as joint receiver of the plate, he being, of course, the most reliable of the seamen.

The lady was not a little disconcerted on receiving the officers. With cool determination they made known their purpose. There was no escape. The lady retired. The butler came; and soon, several silver salvers, and other articles of value, were silently deposited in the parlor in the presence of the officers and Israel.

"Mister Butler," said Israel, "let me go into the dairy and help to carry the milk-pans."

But, scowling upon this rusticity, or roguishness—he knew not which—the butler, in high dudgeon at Israel's republican familiarity, as well as black as a thunder-cloud with the general insult offered to an illustrious household by a party of armed thieves, as he viewed them, declined any assistance. In a quarter of an hour the officers left the house, carrying their booty.

At the porch they were met by a red-cheeked, spiteful-looking lass, who, with her brave lady's compliments, added two child's rattles of silver and coral to their load.

Now, one of the officers was a Frenchman, the other a Spaniard.

The Spaniard dashed his rattle indignantly to the ground. The Frenchman took his very pleasantly, and kissed it, saying to the girl that he would long preserve the coral, as a memento of her rosy cheeks.

When the party arrived on the beach, they found Captain Paul writing with pencil on paper held up against the smooth tableted side of the cliff. Next moment he seemed to be making his signature. With a reproachful glance towards the two officers, he handed the slip to Israel, bidding him hasten immediately with it to the house and place it in Lady Selkirk's own hands.

The note was as follows:

"Madame:

"After so courteous a reception, I am disturbed to make you no better return than you have just experienced from the actions of certain persons under my command.—actions, lady, which my profession of arms obliges me not only to brook, but, in a measure, to countenance. From the bottom of my heart, my dear lady, I deplore this most melancholy necessity of my delicate position. However unhandsome the desire of these men, some complaisance seemed due them from me, for their general good conduct and bravery on former occasions. I had but an instant to consider. I trust, that in unavoidably gratifying them, I have inflicted less injury on your ladyship's property than I have on my own bleeding sensibilities. But my heart will not allow me to say more. Permit me to assure you, dear lady, that when the plate is sold, I shall, at all hazards, become the purchaser, and will be proud to restore it to you, by such conveyance as you may hereafter see fit to appoint.

"From hence I go, Madame, to engage, to-morrow morning, his Majesty's ship, Drake, of twenty guns, now lying at Carrickfergus. I should meet the enemy with more than wonted resolution, could I flatter myself that, through this unhandsome conduct on the part of my officers, I lie not under the disesteem of the sweet lady of the Isle of St. Mary's. But unconquerable as Mars should I be, could I but dare to dream, that in some green retreat of her charming domain, the Countess of Selkirk offers up a charitable prayer for, my dear lady countess, one, who coming to take a captive, himself has been captivated.

"Your ladyship's adoring enemy,
"JOHN PAUL JONES."

147

How the lady received this super-ardent note, history does not relate. But history has not omitted to record, that after the return of the Ranger to France, through the assiduous efforts of Paul in buying up the booty, piece by piece, from the clutches of those among whom it had been divided, and not without a pecuniary private loss to himself, equal to the total value of the plunder, the plate was punctually restored, even to the silver heads of two pepper-boxes; and, not only this, but the Earl, hearing all the particulars, magnanimously wrote Paul a letter, expressing thanks for his politeness. In the opinion of the noble Earl, Paul was a man of honor. It were rash to differ in opinion with such high-born authority.

Upon returning to the ship, she was instantly pointed over towards the Irish coast. Next morning Carrickfergus was in sight. Paul would have gone straight in; but Israel, reconnoitring with his glass, informed him that a large ship, probably the Drake, was just coming out.

"What think you, Israel, do they know who we are? Let me have the glass."

"They are dropping a boat now, sir," replied Israel, removing the glass from his eye, and handing it to Paul.

"So they are—so they are. They don't know us. I'll decoy that boat alongside. Quick—they are coming for us—take the helm now yourself, my lion, and keep the ship's stern steadily presented towards the advancing boat. Don't let them have the least peep at our broadside."

The boat came on, an officer in its bow all the time eyeing the Ranger through a glass. Presently the boat was within hail.

"Ship ahoy! Who are you?"

"Oh, come alongside," answered Paul through his trumpet, in a rapid off-hand tone, as though he were a gruff sort of friend, impatient at being suspected for a foe.

In a few moments the officer of the boat stepped into the Ranger's gangway. Cocking his bonnet gallantly, Paul advanced towards him, making a very polite bow, saying: "Good morning, sir, good morning; delighted to see you. That's a pretty sword you have; pray, let me look at it."

"I see," said the officer, glancing at the ship's armament, and turning pale. "I am your prisoner."

"No—my guest," responded Paul, winningly. "Pray, let me relieve you of your—your—cane."

Thus humorously he received the officer's delivered sword.

"Now tell me, sir, if you please," he continued, "what brings out his Majesty's ship Drake this fine morning? Going a little airing?"

"She comes out in search of you, but when I left her side half an hour since she did not know that the ship off the harbor was the one she sought."

"You had news from Whitehaven, I suppose, last night, eh?"

"Aye: express; saying that certain incendiaries had landed there early that morning."

"What?—what sort of men were they, did you say?" said Paul, shaking his bonnet fiercely to one side of his head, and coming close to the officer. "Pardon me," he added derisively, "I had forgot you are my *guest*. Israel, see the unfortunate gentleman below, and his men forward."

The Drake was now seen slowly coming out under a light air, attended by five small pleasure-vessels, decorated with flags and streamers, and full of gaily-dressed people, whom motives similar to those which drew visitors to the circus, had induced to embark on their adventurous trip. But they little dreamed how nigh the desperate enemy was.

"Drop the captured boat astern," said Paul; "see what effect that will have on those merry voyagers."

No sooner was the empty boat descried by the pleasure-vessels than forthwith, surmising the truth, they with all diligence turned about and re-entered the harbor. Shortly after, alarm-smokes were seen extending along both sides of the channel.

"They smoke us at last, Captain Paul," said Israel.

"There will be more smoke yet before the day is done," replied Paul, gravely.

The wind was right under the land, the tide unfavorable. The Drake worked out very slowly.

Meantime, like some fiery-hearted duellist calling on urgent business at frosty daybreak, and long kept waiting at the door by the dilatoriness of his antagonist, shrinking at the idea of getting up to be cut to pieces in the cold—the Ranger, with a better breeze, impatiently tacked to and fro in the channel. At last, when the English vessel had fairly weathered the point, Paul, ranging ahead, courteously led her forth, as a beau might a belle in a ball-room, to mid-channel, and then suffered her to come within hail.

"She is hoisting her colors now, sir," said Israel.

"Give her the stars and stripes, then, my lad."

Joyfully running to the locker, Israel attached the flag to the halyards. The wind freshened. He stood elevated. The bright flag blew around him, a glorified shroud, enveloping him in its red ribbons and spangles, like up-springing tongues, and sparkles of flame.

As the colors rose to their final perch, and streamed in the air, Paul eyed them exultingly.

"I first hoisted that flag on an American ship, and was the first among men to get it saluted. If I perish this night, the name of Paul Jones shall live. Hark! they hail us."

"What ship are you?"

"Your enemy. Come on! What wants the fellow of more prefaces and introductions?"

The sun was now calmly setting over the green land of Ireland. The sky was serene, the sea smooth, the wind just sufficient to waft the two vessels steadily and gently. After the first firing and a little manœuvring, the two ships glided on freely, side by side; in that mild air exchanging their deadly broadsides, like two friendly horsemen walking their steeds along a plain, chatting as they go. After an hour of this running fight, the conversation ended. The Drake struck. How changed from the big craft of sixty short minutes before! She seemed now, above deck, like a piece of wild western woodland into which choppers had been. Her masts and yards prostrate, and hanging in jack-straws; several of her sails ballooning out, as they dragged in the sea, like great lopped tops of foliage. The black hull and shattered stumps of masts, galled and riddled, looked as if gigantic woodpeckers had been tapping them.

The Drake was the larger ship; more cannon; more men. Her loss in killed and wounded was far the greater. Her brave captain and lieutenant were mortally wounded.

The former died as the prize was boarded, the latter two days after.

It was twilight, the weather still severe. No cannonade, naught that mad man can do, molests the stoical imperturbability of Nature, when Nature chooses to be still. This weather, holding on through the following day, greatly facilitated the refitting of the ships. That done, the two vessels, sailing round the north of Ireland, steered towards Brest. They were repeatedly chased by English cruisers, but safely reached their anchorage in the French waters.

"A pretty fair four weeks' yachting, gentlemen," said Paul Jones, as the Ranger swung to her cable, while some French officers boarded her. "I bring two travellers with me, gentlemen," he continued. "Allow me to introduce you to my particular friend Israel Potter, late of North America, and also to his Britannic Majesty's ship Drake, late of Carrickfergus, Ireland."

This cruise made loud fame for Paul, especially at the court of France, whose king sent Paul a sword and a medal. But poor Israel, who also had conquered a craft, and all unaided too—what had he?

18

The Expedition That Sailed from Groix

Three months after anchoring at Brest, through Dr. Franklin's negotiations with the French king, backed by the bestirring ardor of Paul, a squadron of nine vessels, of various force, were ready in the road of Groix for another descent on the British coasts. These craft were miscellaneously picked up, their crews a mongrel pack, the officers mostly French, unacquainted with each other, and secretly jealous of Paul. The expedition was full of the elements of insubordination and failure. Much bitterness and agony resulted to a spirit like Paul's. But he bore up, and though in many particulars the sequel more than warranted his misgivings, his soul still refused to surrender.

The career of this stubborn adventurer signally illustrates the idea that since all human affairs are subject to organic disorder, since they are created in and sustained by a sort of half-disciplined chaos, hence he who in great things seeks success must never wait for smooth water, which never was and never will be, but, with what straggling method he can, dash with all his derangements at his object, leaving the rest to Fortune.

Though nominally commander of the squadron, Paul was not so in effect. Most of his captains conceitedly claimed independent commands. One of them in the end proved a traitor outright; few of the rest were reliable.

As for the ships, that commanded by Paul in person will be a good example of the fleet. She was an old Indiaman, clumsy and crank, smelling strongly of the savor of tea, cloves, and arrack, the cargoes of former voyages. Even at that day she was, from her venerable grotesqueness, what a cocked hat is, at the present age, among ordinary beavers. Her elephantine bulk was houdahed with a castellated poop like the leaning tower of Pisa. Poor Israel, standing on the top of this poop, spy-glass at his eye, looked more an astronomer than a mariner, having to do, not with the mountains of the billows, but the mountains in the moon. Galileo on Fiesole. She was originally a single-decked ship, that is, carried her armament on one gun-deck; but cutting ports below, in her after part, Paul rammed out there six old eighteen-pounders, whose rusty muzzles peered just above the waterline, like a parcel of dirty mulattoes from a cellarway. Her name was the Duras, but, ere sailing, it was changed to that other appellation, whereby this sad old hulk became afterwards immortal. Though it is not unknown, that a compliment to Doctor Franklin was involved in this change of titles, yet the secret history of the affair will now for the first time be disclosed.

It was evening in the road of Groix. After a fagging day's work, trying to conciliate the hostile jealousy of his officers, and provide, in the face of endless obstacles (for he had to dance attendance on scores of intriguing factors and brokers ashore), the requisite stores for the fleet, Paul sat in his cabin in a half-despondent reverie, while Israel, cross-legged at his commander's feet, was patching up some old signals.

"Captain Paul, I don't like our ship's name.—Duras? What's that mean?—Duras? Being cribbed up in a ship named Duras! a sort of makes one feel as if he were in durance vile."

"Gad, I never thought of that before, my lion. Duras—

Durance vile. I suppose it's superstition, but I'll change it. Come, Yellow-mane, what shall we call her?"

"Well, Captain Paul, don't you like Doctor Franklin? Hasn't he been the prime man to get this fleet together? Let's call her the Doctor Franklin."

"Oh, no, that will too publicly declare him just at present; and Poor Richard wants to be a little shady in this business."

"Poor Richard!—call her Poor Richard, then," cried Israel, suddenly struck by the idea.

"'Gad, you have it," answered Paul, springing to his feet, as all trace of his former despondency left him;— "Poor Richard shall be the name, in honour to the saying, that 'God helps them that help themselves,' as Poor Richard says."

Now this was the way the craft came to be called the *Bon Homme Richard;* for it being deemed advisable to have a French rendering of the new title, it assumed the above form.

A few days after, the force sailed. Ere long, they captured several vessels; but the captains of the squadron proving refractory, events took so deplorable a turn, that Paul, for the present, was obliged to return to Groix. Luckily, however, at this junction a cartel arrived from England with upwards of a hundred exchanged American seamen, who almost to a man enlisted under the flag of Paul.

Upon the resailing of the force, the old troubles broke out afresh. Most of her consorts insubordinately separated from the *Bon Homme Richard.* At length Paul found himself in violent storms beating off the rugged southeastern coast of Scotland, with only two accompanying ships. But neither the mutiny of his fleet, nor the chaos of the elements, made him falter in his purpose. Nay, at this crisis, he projected the most daring of all his descents.

The Cheviot Hills were in sight. Sundry vessels had been described bound in for the Firth of Forth, on whose south shore, well up the Firth, stands Leith, the port of Edinburgh, distant but a mile or two from that capital. He resolved to dash at Leith, and lay it under contribution or in ashes. He called the captains of his two remaining consorts on board his own ship to arrange details. Those worthies had much of fastidious remark to make against the plan. After losing much time in trying to bring to a conclusion their sage deliberations, Paul, by addressing their cupidity, achieved that which all appeals to their gallantry could not accomplish. He proclaimed the grand prize of the Leith lottery at no less a figure than £200,000, that being named as the ransom. Enough: the three ships enter the Firth, boldly and freely, as if carrying Quakers to a Peace-Congress.

Along both startled shores the panic of their approach spread like the cholera. The three suspicious crafts had so long lain off and on, that none doubted they were led by the audacious viking, Paul Jones. At five o'clock, on the following morning, they were distinctly seen from the capital of Scotland, quietly sailing up the bay. Batteries were hastily thrown up at Leith, arms were obtained from the castle at Edinburgh, alarm fires were kindled in all directions. Yet with such tranquillity of effrontery did Paul conduct his ships, concealing as much as possible their warlike character, that more than once his vessels were mistaken for merchantmen, and hailed by passing ships as such.

In the afternoon, Israel, at his station on the tower of Pisa, reported a boat with five men coming off to the *Richard* from the coast of Fife.

"They have hot oak-cakes for us," said Paul; "let 'em come. To encourage them, show them the English ensign, Israel, my lad."

Soon the boat was alongside.

"Well, my good fellows, what can I do for you this afternoon?" said Paul, leaning over the side with a patronizing air.

"Why, captain, we come from the Laird of Crokarky, who wants some powder and ball for his money."

"What would you with powder and ball, pray?"

"Oh! haven't you heard that that bloody pirate, Paul Jones, is somewhere hanging round the coasts?"

"Aye, indeed, but he won't hurt you. He's only going

round among the nations, with his old hat, taking up contributions. So, away with ye; ye don't want any powder and ball to give him. He wants contributions of silver, not lead. Prepare yourselves with silver, I say."

"Nay, captain, the Laird ordered us not to return without powder and ball. See, here is the price. It may be the taking of the bloody pirate, if you let us have what we want."

"Well, pass 'em over a keg," said Paul, laughing, but modifying his order by a sly whisper to Israel: "Oh, put up your price, it's a gift to ye."

"But ball, captain; what's the use of powder without ball?" roared one of the fellows from the boat's bow, as the keg was lowered in. "We want ball."

"Bless my soul, you bawl loud enough as it is. Away with ye, with what you have. Look to your keg, and hark ye, if ye catch that villain, Paul Jones, give him no quarter."

"But, captain, here," shouted one of the boatmen, "there's a mistake. This is a keg of pickles, not powder. Look," and poking into the bung-hole, he dragged out a green cucumber dripping with brine. "Take this back, and give us the powder."

"Pooh," said Paul, "the powder is at the bottom, pickled powder, best way to keep it. Away with ye, now, and after that bloody embezzler, Paul Jones."

This was Sunday. The ships held on. During the afternoon, a long tack of the *Richard* brought her close towards the shores of Fife, near the thriving little port of Kirkaldy.

"There's a great crowd on the beach, Captain Paul," said Israel, looking through his glass. "There seems to be an old woman standing on a fish-barrel there, a sort of selling things at auction to the people, but I can't be certain yet."

"Let me see," said Paul, taking the glass as they came nigher. "Sure enough, it's an old lady—an old quack-doctress, seems to me, in a black gown, too. I must hail her."

Ordering the ship to be kept on towards the port, he shortened sail within easy distance, so as to glide slowly by, and seizing the trumpet, thus spoke:

"Old lady, ahoy! What are you talking about? What's your text?"

"The righteous shall rejoice when he seeth the vengeance. He shall wash his feet in the blood of the wicked."

"Ah, what a lack of charity. Now hear mine:— God helpeth them that help themselves, as Poor Richard says."

"Reprobate pirate, a gale shall yet come to drive thee in wrecks from our waters."

"The strong wind of your hate fills my sails well. Adieu," waving his bonnet—"tell us the rest at Leith."

Next morning the ships were almost within cannonshot of the town. The men to be landed were in the boats. Israel had the tiller of the foremost one, waiting for his commander to enter, when just as Paul's foot was on the gangway, a sudden squall struck all three ships, washing the boats against them, and causing indescribable confusion. The squall ended in a violent gale. Getting his men on board with all dispatch, Paul essayed his best to withstand the fury of the wind, but it blew adversely, and with redoubled power. A ship at a distance went down beneath it. The disappointed invader was obliged to turn before the gale, and renounce his project.

To this hour, on the shores of the Firth of Forth, it is the popular persuasion, that the Rev. Mr. Shirrer's (of Kirkaldy) powerful intercession was the direct cause of the elemental repulse experienced off the endangered harbor of Leith.

Through the ill qualities of Paul's associate captains: their timidity, incapable of keeping pace with his daring; their jealousy, blind to his superiority to rivalship; together with the general reduction of his force, now reduced by desertion, from nine to three ships; and last of all, the enmity of seas and winds; the invader, driven, not by a fleet, but a gale, out of the Scottish waters, had the mortification in prospect of terminating a cruise, so formidable in appearance at the onset, without one added deed to sustain the reputation gained by former exploits. Nevertheless, he was not disheartened. He sought to conciliate fortune, not by despondency, but by resolution. And, as if won by his confident bearing, that fickle power suddenly went over to him from the ranks of the enemy—suddenly as plumed Marshal Ney to the stubborn standard of Napoleon from Elba, marching regenerated on Paris. In a word, luck—that's the word—shortly threw in Paul's way the great action of his life: the most extraordinary of all naval engagements; the unparalleled deathlock with the Serapis.

19

They Fight the Serapis

The battle between the *Bon Homme Richard* and the Serapis stands in history as the first signal collision on the sea between the Englishman and the American. For obstinacy, mutual hatred, and courage, it is without precedent or subsequent in the story of ocean. The strife long hung undetermined, but the English flag struck in the end.

There would seem to be something singularly indicatory in this engagement. It may involve at once a type, a parallel, and a prophecy. Sharing the same blood with England, and yet her proved foe in two wars—not wholly inclined at bottom to forget an old grudge—intrepid, unprincipled, reckless, predatory, with boundless ambition, civilized in externals but a savage at heart, America is, or may yet be, the Paul Jones of nations.

Regarded in this indicatory light, the battle between the *Bon Homme Richard* and the Serapis—in itself so curious—may well enlist our interest.

Never was there a fight so snarled. The intricacy of those incidents which defy the narrator's extrication, is not illy figured in that bewildering intertanglement of all the yards and anchors of the two ships, which confounded them for the time in one chaos of devastation.

Elsewhere than here the reader must go who seeks an elaborate version of the fight, or, indeed, much of any regular account of it whatever. The writer is but brought to mention the battle because he must needs follow, in all events, the fortunes of the humble adventurer whose life he records. Yet this necessarily involves some general view of each conspicuous incident in which he shares.

Several circumstances of the place and time served to invest the fight with a certain scenic atmosphere casting a light almost poetic over the wild gloom of its tragic results. The battle was fought between the hours of seven and ten at night; the height of it was under a full harvest moon, in view of thousands of distant spectators crowning the high cliffs of Yorkshire.

From the Tees to the Humber, the eastern coast of Britain, for the most part, wears a savage, melancholy, and Calabrian aspect. It is in course of incessant decay. Every year the isle which repulses nearly all other foes, succumbs to the Attila assaults of the deep. Here and there the base of the cliffs is strewn with masses of rock, undermined by the waves, and tumbled headlong below, where, sometimes, the water completely surrounds them, showing in shattered confusion detached rocks, pyramids, and obelisks, rising half-revealed from the surf—the Tadmores of the wasteful desert of the sea. Nowhere is this desolation more marked than for those fifty miles of coast between Flamborough Head and the Spurm.

Weathering out the gale which had driven them from Leith, Paul's ships for a few days were employed in giving chase to various merchantmen and colliers; capturing some, sinking others, and putting the rest to flight. Off the mouth of the Humber they ineffectually manœuvred with a view of drawing out a king's frigate, reported to be lying at anchor within. At another time a large fleet was encountered, under convoy of some ships of force. But their panic caused the fleet to hug the edge of perilous shoals very nigh the land, where, by reason of his having no competent pilot, Paul durst not approach to molest them.

The same night he saw two strangers further out at sea, and chased them until three in the morning, when, getting pretty nigh, he surmised that they must needs be vessels of his own squadron, which, previous to his entering the Firth of Forth, had separated from his command. Daylight proved this supposition correct. Five vessels of the original squadron were now once more in company. About noon a fleet of forty merchantmen appeared coming round Flamborough Head, protected by two English men-of-war, the Serapis and Countess of Scarborough. Descrying the five cruisers sailing down, the forty sail, like forty chickens, fluttered in a panic under the wing of the shore. Their armed protectors bravely steered from the land, making the disposition for battle. Promptly accepting the challenge, Paul, giving the signal to his consorts, earnestly pressed forward. But, earnest as he was, it was seven in the evening ere the encounter began. Meantime his comrades, heedless of his signals, sailed independently along. Dismissing them from present consideration, we confine ourselves, for a while, to the Richard and the Serapis, the grand duellists of the fight.

The Richard carried a motley crew, to keep whom in order one hundred and thirty-five soldiers—themselves a hybrid band—had been put on board, commanded by French officers of inferior rank. Her armament was similarly heterogeneous; guns of all sorts and calibres; but about equal on the whole to those of a thirty-two-gun frigate. The spirit of baneful intermixture pervaded this craft throughout.

The Serapis was a frigate of fifty guns, more than half of which individually exceeded in calibre any one gun of the Richard. She had a crew of some three hundred and twenty trained man-of-war's men.

There is something in a naval engagement which radically distinguishes it from one on the land. The ocean, at times, has what is called its *sea* and its *trough of the sea;* but it has neither rivers, woods, banks, towns, nor mountains. In mild weather it is one hammered plain. Stratagems, like those of disciplined armies—ambuscades, like those of Indians, are impossible. All is clear, open, fluent. The very element which sustains the combatants, yields at the stroke of a feather. One wind and one tide at one time operate upon all who here engage. This simplicity renders a battle between two men-of-war, with their huge white wings, more akin to the Miltonic contests of archangels than to *the comparatively squalid* tussles of earth.

As the ships neared, a hazy darkness overspread the water. The moon was not yet risen. Objects were perceived with difficulty. Borne by a soft moist breeze over gentle waves, they came within pistol-shot. Owing to the obscurity, and the known neighborhood of other vessels, the Serapis was uncertain who the Richard was. Through the dim mist each ship loomed forth to the other vast, but indistinct, as the ghost of Morven. Sounds of the trampling of resolute men echoed from either hull, whose tight decks dully resounded like drum-heads in a funeral march.

The Serapis hailed. She was answered by a broadside. For half an hour the combatants deliberately manœuvred, continually changing their position, but always within shot fire. The Serapis—the better sailer of the two—kept critically circling the Richard, making lounging advances now and then, and as suddenly steering off; hate causing her to act not unlike a wheeling cock about a hen, when stirred by the contrary passion. Meantime, though within easy speaking distance, no further syllable was exchanged; but an incessant cannonade was kept up.

At this point, a third party, the Scarborough, drew near, seemingly desirous of giving assistance to her consort. But thick smoke was now added to the night's natural obscurity. The Scarborough imperfectly discerned two ships, and plainly saw the common fire they made; but which was which, she could not tell. Eager to befriend the Serapis, she durst not fire a gun, lest she might unwittingly act the part of a foe, As when a hawk and a crow are clawing and beaking high in the air, a second crow flying near, will seek to join the battle, but finding no fair chance to engage, at last flies away to the woods; just so did the Scarborough now. Prudence dictated the step; because several chance shots—from which of the combatants could not be known—had already struck the

Scarborough. So, unwilling uselessly to expose herself, off went for the present this baffled and ineffectual friend.

Not long after, an invisible hand came and set down a great yellow lamp in the east. The hand reached up unseen from below the horizon, and set the lamp down right on the rim of the horizon, as on a threshold; as much as to say, Gentlemen warriors, permit me a little to light up this rather gloomy looking subject. The lamp was the round harvest moon; the one solitary foot-light of the scene. But scarcely did the rays from the lamp pierce that languid haze. Objects before perceived with difficulty, now glimmered ambiguously. Bedded in strange vapors, the great foot light cast a dubious, half demoniac glare across the waters, like the phantasmagoric stream sent athwart a London flagging in a night-rain from an apothecary's blue and green window. Through this sardonical mist, the face of the Man-in-the-Moon—looking right towards the combatants, as if he were standing in a trap-door of the sea, leaning forward leisurely with his arms complacently folded over upon the edge of the horizon—this queer face wore a serious, apishly self-satisfied leer, as if the Man-in-the-Moon had somehow secretly put up the ships to their contest, and in the depths of his malignant old soul was not unpleased to see how well his charms worked. There stood the grinning Man-in-the-Moon, his head just dodging into view over the rim of the sea:—Mephistopheles prompter of the stage.

Aided now a little by the planet, one of the consorts of the Richard, the Pallas, hovering far outside the fight, dimly discerned the suspicious form of a lonely vessel unknown to her. She resolved to engage it, if it proved a foe. But ere they joined, the unknown ship—which proved to be the Scarborough—received a broadside at long gun's distance from another consort of the Richard, the Alliance. The shot whizzed across the broad interval like shuttlecocks across a great hall. Presently the battledores of both batteries were at work, and rapid compliments of shuttlecocks were very promptly exchanged. The adverse consorts of the two main belligerents fought with all the rage of those fiery seconds who in some desperate duels make their principal's quarrel their own. Diverted from the Richard and the Serapis by this little by-play, the Man-in-the-Moon, all eager to see what it was, somewhat raised himself from his trap-door with an added grin on his face. By this time, off sneaked the Alliance, and down swept the Pallas, at close quarters engaging the Scarborough; an encounter destined in less than an hour to end in the latter ship's striking her flag.

Compared to the Serapis and the Richard, the Pallas and the Scarborough were as two pages to two knights. In their immature way they showed the same traits as their fully developed superiors.

The Man-in-the-Moon now raised himself still higher to obtain a better view of affairs.

But the Man-in-the-Moon was not the only spectator. From the high cliffs of the shore, and especially from the great promontory of Flamborough Head, the scene was witnessed by crowds of the islanders. Any rustic might be pardoned his curiosity in view of the spectacle presented. Far in the indistinct distance fleets of frightened merchantmen filled the lower air with their sails, as flakes of snow in a snow-storm by night. Hovering undeterminedly, in another direction, were several of the scattered consorts of Paul, taking no part in the fray. Nearer, was an isolated mist, investing the Pallas and Scarborough—a mist slowly adrift on the sea, like a floating isle, and at intervals irradiated with sparkles of fire and resonant with the boom of cannon. Further away, in the deeper water, was a lurid cloud, incessantly torn in shreds of lightning, then fusing together again, once more to be rent. As yet this lurid cloud was neither stationary nor slowly adrift, like the first-mentioned one; but, instinct with chaotic vitality, shifted hither and thither, foaming with fire, like a valiant water-spout careering off the coast of Malabar.

To get some idea of the events enacting in that cloud, it will be necessary to enter it; to go and possess it, as a ghost may rush into a body, or the devils into the swine, which running down the steep place perished in the sea; just as the Richard is yet to do.

Thus far the Serapis and the Richard had been manœuvring and chasséing to each other like partners in a cotillion, all the time indulging in rapid repartee.

But finding at last that the superior manageableness of the enemy's ship enabled him to get the better of the clumsy old Indiaman, the Richard, in taking position, Paul, with his wonted resolution, at once sought to neutralize this, by hugging him close. But the attempt to lay the Richard right across the head of the Serapis ended quite otherwise, in sending the enemy's jib-boom just over the Richard's great tower of Pisa, where Israel was stationed; who, catching it eagerly, stood for an instant holding to the slack of the sail, like one grasping a horse by the mane prior to vaulting into the saddle.

"Aye, hold hard, lad," cried Paul, springing to his side with a coil of rigging. With a few rapid turns he knitted himself to his foe. The wind now acting on the sails of the Serapis forced her, heel and point, her entire length, cheek by jowl, alongside the Richard. The projecting cannon scraped; the yards interlocked; but the hulls did not touch. A long lane of darkling water lay wedged between, like that narrow canal in Venice which dozes between two shadowy piles, and high in air is secretly crossed by the Bridge of Sighs. But where the six yard-arms reciprocally arched overhead, three bridges of sighs were both seen and heard, as the moon and wind kept rising.

Into that Lethean canal—pond-like in its smoothness as compared with the sea without—fell many a poor soul that night; fell, forever forgotten.

As some heaving rent coinciding with a disputed frontier on a volcanic plain, that boundary abyss was the jaws of death to both sides. So contracted was it, that in many cases the gun-rammers had to be thrust into the opposite ports, in order to enter to muzzles of their own cannon. It seemed more an intestine feud, than a fight between strangers. Or rather, it was as if the Siamese Twins, oblivious of their fraternal bond, should rage in unnatural fight.

19 *Continued*

They Fight the Serapis

Ere long, a horrible explosion was heard, drowning for the instant the cannonade. Two of the old eighteen-pounders—before spoken of, as having been hurriedly set up below the main deck of the Richard—burst all to pieces, killing the sailors who worked them, and shattering all that part of the hull, as if two exploded steam-boilers had shot out of its opposite sides. The effect was like the fall of the walls of a house. Little now upheld the great tower of Pisa but a few naked crow stanchions. Thenceforth, not a few balls from the Serapis must have passed straight through the Richard without grazing her. It was like firing buck-shot through the ribs of a skeleton.

But, further forward, so deadly was the broadside from the heavy batteries of the Serapis—levelled point-blank, and right down the throat and bowels, as it were, of the Richard—that it cleared everything before it. The men on the Richard's covered gun-deck ran above, like miners from the fire-damp. Collecting on the forecastle, they continued to fight with grenades and muskets. The soldiers also were in the lofty tops, whence they kept up incessant volleys, cascading their fire down as pouring lava from cliffs.

The position of the men in the two ships was now exactly reversed. For while the Serapis was tearing the Richard all to pieces below deck, and had swept that covered part almost of the last man, the Richard's crowd of musketry had complete control of the upper deck of the Serapis, where it was almost impossible for man to remain unless as a corpse. Though in the beginning, the tops of the Serapis had not been unsupplied with marksmen, yet they had long since been cleared by the overmastering musketry of the Richard. Several, with leg or arm broken by a ball, had been seen going dimly downward from their giddy perch, like falling pigeons shot on the wing.

As busy swallows about barn-eaves and ridge-poles, some of the Richard's marksmen, quitting their tops, now went far out on their yard-arms, where they overhung the Scrapis. From thence they dropped hand-grenades upon her decks, like apples, which growing in one field fall over the fence into another. Others of their band flung the same sour fruit into the open ports of the Serapis. A hail-storm of aerial combustion descended and slanted on the Serapis, while horizontal thunderbolts rolled crosswise through the subterranean vaults of the Richard. The belligerents were no longer, in the ordinary sense of things, an English ship and an American ship. It was a co-partnership and joint-stock combustion-company of both ships; yet divided, even in participation. The two vessels were as two houses, through whose party-wall doors have been cut; one family (the Guelphs) occupying the whole lower story; another family (the Ghibellines) the whole upper story.

Meanwhile, determined Paul flew hither and thither like the meteoric corposant-ball, which shiftingly dances on the tips and verges of ships' rigging in storms. Wherever he went, he seemed to cast a pale light on all faces. Blacked and burnt, his Scotch bonnet was compressed to a gun-wad on his head. His Parisian coat, with its gold-laced sleeve laid aside, disclosed to the full the blue tattooing on his arm, which sometimes in fierce gestures streamed in the haze of the cannonade, cabalistically terrific as the charmed standard of Satan. Yet his frenzied manner was less a testimony of his internal commotion than intended to inspirit and madden his men, some of whom seeing him, in transports of intrepidity stripped themselves to their trowsers, exposing their naked bodies to the as naked shot. The same was done on the Serapis, where several guns were seen surrounded by their buff crews as by fauns and satyrs.

At the beginning of the fray, before the ships interlocked, intervals of smoke which swept over the ships as mist over mountain-tops, affording open rents here and there—the gundeck of the Serapis, at certain points, showed, congealed for the instant in all attitudes of dauntlessness, a gallery of marble statues—fighting gladiators.

Stooping low and intent, with one braced leg thrust behind, and one arm thrust forward, curling round towards the muzzle of the gun, there was seen the *loader,* performing his allotted part; on the other side of the carriage, in the same stooping posture, but with both hands holding his long black pole, pike-wise, ready for instant use—stood the eager *rammer and sponger;* while at the breech, crouched the wary *captain of the gun,* his keen eye, like the watching leopard's, burning along the range; and behind all, tall and erect, the Egyptian symbol of death, stood the *matchman,* immovable for the moment, his long-handled match reversed. Up to their two long death-dealing batteries, the trained men of the Serapis stood and toiled in mechanical magic of discipline. They tended those rows of guns, as Lowell girls the rows of looms in a cotton factory. The Parcæ were not more methodical; Atropos not more fatal; the automaton chess-player not more irresponsible.

"Look, lad; I want a grenade, now, thrown down their main hatchway. I saw long piles of cartridges there. The powder monkeys have brought them up faster than they can be used. Take a bucket of combustibles, and let's hear from you presently."

These words were spoken by Paul to Israel. Israel did

168

as ordered. In a few minutes, bucket in hand, begrimed with powder, sixty feet in air, he hung like Apollyon from the extreme tip of the yard over the fated abyss of the hatchway. As he looked down between the eddies of smoke into that slaughterous pit, it was like looking from the verge of a cataract down into the yeasty pool at its base. Watching his chance, he dropped one grenade with such faultless precision, that, striking its mark, an explosion rent the Serapis like a volcano. The long row of heaped cartridges was ignited. The fire ran horizontally, like an express on a railway. More than twenty men were instantly killed: nearly forty wounded. This blow restored the chances of battle, before in favor of the Serapis.

But the drooping spirits of the English were suddenly revived, by an event which crowned the scene by an act on the part of one of the consorts of the Richard, the incredible atrocity of which has induced all humane minds to impute it rather to some incomprehensible mistake than to the malignant madness of the perpetrator.

The cautious approach and retreat of a consort of the Serapis, the Scarborough, before the moon rose, has already been mentioned. It is now to be related how that, when the moon was more than an hour high, a consort of the Richard, the Alliance, likewise approached and retreated. This ship, commanded by a Frenchman, infamous in his own navy, and obnoxious in the service to which he at present belonged; this ship, foremost in insurgency to Paul hitherto, and which, for the most part, had crept like a poltroon from the fray; the Alliance now was at hand. Seeing her, Paul deemed the battle at an end. But to his horror, the Alliance threw a broadside full into the stern of the Richard, without touching the Serapis. Paul called to her, for God's sake to forbear destroying the Richard. The reply was, a second, a third, a fourth broadside, striking the Richard ahead, astern, and amidships. One of the volleys killed several men and one officer. Meantime, like carpenters' augers, and the sea-worm called Remora, the guns of the Serapis were drilling away at the same doomed hull. After performing her nameless exploit, the Alliance sailed away, and did no more. She was like the great fire of London, breaking out on the heel of the great Plague. By this time, the Richard had so many shot-holes low down in her hull, that like a sieve she began to settle.

"Do you strike?" cried the English captain.

"I have not yet begun to fight," howled sinking Paul.

This summons and response were whirled on eddies of smoke and flame. Both vessels were now on fire. The men of either knew hardly which to do; strive to destroy the enemy, or save themselves. In the midst of this, one hundred human beings, hitherto invisible strangers, were suddenly added to the rest. Five score English prisoners, till now confined in the Richard's hold, liberated in his consternation by the master at arms, burst up the hatchways. One of them, the captain of a letter of marque, captured by Paul, off the Scottish coast, crawled through a port, as a burglar through a window, from the one ship to the other, and reported affairs to the English captain.

While Paul and his lieutenants were confronting these prisoners, the gunner, running up from below, and not perceiving his official superiors, and deeming them dead, believing himself now left sole surviving officer, ran to the tower of Pisa to haul down the colors. But they were already shot down and trailing in the water astern, like a sailor's towing shirt. Seeing the gunner there, groping about in the smoke, Israel asked what he wanted.

At this moment the gunner, rushing to the rail, shouted "Quarter! Quarter!" to the Serapis.

"I'll quarter ye," yelled Israel, smiting the gunner with the flat of his cutlass.

"Do you strike?" now came from the Serapis.

"Aye, aye, aye!" involuntarily cried Israel, fetching the gunner a shower of blows.

"Do you strike?" again was repeated from the Serapis; whose captain, judging from the augmented confusion on board the Richard, owing to the escape of the prisoners, and also influenced by the report made to him by his late guest of the port-hole, doubted not that the enemy must needs be about surrendering.

"Do you strike?"

"Aye!—I strike *back*," roared Paul, for the first time now hearing the summons.

But judging this frantic response to come, like the others, from some unauthorized source, the English captain directed his boarders to be called, some of whom presently leaped on the Richard's rail, but, throwing out his tattooed arm at them, with a sabre at the end of it, Paul showed them how boarders repelled boarders. The English retreated, but not before they had been thinned out again, like spring radishes, by the unfaltering fire from the Richard's tops.

An officer of the Richard, seeing the mass of prisoners delirious with sudden liberty and fright, pricked them with his sword to the pumps, thus keeping the ship afloat by the very blunder which had promised to have been fatal. The vessels now blazed so in the rigging that both parties desisted from hostilities to subdue the common foe.

When some faint order was again restored upon the Richard her chances of victory increased, while those of the English, driven under cover, proportionably waned. Early in the contest, Paul, with his own hand, had brought one of his largest guns to bear against the enemy's mainmast. That shot had hit. The mast now plainly tottered. Nevertheless, it seemed as if, in this fight, neither party could be victor. Mutual obliteration from the face of the waters seemed the only natural sequel to hostilities like these. It is, therefore, honor to him as a man, and not reproach to him as an officer, that, to stay such carnage, Captain Pearson, of the Serapis, with his own hands hauled down his colors. But just as an officer from the Richard swung himself on board the Serapis, and accosted the English captain, the first lieutenant of the Serapis came up from below inquiring whether the Richard had struck, since her fire had ceased.

So equal was the conflict that, even after the surrender, it could be, and was, a question to one of the warriors engaged (who had not happened to see the English flag hauled down) whether the Serapis had struck to the Richard, or the Richard to the Serapis. Nay, while the Richard's officer was still amicably conversing with the English

171

captain, a midshipman of the Richard, in act of following his superior on board the surrendered vessel, was run through the thigh by a pike in the hand of an ignorant boarder of the Serapis. While, equally ignorant, the cannons below deck were still thundering away at the nominal conqueror from the batteries of the nominally conquered ship.

But though the Serapis had submitted, there were two misanthropical foes on board the Richard which would not so easily succumb—fire and water. All night the victors were engaged in suppressing the flames. Not until daylight were the flames got under; but though the pumps were kept continually going, the water in the hold still gained. A few hours after sunrise the Richard was deserted for the Serapis and the other vessels of the squadron of Paul. About ten o'clock the Richard, gorged with slaughter, wallowed heavily, gave a long roll, and blasted by tornadoes of sulphur, slowly sunk, like Gomorrah, out of sight.

The loss of life in the two ships was about equal; one-half of the total number of those engaged being either killed or wounded.

In view of this battle one may ask—What separates the enlightened man from the savage? Is civilization a thing distinct, or is it an advanced stage of barbarism?

20

The Shuttle

For a time back, across the otherwise blue-jean career of Israel, Paul Jones flits and re-flits like a crimson thread. One more brief intermingling of it, and to the plain old homespun we return.

The battle won, the squadron started for the Texel, where they arrived in safety. Omitting all mention of intervening harassments, suffice it, that after some months of inaction as to anything of a warlike nature, Paul and Israel (both, from different motives, eager to return to America) sailed for that country in the armed ship Ariel, Paul as commander, Israel as quartermaster.

Two weeks out, they encountered by night a frigate-like craft, supposed to be an enemy. The vessels came within hail, both showing English colors, with purposes of mutual deception, affecting to belong to the English Navy. For an hour, through their speaking trumpets, the captains equivocally conversed. A very reserved, adroit, hood-winking, statesman-like conversation, indeed. At last, professing some little incredulity as to the truthfulness of the stranger's statement, Paul intimated a desire that he should put out a boat and come on board to show his commission, to which the stranger very affably replied, that unfortunately his boat was exceedingly leaky. With equal politeness, Paul begged him to consider the danger attending a refusal, which rejoinder nettled the other, who suddenly retorted that he would answer for twenty guns, and that both himself and men were knock-down Englishmen. Upon this, Paul said that he would allow him exactly five minutes for a sober, second thought. That brief period passed, Paul, hoisting the American colors, ran close under the other ship's stern, and engaged her. It was about eight o'clock at night that this strange quarrel was picked in the middle of the ocean. Why cannot men be peaceable on that great common? Or does nature in those fierce night-brawlers, the billows, set mankind but a sorry example?

After ten minutes' cannonading, the stranger struck, shouting out that half his men were killed. The Ariel's crew hurrahed. Boarders were called to take possession. At this juncture, the prize shifting her position so that she headed away, and to leeward of the Ariel, thrust her long spanker-boom diagonally over the latter's quarter; when Israel, who was standing close by, instinctively caught hold of it—just as he had grasped the jib-boom of the Serapis—and, at the same moment, hearing the call to take possession, in the valiant excitement of the occasion, he leaped upon the spar, and made a rush for the stranger's deck, thinking, of course, that he would be immediately followed by the regular boarders. But the sails of the strange ship suddenly filled; she began to glide through the sea; her spanker-boom, not having at all entangled itself, offering no hindrance. Israel, clinging midway along the boom, soon found himself divided from the Ariel by a space impossible to be leaped. Meantime, suspecting foul play, Paul set every sail; but the stranger, having already the advantage, contrived to make good her escape, though perseveringly chased by the cheated conqueror.

In the confusion, no eye had observed our hero's spring. But, as the vessels separated more, an officer of the strange ship spying a man on the boom, and taking him for one of his own men, demanded what he did there.

"Clearing the signal halyards, sir," replied Israel, fumbling with the cord which happened to be dangling near by.

"Well, bear a hand and come in, or you will have a bow-chaser at you soon," referring to the bow guns of the Ariel.

"Aye, aye, sir," said Israel, and in a moment he sprang to the deck, and soon found himself mixed in among some two hundred English sailors of a large letter of marque. At once he perceived that the story of half the crew being killed was a mere hoax, played off for the sake of making an escape. Orders were continually being given to pull on this and that rope, as the ship crowded all sail in flight. To these orders Israel, with the rest, promptly responded, pulling at the rigging stoutly as the best of them; though Heaven knows his heart sunk deeper and deeper at every pull which thus helped once again to widen the gulf between him and home.

In intervals he considered with himself what to do. Favored by the obscurity of the night and the number of the crew, and wearing much the same dress as theirs, it was very easy to pass himself off for one of them till morning. But daylight would be sure to expose him, unless some cunning plan could be hit upon. If discovered for what he was, nothing short of a prison awaited him upon the ship's arrival in port.

It was a desperate case, only as desperate a remedy could serve. One thing was sure, he could not hide. Some audacious parade of himself promised the only hope. Marking that the sailors, not being of the regular navy, wore no uniform, and perceiving that his jacket was the only garment on him which bore any distinguishing badge, our adventurer took it off, and privily dropped it overboard, remaining now in his dark blue woolen shirt and blue cloth waistcoat.

What the more inspirited Israel to the added step now contemplated, was the circumstance that the ship was not a Frenchman's or other foreigner, but her crew, though enemies, spoke the same language that he did.

So very quietly, at last, he goes aloft into the maintop,

and sitting down on an old sail there, beside some eight or ten topmen, in an off-handed way asks one for tobacco.

"Give us a quid, lad," as he settled himself in his seat.

"Halloo," said the strange sailor, "who be you? Get out of the top! The fore and mizzen-top men won't let us go into their tops, and blame me if we'll let any of their gangs come here. So, away ye go."

"You're blind, or crazy, old boy," rejoined Israel. "I'm a topmate; ain't I, lads?" appealing to the rest.

"There's only ten maintopmen belonging to our watch; if you are one, then there'll be eleven," said a second sailor. "Get out of the top!"

"This is too bad, maties," cried Israel, "to serve an old topmate this way. Come, come, you are foolish. Give us a quid." And, once more, with the utmost sociability, he addressed the sailor next to him.

"Look ye," returned the other, "if you don't make away with yourself, you skulking spy from the mizzen, we'll drop you to deck like a jewel-block."

Seeing the party thus resolute, Israel, with some affected banter, descended.

The reason why he had tried the scheme—and, spite of the foregoing failure, meant to repeat it—was this: As customary in armed ships, the men were in companies allotted to particular places and functions. Therefore, to escape final detection, Israel must some way get himself recognized as belonging to some one of those bands; otherwise, as an isolated nondescript, discovery ere long would be certain, especially upon the next general muster. To be sure, the hope in question was a forlorn sort of hope, but it was his sole one, and must therefore be tried.

Mixing in again for a while with the general watch, he at last goes on the forecastle among the sheet-anchor-men there, at present engaged in critically discussing the merits of the late valiant encounter, and expressing their opinion that by daybreak the enemy in chase would be hull-down out of sight.

"To be sure she will," cried Israel, joining in with the group, "old ballyhoo that she is, to be sure. But didn't we pepper her, lads? Give us a chew of tobacco, one of ye.

How many have we wounded, do ye know? None killed that I've heard of. Wasn't that a fine hoax we played on 'em? Ha! ha! But give us a chew."

In the prodigal fraternal patriotism of the moment, one of the old worthies freely handed his plug to our adventurer, who, helping himself, returned it, repeating the question as to the killed and wounded.

"Why," said he of the plug, "Jack Jewboy told me, just now, that there's only seven men carried down to the surgeon, but not a soul killed."

"Good, boys, good!" cried Israel, moving up to one of the gun-carriages, where three or four men were sitting —"slip along, chaps, slip along, and give a watchmate a seat with ye."

"All full here, lad; try the next gun."

"Boys, clear a place here," said Israel, advancing, like one of the family, to that gun.

"Who the devil are *you,* making this row here?" demanded a stern-looking old fellow, captain of the fore-castle, "seems to me you make considerable noise. Are you a forecastleman?"

"If the bowsprit belongs here, so do I," rejoined Israel, composedly.

"Let's look at ye, then!" and seizing a battle-lantern, before thrust under a gun, the old veteran came close to Israel before he had time to elude the scrutiny.

"Take that!" said his examiner, and fetching Israel a terrible thump, pushed him ignominiously off the fore-castle as some unknown interloper from distant parts of the ship.

With similar perseverence of effrontery, Israel tried other quarters of the vessel. But with equal ill success. Jealous with the spirit of class, no social circle would receive him. As a last resort, he dived down among the *holders.*

A group of them sat round a lantern, in the dark bowels of the ship, like a knot of charcoal burners in a pine forest at midnight.

"Well, boys, what's the good word?" said Israel, advancing very cordially, but keeping as much as possible in the shadow.

"The good word is," rejoined a censorious old *holder,* "that you had best go where you belong—on deck—and not be a skulking down here where you *don't* belong. I suppose this is the way you skulked during the fight."

"Oh, you're growly to-night, shipmate," said Israel, pleasantly—"supper sits hard on your conscience."

"Get out of the hold with ye," roared the other. "On deck, or I'll call the master-at-arms."

Once more Israel decamped.

Sorely against his grain, as a final effort to blend himself openly with the crew, he now went among the *waisters:* the vilest caste of an armed ship's company, mere dregs and settlings—sea-Pariahs, comprising all the lazy, all the inefficient, all the unfortunate and fated, all the melancholy, all the infirm, all the rheumatical scamps, scapegraces, ruined prodigal sons, sooty faces, and swineherds of the crew, not excluding those with dismal wardrobes.

An unhappy, tattered, moping row of them sat along dolefully on the gun-deck, like a parcel of crest-fallen buzzards, exiled from civilized society.

"Cheer up, lads," said Israel, in a jovial tone, "homeward-bound, you know. Give us a seat among ye, friends."

"Oh, sit on your head!" answered a sullen fellow in the corner.

"Come, come, no growling; we're homeward-bound. Whoop, my hearties!"

"Workhouse bound, you mean," grumbled another sorry chap, in a darned shirt.

"Oh, boys, don't be down-hearted. Let's keep up our spirits. Sing us a song, one of ye, and I'll give the chorus."

"Sing if ye like, but I'll plug my ears, for one," said still another sulky varlet, with the toes out of his seaboots, while all the rest with one roar of misanthropy joined him.

But Israel, not to be daunted, began:

" 'Cease, rude Boreas, cease your growling!' "

"And you cease your squeaking, will ye?" cried a fellow in a banged tarpaulin. "Did ye get a ball in the windpipe, that ye cough that way, worse nor a broken-nosed old bellows? Have done with your groaning, it's worse nor the death-rattle."

"Boys, is this the way you treat a watchmate," demanded Israel reproachfully, "trying to cheer up his friends? Shame on ye, boys. Come, let's be sociable. Spin us a yarn, one of ye. Meantime, rub my back for me, another," and very confidently he leaned against his neighbor.

"Lean off me, will ye?" roared his friend, shoving him away.

"But who *is* this ere singing, leaning, yarn-spinning chap? Who are ye? Be you a waister, or be you not?"

So saying, one of this peevish, sottish band staggered close up to Israel. But there was a deck above and a deck below, and the lantern swung in the distance. It was too dim to see with critical exactness.

"No such singing chap belongs to our gang, that's flat," he dogmatically exclaimed at last, after an ineffectual scrutiny. "Sail out of this!"

And with a shove once more, poor Israel was ejected.

Blackballed out of every club, he went disheartened on deck. So long, while night screened him at least, as he contented himself with promiscuously circulating, all was safe; it was the endeavor to fraternize with any one set which was sure to endanger him. At last, wearied out, he happened to find himself on the berth deck, where the watch below were slumbering. Some hundred and fifty hammocks were on that deck. Seeing one empty, he leaped in, thinking luck might yet some way befriend him. Here, at last, the sultry confinement put him fast asleep. He was wakened by a savage whiskerando of the other watch, who, seizing him by his waistband, dragged him most indecorously out, furiously denouncing him for a skulker.

Springing to his feet, Israel perceived from the crowd and tumult of the berth deck, now all alive with men leaping into their hammocks, instead of being full of sleepers quietly dosing therein, that the watches were changed. Going above, he renewed in various quarters his offers of intimacy with the fresh men there assembled;

but was successively repulsed as before. At length, just as day was breaking, an irascible fellow whose stubborn opposition our adventurer had long in vain sought to conciliate—this man suddenly perceiving, by the gray morning light, that Israel had somehow an alien sort of general look, very savagely pressed him for explicit information as to who he might be. The answers increased his suspicion. Others began to surround the two. Presently, quite a circle was formed. Sailors from distant parts of the ship drew near. One, and then another, and another, declared that they, in their quarters, too, had been molested by a vagabond claiming fraternity, and seeking to palm himself off upon decent society. In vain Israel protested. The truth, like the day, dawned clearer and clearer. More and more closely he was scanned. At length the hour for having all hands on deck arrived; when the other watch which Israel had first tried, reascending to the deck, and hearing the matter in discussion, they endorsed the charge of molestation and attempted imposture through the night, on the part of some person unknown, but who, likely enough, was the strange man now before them. In the end, the master-at-arms appeared with his bamboo, who summarily collaring poor Israel, led him as a mysterious culprit to the officer of the deck, which gentleman having heard the charge, examined him in great perplexity, and, saying that he did not at all recognize that countenance, requested the junior officers to contribute their scrutiny. But those officers were equally at fault.

"Who the deuce *are* you?" at last said the officer-of-the-deck, in added bewilderment. "Where did you come from? What's your business? Where are you stationed? What's your name? Who are you, any way? How did you get here? and where are you going?"

"Sir," replied Israel very humbly, "I am going to my regular duty, if you will but let me. I belong to the maintop, and ought to be now engaged in preparing the topgallant stu'n'-sail for hoisting."

"Belong to the maintop? Why, these men here say you have been trying to belong to the foretop, and the mizzentop, and the forecastle, and the hold, and the waist, and

180

every other part of the ship. This is extraordinary," he added, turning upon the junior officers.

"He must be out of his mind," replied one of them, the sailing-master.

"Out of his mind?" rejoined the officer-of-the-deck. "He's out of all reason; out of all men's knowledge and memories! Why, no one knows him; no one has ever seen him before; no imagination, in the wildest flight of a morbid nightmare, has ever so much as dreamed of him. Who *are* you?" he again added, fierce with amazement. "What's your name? Are you down in the ship's books, or at all in the records of nature?"

"My name, sir, is Peter Perkins," said Israel, thinking it most prudent to conceal his real appellation.

"Certainly, I never heard that name before. Pray, see if Peter Perkins is down on the quarter-bills," he added to a midshipman. "Quick, bring the book here."

Having received it, he ran his fingers along the columns, and dashing down the book, declared that no such name was there.

"You are not down, sir. There is no Peter Perkins here. Tell me at once who are you?"

"It might be, sir," said Israel, gravely, "that seeing I shipped under the effects of liquor, I might, out of absent-mindedness like, have given in some other person's name instead of my own."

"Well, what name have you gone by among your ship-mates since you've been aboard?"

"Peter Perkins, sir."

Upon this the officer turned to the men around, inquiring whether the name of Peter Perkins was familiar to them as that of a shipmate. One and all answered no.

"This won't do, sir," now said the officer. "You see it won't do. Who are you?"

"A poor persecuted fellow at your service, sir."

"*Who* persecutes you?"

"Every one, sir. All hands seem to be against me; none of them willing to remember me."

"Tell me," demanded the officer earnestly, "how long do you remember yourself? Do you remember yesterday

181

morning? You must have come into existence by some sort of spontaneous combustion in the hold. Or were you fired aboard from the enemy, last night, in a cartridge? Do you remember yesterday?"

"Oh, yes, sir."

"What was you doing yesterday?"

"Well, sir, for one thing, I believe I had the honor of a little talk with yourself."

"With *me?*"

"Yes, sir; about nine o'clock in the morning—the sea being smooth and the ship running, as I should think, about seven knots—you came up into the maintop, where I belong, and was pleased to ask my opinion about the best way to set a topgallant stu'n'-sail."

"He's mad! He's mad!" said the officer, with delirious conclusiveness. "Take him away, take him away, take him away—put him somewhere, master-at-arms. Stay, one test more. What mess do you belong to?"

"Number 12, sir."

"Mr. Tidds," to a midshipman, "send mess No. 12 to the mast."

Ten sailors replied to the summons, and arranged themselves before Israel.

"Men, does this man belong to your mess?"

"No, sir; never saw him before this morning."

"What are those men's names?" he demanded of Israel.

"Well, sir, I am so intimate with all of them," looking upon them with a kindly glance, "I never call them by their real names, but by nicknames. So, never using their real names, I have forgotten them. The nicknames that I know them by, are Towser, Bowser, Rowser, Snowser."

"Enough. Mad as a March hare. Take him away. Hold," again added the officer, whom some strange fascination still bound to the bootless investigation. "What's *my* name, sir?"

"Why, sir, one of my messmates here called you Lieutenant Williamson, just now, and I never heard you called by any other name."

"There's method in his madness," thought the officer to himself. "What's the captain's name?"

"Why, sir, when we spoke the enemy, last night, I heard him say, through his trumpet, that he was Captain Parker; and very likely he knows his own name."

"I have you now. That ain't the captain's real name."

"He's the best judge himself, sir, of what his name is, I should think."

"Were it not," said the officer, now turning gravely upon his juniors, "were it not that such a supposition were on other grounds absurd, I should certainly conclude that this man, in some unknown way, got on board here from the enemy last night."

"How could he, sir?" asked the sailing-master.

"Heaven knows. But our spanker-boom geared the other ship, you know, in manœuvring to get headway."

"But supposing he *could* have got here that fashion, which is quite impossible under all the circumstances, what motive could have induced him voluntarily to jump among enemies?"

"Let him answer for himself," said the officer, turning suddenly upon Israel, with the view of taking him off his guard, by the matter of course assumption of the very point at issue.

"Answer, sir. Why did you jump on board here, last night, from the enemy?"

"Jump on board, sir, from the enemy? Why, sir, my station at general quarters is a gun No. 3, of the lower deck, here."

"He's cracked—or else I am turned—or all the world is;—take him away!"

"But where am I to take him, sir?" said the master-at-arms. "He don't seem to belong anywhere, sir. Where—where am I to take him?"

"Take him out of sight," said the officer, now incensed with his own perplexity. "Take him out of sight, I say."

"Come along, then, my ghost," said the master-at-arms. And, collaring the phantom, he led it hither and thither, not knowing exactly what to do with it.

Some fifteen minutes passed, when the captain coming from his cabin, and observing the master-at-arms leading Israel about in this indefinite style, demanded the reason of that procedure, adding that it was against his express orders for any new and degrading punishments to be invented for his men.

"Come here, master-at-arms. To what end do you lead that man about?"

"To no end in the world, sir. I keep leading him about because he has no final destination."

"Mr. Officer-of-the-deck, what does this mean? Who is this strange man? I don't know that I remember him. Who is he? And what is signified by his being led about?"

Hereupon the officer-of-the-deck, throwing himself into a tragical posture, set forth the entire mystery; much to the captain's astonishment, who at once indignantly turned upon the phantom.

"You rascal—don't try to deceive me. Who are you? and where did you come from last?"

"Sir, my name is Peter Perkins, and I last came from the forecastle, where the master-at-arms last led me, before coming here."

"No joking, sir, no joking."

"Sir, I'm sure it's too serious a business to joke about."

"Do you have the assurance to say, that you, as a regularly shipped man, have been on board this vessel ever since she sailed from Falmouth, ten months ago?"

"Sir, anxious to secure a berth under so good a commander, I was among the first to enlist."

"What ports have we touched at, sir?" said the captain, now in a little softer tone.

"Ports, sir, ports?"

"Yes, sir, *ports.*"

Israel began to scratch his yellow hair.

"What *ports,* sir?"

"Well, sir:—Boston, for one."

"Right there," whispered a midshipman.

"What was the next port, sir?"

"Why, sir, I was saying Boston was the *first* port, I believe; wasn't it?—and"—

"The *second* port, sir, is what I want."

"Well—New York."

"Right again," whispered the midshipman.

184

"And what port are we bound to, now?"

"Let me see—homeward-bound—Falmouth, sir."

"What sort of a place is Boston?"

"Pretty considerable of a place, sir."

"Very straight streets, ain't they?"

"Yes, sir; cow-paths, cut by sheep-walks, and intersected with hen-tracks."

"When did we fire the first gun?"

"Well, sir, just as we were leaving Falmouth, ten months ago—signal-gun, sir."

"Where did we fire the first *shotted* gun, sir?—and what was the name of the privateer we took upon that occasion?"

" 'Pears to me, sir, at that time I was on the sick list. Yes, sir, that must have been the time; I had the brain fever, and lost my mind for a while."

"Master-at-arms, take this man away."

"Where shall I take him, sir?" touching his cap.

"Go, and air him on the forecastle."

So they resumed their devious wanderings. At last, they descended to the berth-deck. It being now breakfast-time, the master-at-arms, a good-humored man, very kindly introduced our hero to his mess, and presented him with breakfast, during which he in vain endeavored, by all sorts of subtle blandishments, to worm out his secret.

At length Israel was set at liberty; and whenever there was any important duty to be done, volunteered to it with such cheerful alacrity, and approved himself so docile and excellent a seaman, that he conciliated the approbation of all the officers, as well as the captain; while his general sociability served, in the end, to turn in his favor the suspicious hearts of the mariners. Perceiving his good qualities, both as a sailor and man, the captain of the maintop applied for his admission into that section of the ship; where, still improving upon his former reputation, our hero did duty for the residue of the voyage.

One pleasant afternoon, the last of the passage, when the ship was nearing the Lizard, within a few hours' sail of her port, the officer-of-the-deck, happening to glance upwards towards the maintop, descried Israel there, leaning very leisurely over the rail, looking mildly down where the officer stood.

"Well, Peter Perkins, you seem to belong to the main-top, after all."

"I always told you so, sir," smiled Israel benevolently down upon him, "though, at first, you remember, sir, you would not believe it."

21

Samson among the Philistines

At length, as the ship, gliding on past three or four vessels at anchor in the roadstead—one, a man-of-war just furling her sails—came nigh Falmouth town, Israel, from his perch, saw crowds in violent commotion on the shore, while the adjacent roofs were covered with sightseers. A large man-of-war cutter was just landing its occupants, among whom were a corporal's guard and three officers, besides the naval lieutenant and boat's crew. Some of this company having landed, and formed a sort of lane among the mob, two trim soldiers, armed to the teeth, rose in the stern-sheets; and between them, a martial man of Patagonian stature, their ragged and handcuffed captive, whose defiant head overshadowed theirs, as St. Paul's dome its inferior steeples. Immediately the mob raised a shout, pressing in curiosity towards the colossal stranger; so that, drawing their swords, four of the soldiers had to force a passage for their comrades, who followed on, conducting the giant.

As the letter of marque drew still nigher, Israel heard the officer in command of the party ashore shouting, "To the castle! to the castle!" and so, surrounded by shouting throngs, the company moved on, preceded by the three drawn swords, ever and anon flourished at the rioters, towards a large grim pile on a cliff about a mile from the landing. Long as they were in sight, the bulky form of the captive was seen at times swayingly towering over the flashing bayonets and cutlasses, like a great whale breaching amid a hostile retinue of sword-fish. Now and then, too, with barbaric scorn, he taunted them with cramped gestures of his manacled hands.

When at last the vessel had gained her anchorage, opposite a distant detached warehouse, all was still; and the work of breaking out in the hold immediately commencing, and continuing till nightfall, absorbed all further attention for the present.

Next day was Sunday; and about noon Israel, with others, was allowed to go ashore for a stroll. The town was quiet. Seeing nothing very interesting there, he passed out, alone, into the fields alongshore, and presently found himself climbing the cliff whereon stood the grim pile before spoken of.

"What place is yon?" he asked of a rustic passing.

"Pendennis Castle."

As he stepped upon the short crisp sward under its walls, he started at a violent sound from within, as of the roar of some tormented lion. Soon the sound became articulate, and he heard the following words bayed out with an amazing vigor:

"Brag no more, Old England; consider you are but an island! Order back your broken battalions! home, and repent in ashes! Long enough have your hired tories across the sea forgotten the Lord their God, and bowed down to Howe and Kniphausen—the Hessian!——Hands off, red-skinned jackal! Wearing the king's plate,* as I do, I have treasures of wrath against you British."

* Meaning, probably, certain manacles.

Then came a clanking, as of a chain; many vengeful sounds, all confusedly together; with strugglings. Then again the voice:

"Ye brought me out here, from my dungeon to this green—affronting yon Sabbath sun—to see how a rebel looks. But I show ye how a true gentleman and Christian can conduct in adversity. Back, dogs! Respect a gentleman and a Christian, though he *be* in rags and smell of bilge-water."

Filled with astonishment at these words, which came from over a massive wall, enclosing what seemed an open parade-space, Israel pressed forward, and soon came to a black archway, leading far within, underneath, to a grassy tract, through a tower. Like two boar's tusks, two sentries stood on guard at either side of the open jaws of the arch. Scrutinizing our adventurer a moment, they signed him permission to enter.

Arrived at the end of the arched-way, where the sun shone, Israel stood transfixed at the scene.

Like some baited bull in the ring, crouched the Patagonian-looking captive, handcuffed as before; the grass of the green trampled, and gored up all about him, both by his own movements and those of the people around. Except some soldiers and sailors, these seemed mostly townspeople, collected here out of curiosity. The stranger was outlandishly arrayed in the sorry remains of a half-Indian, half-Canadian sort of a dress, consisting of a fawnskin jacket—the fur outside and hanging in ragged tufts—a half-rotten, bark-like belt of wampum; aged breeches of sagathy; bedarned worsted stockings to the knee; old moccasins riddled with holes, their metal tags yellow with salt-water rust; a faded red woollen bonnet, not unlike a Russian night-cap, or a portentous, ensanguined full-moon, all soiled, and stuck about with bits of half-rotted straw. He seemed just broken from the dead leases in David's outlawed Cave of Adullam. Unshaven, beard and hair matted, and profuse as a corn-field beaten down by hailstorms, his whole marred aspect was that of

189

some wild beast; but of a royal sort, and unsubdued by the cage.

"Aye, stare, stare! Though but last night dragged out of a ship's hold, like a smutty tierce; and this morning out of your littered barracks here, like a murderer; for all that, you may well stare at Ethan Ticonderoga Allen, the unconquered soldier, * * * You Turks never saw a Christian before. Stare on! I am he, who, when your Lord Howe wanted to bribe a patriot to fall down and worship him by an offer of a major-generalship and five thousand acres of choice land in old Vermont—(Ha! three-times-three for glorious old Vermont, and my Green-Mountain boys! Hurrah! Hurrah! Hurrah!) I am he, I say, who answered your Lord Howe, 'You, *you* offer *our* land? You are like the devil in Scripture, offering all the kingdoms in the world, when the * * * * * had not a corner-lot on earth! Stare on!' "

"Look you, rebel, you had best heed how you talk against General Lord Howe," here said a thin, wasp-waisted, epauletted officer of the castle, coming near and flourishing his sword like a schoolmaster's ferule.

"General Lord Howe? Heed how I talk of that toad-hearted king's lick-spittle of a scarlet poltroon; the vilest wriggler in God's worm-hole below? I tell you, that herds of red-haired devils are impatiently snorting to ladle Lord Howe with all his gang (you included) into the seethingest syrups of Tophet's flames!"

As this blast, the wasp-waisted officer was blown backwards as from before the suddenly burst head of a steam-boiler.

Staggering away, with a snapped spine, he muttered something about its being beneath his dignity to bandy further words with a low-lived rebel.

"Come, come, Colonel Allen," here said a mild-looking man in a sort of clerical undress, "respect the day better than to talk thus of what lies beyond. Were you to die this hour, or what is more probable, be hung next week at Tower-wharf, you know not what might become, in eternity, of yourself."

"Reverend Sir," with a mocking bow, "when not better

employed braiding my beard, I have a little dabbled in your theologies. And let me tell you, Reverend Sir," lowering and intensifying his voice, "that as to the world of spirits, of which you hint, though I know nothing of the mode or manner of that world, no more than do you, yet I expect when I shall arrive there to be treated as well as any other gentleman of my merit. That is to say, far better than you British know how to treat an American officer and meek-hearted Christian captured in honorable war, * * * Every one tells me, as you yourself just breathed, and as, crossing the sea, every billow dinned into my ear, that I, Ethan Allen, am to be hung like a thief. If I am, the great Jehovah and the Continental Congress shall avenge me; while I, for my part, shall show you, even on the tree, how a Christian gentleman can die. Meantime, sir, if you are the clergyman you look, act out your consolatory function, by getting an unfortunate Christian gentleman about to die, a bowl of punch."

The good-natured stranger, not to have his religious courtesy appealed to in vain, immediately dispatched his servant, who stood by, to procure the beverage.

At this juncture, a faint rustling sound, as of the advance of an army with banners, was heard. Silks, scarfs, and ribbons fluttered in the background. Presently, a bright squadron of fair ladies drew nigh, escorted by certain outriding gallants of Falmouth.

"Ah," sighed a soft voice, "what a strange sash, and furred vest, and what leopard-like teeth, and what flaxen hair, but all mildewed;—is that he?"

"Yea, is it, lovely charmer," said Allen, like an Ottoman, bowing over his broad, bovine forehead, and breathing the words out like a lute; "it is he—Ethan Allen, the soldier; now, since ladies' eyes visit him, made trebly a captive."

"Why, he talks like a beau in a parlor, this wild, mossed American from the woods," sighed another fair lady to her mate; "but can this be he we came to see? I must have a lock of his hair."

"It is he, adorable Delilah; and fear not, even though incited by the foe, by clipping my locks, to dwindle my

191

strength. Give me your sword, man," turning to an officer:
—"Ah! I'm fettered. Clip it yourself, lady."

"No, no—I am——"

"Afraid, would you say? Afraid of the vowed friend
and champion of all ladies all round the world? Nay, nay,
come hither."

The lady advanced; and soon, overcoming her timidity,
her white hand shone like whipped foam amid the matted
waves of flaxen hair.

"Ah, this is like clipping tangled tags of gold-lace,"
cried she; "but see, it is half straw."

"But the wearer is no man-of-straw, lady; were I free,
and you had ten thousand foes—horse, foot, and dragoons
—how like a friend I could fight for you! Come, you have
robbed me of my hair; let me rob your dainty hand of its
price. What, afraid again?"

"No, not that; but——"

"I see, lady; I may do it, by your leave, but not by
your word; the wonted way of ladies. There, it is done.
Sweeter that kiss, than the bitter heart of a cherry."

When at length this lady left, no small talk was had by
her with her companions about someway relieving the
hard lot of so knightly an unfortunate. Whereupon a
worthy, judicious gentleman, of middle-age, in attendance,
suggested a bottle of good wine every day, and clean linen
once every week. And these the gentle Englishwoman—
too polite and too good to be fastidious—did indeed
actually send to Ethan Allen, so long as he tarried a captive
in her land.

The withdrawal of this company was followed by a
different scene.

A perspiring man in top-boots, a riding-whip in his
hand, and having the air of a prosperous farmer, brushed
in, like a stray bullock, among the rest, for a peep at the
giant; having just entered through the arch, as the ladies
passed out.

"Hearing that the man who took Ticonderoga was here
in Pendennis Castle, I've ridden twenty-five miles to see
him; and to-morrow my brother will ride forty for the
same purpose. So let me have first look. Sir," he continued,

addressing the captive, "will you let me ask you a few plain questions, and be free with you?"

"Be free with me? With all my heart. I love freedom of all things. I'm ready to die for freedom; I expect to. So be free as you please. What is it?"

"Then, sir, permit me to ask what is your occupation in life—in time of peace, I mean?"

"You talk like a tax-gatherer," rejoined Allen, squinting diabolically at him; "what is my occupation in life? Why, in my younger days I studied divinity, but at present I am a conjurer by profession."

Hereupon everybody laughed, equally at the manner as the words, and the nettled farmer retorted:

"Conjurer, eh? well, you conjured wrong that time you were taken."

"Not so wrong, though, as you British did, that time I took Ticonderoga, my friend."

At this juncture the servant came with the punch, when his master bade him present it to the captive.

"No!—give it me, sir, with your own hands, and pledge me as gentleman to gentleman."

"I cannot pledge a state-prisoner, Colonel Allen; but I will hand you the punch with my own hands, since you insist upon it."

"Spoken and done like a true gentleman, sir; I am bound to you."

Then receiving the bowl into his gyved hands, the iron ringing against the china, he put it to his lips, and saying, "I hereby give the British nation credit for half a minute's good usage," at one draught emptied it to the bottom.

"The rebel gulps it down like a swilling hog at a trough," here scoffed a lusty private of the guard, off duty.

"Shame to you!" cried the giver of the bowl.

"Nay, sir; his red coat is a standing blush to him, as it is to the whole scarlet-blushing army." Then turning derisively upon the private: "You object to my way of taking things, do ye? I fear I shall never please ye. You objected to the way, too, in which I took Ticonderoga, and the way in which I meant to take Montreal. Selah! But pray, now that I look at you, are not you the hero I caught dodging round, in his shirt, in the cattlepen, inside the fort? It was the break of day, you remember."

"Come, Yankee," here swore the incensed private; "cease this, or I'll darn your old fawn-skins for ye with the flat of this sword"; for a specimen, laying it lashwise, but not heavily, across the captive's back.

Turning like a tiger, the giant, catching the steel between his teeth, wrenched it from the private's grasp, and striking it with his manacles, sent it spinning like a juggler's dagger into the air, saying, "Lay your dirty coward's iron on a tied gentleman again, and these," lifting his handcuffed fists, "shall be the beetle of mortality to you!"

The now furious soldier would have struck him with all his force, but several men of the town interposed, reminding him that it were outrageous to attack a chained captive.

"Ah," said Allen, "I am accustomed to that, and therefore I am beforehand with them; and the extremity of what I say against Britain, is not meant for you, kind friends, but for my insulters, present and to come." Then recognizing among the interposers the giver of the bowl, he turned with a courteous bow, saying, "Thank you again and again, my good sir; you may not be the worse for this; ours is an unstable world; so that one gentleman never knows when it may be his turn to be helped of another."

But the soldier still making a riot, and the commotion growing general, a superior officer stepped up, who terminated the scene by remanding the prisoner to his cell, dismissing the townspeople, with all strangers, Israel among the rest, and closing the castle gates after them.

22

*Something Further of Ethan Allen;
with Israel's Flight Towards the Wilderness*

Among the episodes of the Revolutionary War none is stranger than that of Ethan Allen in England; the event and the man being equally uncommon.

Allen seems to have been a curious combination of a Hercules, a Joe Miller, a Bayard, and a Tom Hyer; had a person like the Belgian giants; mountain music in him like a Swiss; a heart plump as Cœur de Lion's. Though born in New England, he exhibited no trace of her character. He was frank, bluff, companionable as a Pagan, convivial, a Roman, hearty as a harvest. His spirit was essentially Western; and herein is his peculiar Americanism; for the Western spirit is, or will yet be (for no other is, or can be), the true American one.

For the most part, Allen's manner while in England was scornful and ferocious in the last degree; however, qualified by that wild, heroic sort of levity, which in the hour of oppression or peril seems inseparable from a nature like his; the mode whereby such a temper best evinces its barbaric disdain of adversity, and how cheaply and waggishly it holds the malice, even though triumphant, of its foes! Aside from that inevitable egotism relatively pertaining to pine trees, spires, and giants, there were, perhaps, two special incidental reasons for the Titanic Vermonter's singular demeanor abroad. Taken captive while heading a forlorn hope before Montreal, he was treated with inexcusable cruelty and indignity; something as if he had fallen into the hands of the Dyaks. Immediately upon his capture he would have been deliberately suffered to have been butchered by the Indian allies in cold blood on the spot, had he not, with desperate intrepidity, availed himself of his enormous physical strength, by twitching a British officer to him, and using him for a living target, whirling him round and round against the murderous tomahawks of the savages. Shortly afterwards, led into the town, fenced about by bayonets of the guard, the commander of the enemy, one Colonel McCloud, flourished his cane over the captive's head, with brutal insults promising him a rebel's halter at Tyburn. During his passage to England in the same ship wherein went passenger Colonel Guy Johnson, the implacable tory, he was kept heavily ironed in the hold, and in all ways treated as a common mutineer; or, it may be, rather as a lion of Asia; which, though caged, was still too dreadful to behold without fear and trembling, and consequent cruelty. And no wonder, at least for the fear; for on one occasion, when chained hand and foot, he was insulted on shipboard by an officer; with his teeth he twisted off the nail that went through the mortise of his handcuffs, and so, having his arms at liberty, challenged his insulter to combat. Often, as at Pendennis Castle, when no other avengement was at hand, he would hurl on his foes such howling tempests of anathema as fairly to shock them into retreat. Prompted by somewhat similar motives, both on shipboard and in England, he would often make the most vociferous allusions to Ticonderoga, and the part he played in its capture, well knowing, that of all American names, Ticonderoga was, at that period, by far the most famous and galling to Englishmen.

Parlor-men, dancing-masters, the graduates of the Albe Bellgarde, may shrug their laced shoulders at the boisterousness of Allen in England. True, he stood upon no punctilios with his jailers; for where modest gentlemanhood is all on one side, it is a losing affair; as if my Lord Chesterfield should take off his hat, and smile, and bow, to a mad bull, in hopes of a reciprocation of politeness. When among wild beasts, if they menace you, be a wild beast. Neither is it unlikely that this was the view taken by Allen. For, besides the exasperating tendency to self-assertion which such treatment as his must have bred on a man like him, his experience must have taught him, that by assuming the part of a jocular, reckless, and even braggart barbarian, he would better sustain himself against bullying turnkeys than by submissive quietude. Nor should it be forgotten, that besides the petty details of personal malice, the enemy violated every international usage of right and decency, in treating a distinguished prisoner of war as if he had been a Botany-Bay convict. If, at the present day, in any similar case between the same States, the repetition of such outrages would be more than unlikely, it is only because it is among nations as among individuals: imputed indigence provokes oppression and scorn; but that same indigence being risen to opulence, receives a polite consideration even from its former insulters.

As the event proved, in the course Allen pursued, he was right. Because, though at first nothing was talked of by his captors, and nothing anticipated by himself, but his ignominious execution, or at the least, prolonged and squalid incarceration, nevertheless, these threats and prospects evaporated, and by his facetious scorn for scorn, under the extremest sufferings, he finally wrung repentant usage from his foes; and in the end, being liberated from his irons, and walking the quarter-deck where before he had been thrust into the hold, was carried back to America, and in due time, at New York, honorably included in a regular exchange of prisoners.

It was not without strange interest that Israel had been an eye-witness of the scenes on the Castle Green. Neither was this interest abated by the painful necessity of concealing, for the present, from his brave countryman and

197

fellow-mountaineer, the fact of a friend being nigh. When at last the throng was dismissed, walking towards the town with the rest, he heard that there were some forty or more Americans, privates, confined on the cliff. Upon this, inventing a pretence, he turned back, loitering around the walls for any chance glimpse of the captives. Presently, while looking up at a grated embrasure in the tower, he started at a voice from it familiarly hailing him:

"Potter, is that you? In God's name how came you here?"

At these words, a sentry below had his eye on our astonished adventurer. Bringing his piece to bear, he bade him stand. Next moment Israel was under arrest. Being brought into the presence of the forty prisoners, where they lay in litters of mouldy straw, strewn with gnawed bones, as in a kennel, he recognized among them one Singles, now Sergeant Singles, the man who, upon our hero's return home from his last Cape Horn voyage, he had found wedded to his mountain Jenny. Instantly a rush of emotions filled him. Not as when Damon found Pythias. But far stranger, because very different. For not only had this Singles been an alien to Israel (so far as actual intercourse went), but impelled to it by instinct, Israel had all but detested him, as a successful, and perhaps insidious rival. Nor was it altogether unlikely that Singles had reciprocated the feeling. But now, as if the Atlantic rolled, not between two continents, but two worlds —this, and the next—these alien souls, oblivious to hate, melted down into one.

At such a juncture, it was hard to maintain a disguise, especially when it involved the seeming rejection of advances like the Sergeant's. Still, converting his real amazement into affected surprise, Israel, in presence of the sentries, declared to Singles that he (Singles) must labor under some unaccountable delusion; for he (Potter) was no Yankee rebel, thank Heaven, but a true man to his King; in short, an honest Englishman, born in Kent, and now serving his country, and doing what damage he might to her foes, by being first captain of a carronade on board a letter of marque, that moment in the harbor.

For a moment the captive stood astounded, but observing Israel more narrowly, detecting his latent look, and bethinking him of the useless peril he had thoughtlessly caused to a countryman, no doubt unfortunate as himself, Singles took his cue, and pretending sullenly to apologize for his error, put on a disappointed and crest-fallen air. Nevertheless, it was not without much difficulty, and after many supplemental scrutinies and inquisitions from a board of officers before whom he was subsequently brought, that our wanderer was finally permitted to quit the cliff.

This luckless adventure not only nipped in the bud a little scheme he had been revolving, for materially befriending Ethan Allen and his comrades, but resulted in making his further stay at Falmouth perilous in the extreme. And as if this were not enough, next day, while hanging over the side, painting the hull, in trepidation of a visit from the castle soldiers, rumor came to the ship that the man-of-war in the haven purposed impressing one-third of the letter of marque's crew; though, indeed, the latter vessel was preparing for a second cruise. Being on board a private armed ship, Israel had little dreamed of its liability to the same governmental hardships with the meanest merchantman. But the system of impressment is no respecter either of pity or person.

His mind was soon determined. Unlike his shipmates, braving immediate and lonely hazard, rather than wait for a collective and ultimate one, he cunningly dropped himself overboard the same night, and after the narrowest risk from the muskets of the man-of-war's sentries (whose gangways he had to pass), succeeded in swimming to shore, where he fell exhausted, but recovering, fled inland, doubly haunted by the thought, that whether as an Englishman, or whether as an American, he would, if caught, be now equally subject to enslavement.

Shortly after the break of day, having gained many miles, he succeeded in ridding himself of his seaman's clothing, having found some mouldy old rags on the banks of a stagnant pond, nigh a rickety building, which looked like a poorhouse—clothing not improbably, as he surmised, left there on the bank by some pauper suicide. Marvel not that he should with avidity seize these rags; what the suicides abandon, the living hug.

Once more in beggar's garb, the fugitive sped towards London, prompted by the same instinct which impels the hunted fox to the wilderness; for solitudes befriend the endangered wild beast, but crowds are the security, because the true desert, of persecuted man. Among the things of the capital, Israel for more than forty years was yet to disappear, as one entering at dusk into a thick wood. Nor did ever the German forest, nor Tasso's enchanted one, contain in its depths more things of horror than eventually were revealed in the secret clefts, gulfs, caves and dens of London.

But here we anticipate a page.

23

Israel in Egypt

It was a gray, lowering afternoon that, worn out, half starved, and haggard, Israel arrived within some ten or fifteen miles of London, and saw scores and scores of forlorn men engaged in a great brickyard.

For the most part, brickmaking is all mud and mire. Where, abroad, the business is carried on largely, as to supply the London market, hordes of the poorest wretches are employed, their grimy tatters naturally adapting them to an employ where cleanliness is as much out of the question as with a drowned man at the bottom of the lake in the Dismal Swamp.

Desperate with want, Israel resolved to turn brickmaker, nor did he fear to present himself as a stranger, nothing doubting that to such a vocation his rags would be accounted the best letters of introduction.

To be brief, he accosted one of the many surly overseers, or taskmasters of the yard, who, with no few pompous airs, finally engaged him at six shillings a week, almost equivalent to a dollar and a half. He was appointed to one of the mills for grinding up the ingredients. This mill stood in the open air. It was of a rude, primitive, Eastern aspect, consisting of a sort of hopper, emptying into a barrel-shaped receptacle. In the barrel was a clumsy machine turned round at its axis by a great bent beam, like a well-sweep, only it was horizontal; to this beam, at its outer end, a spavined old horse was attached. The muddy mixture was shovelled into the hopper by spavined-looking old men, while, trudging wearily round and round, the spavined old horse ground it all up till it slowly squashed out at the bottom of the barrel, in a doughy compound, all ready for the moulds. Where the dough squeezed out of the barrel a pit was sunken, so as to bring the moulder here stationed down to a level with the trough, into which the dough fell. Israel was assigned to this pit. Men came to him continually, reaching down rude wooden trays, divided into compartments, each of the size and shape of a brick. With a flat sort of big ladle, Israel slapped the dough into the trays from the trough; then, with a bit of smooth board, scraped the top even, and handed it up. Half buried there in the pit, all the time handing those desolate trays, poor Israel seemed some gravedigger, or churchyard man, tucking away dead little innocents in their coffins on one side, and cunningly disinterring them again to resurrectionists stationed on the other.

Twenty of these melancholy old mills were in operation. Twenty heartbroken old horses, rigged out deplorably in cast-off old cart harness, incessantly tugged at twenty great shaggy beams; while from twenty half-burst old barrels, twenty wads of mud, with a lava-like course, gouged out into twenty old troughs, to be slapped by twenty tattered men into the twenty-times-twenty battered old trays.

Ere entering his pit for the first, Israel had been struck by the dismally devil-may-care gestures of the moulders. But hardly had he himself been a moulder three days, when his previous sedateness of concern at his unfortunate lot, began to conform to the reckless sort of half jolly despair expressed by the others. The truth indeed was, that this continual, violent, helter-skelter slapping of the dough into the moulds, begat a corresponding disposition

202

in the moulder, who, by heedlessly slapping that sad dough, as stuff of little worth, was thereby taught, in his meditations, to slap, with similar heedlessness, his own sadder fortunes, as of still less vital consideration. To these muddy philosophers, men and bricks were equally of clay. "What signifies who we be—dukes or ditchers?" thought the moulders; "all is vanity and clay." So slap, slap, slap, care-free and negligent, with bitter unconcern, these dismal desperadoes flapped down the dough. If this recklessness were vicious of them, be it so; but their vice was like that weed which but grows on barren ground; enrich the soil, and it disappears.

For thirteen weary weeks, lorded over by the taskmaster, Israel toiled in his pit. Though this condemned him to a sort of earthy dungeon, or gravedigger's hole, while he worked, yet even when liberated to his meals, naught of a cheery nature greeted him. The yard was encamped, with all its endless rows of tented sheds, and kilns, and mills, upon a wild waste moor, belted round by bogs and fens. The blank horizon, like a rope, coiled round the whole.

Sometimes the air was harsh and bleak; the ridged and mottled sky looked scourged, or cramping fogs set in from sea, for leagues around, ferreting out each rheumatic human bone, and racking it; the sciatic limpers shivered; their aguish rags sponged up the mists. No shelter, though it hailed. The sheds were for the bricks. Unless, indeed, according to the phrase, each man was a "brick," which, in sober scripture, was the case; brick is no bad name for any son of Adam; Eden was but a brickyard; what is a mortal but a few luckless shovelfuls of clay, moulded in a mould, laid out on a sheet to dry, and ere long quickened into his queer caprices by the sun? Are not men built in communities just like bricks into a wall? Consider the great wall of China: ponder the great populace of Pekin. As man serves bricks, so God him, building him up by billions into edifices of his purposes. Man attains not to the nobility of a brick, unless taken in the aggregate. Yet is there a difference in brick, whether quick or dead; which, for the last, we now shall see.

23 *Continued*

Israel in Egypt

All night long, men sat before the mouth of the kilns, feeding them with fuel. A dull smoke—a smoke of their torments—went up from their tops. It was curious to see the kilns under the action of the fire, gradually changing color, like boiling lobsters. When, at last, the fires would be extinguished, the bricks being duly baked, Israel often took a peep into the low vaulted ways at the base, where the flaming fagots had crackled. The bricks immediately lining the vaults would be all burnt to useless scrolls, black as charcoal, and twisted into shapes the most grotesque; the next tier would be a little less withered, but hardly fit for service; and gradually, as you went higher and higher along the successive layers of the kiln, you came to the midmost ones, sound, square, and perfect bricks, bringing the highest prices; from these the contents of the kiln gradually deteriorated in the opposite direction, upward. But the topmost layers, though inferior to the best, by no means presented the distorted look of the furnace-bricks. The furnace bricks were haggard, with the immediate blistering of the fire—the mid-most ones were ruddy with a genial and tempered glow—the summit ones were pale with the languor of too exclusive an exemption from the burden of the blaze.

These kilns were a sort of temporary temples constructed in the yard, each brick being set against its neighbor almost with the care taken by the mason. But as soon as the fire was extinguished, down came the kiln in a tumbled ruin, carted off to London, once more to be set up in ambitious edifices, to a true brickyard philosopher, little less transient than the kilns.

Sometimes, lading out his dough, Israel could not but bethink him of what seemed enigmatic in his fate. He whom love of country made a hater of her foes—the foreigners among whom he now was thrown—he who, as soldier and sailor, had joined to kill, burn and destroy both them and theirs—here he was at last, serving that very people as a slave, better succeeding in making their bricks than firing their ships. To think that he should be thus helping, with all his strength, to extend the walls of the Thebes of the oppressor, made him half mad. Poor Israel! well-named—bondsman in the English Egypt. But he drowned the thought by still more recklessly spattering with his ladle: "What signifies who we be, or where we are, or what we do?" Slap-dash! "Kings as clowns are codgers—who ain't a nobody?" Splash! "All is vanity and clay."

24

In the City of Dis

At the end of his brickmaking, our adventurer found himself with a tolerable suit of clothes—somewhat darned—on his back, several blood-blisters in his palms, and some verdigris coppers in his pocket. Forthwith, to seek his fortune, he proceeded on foot to the capital, entering, like the King, from Windsor, from the Surrey side.

It was late on a Monday morning, in November—a Blue Monday—a Fifth of November—Guy Fawkes' Day! —very blue, foggy, doleful and gunpowdery, indeed, as shortly will be seen, that Israel found himself wedged in among the greatest everyday crowd which grimy London presents to the curious stranger: that hereditary crowd—gulf-stream of humanity—which, for continuous centuries, has never ceased pouring, like an endless shoal of herring, over London Bridge.

At the period here written of, the bridge, specifically known by that name, was a singular and sombre pile, built by a cowled monk—Peter of Colchurch—some five hundred years before. Its arches had long been crowded at the sides with strange old rookeries of disproportioned and toppling height, converting the bridge at once into the most densely occupied ward and most jammed thoroughfare of the town, while, as the skulls of bullocks are hung out for signs to the gateways of shambles, so the withered heads and smoked quarters of traitors, stuck on pikes, long crowned the Southwark entrance.

Though these rookeries, with their grisly heraldry, had been pulled down some twenty years prior to the present visit, still enough of grotesque and antiquity clung to the structure at large to render it the most striking of objects, especially to one like our hero, born in a virgin clime, where the only antiquities are the forever youthful heavens and the earth.

On his route from Brentford to Paris, Israel had passed through the capital, but only as a courier; so that now, for the first time, he had time to linger, and loiter, and lounge—slowly absorb what he saw—meditate himself into boundless amazement. For forty years he never recovered from that surprise—never, till dead, had done with his wondering.

Hung in long, sepulchral arches of stone, the black, besmoked bridge seemed a huge scarf of crape, festooning the river across. Similar funeral festoons spanned it to the west, while eastward, towards the sea, tiers and tiers of jetty colliers lay moored, side by side, fleets of black swans.

The Thames, which far away, among the green fields of Berks, ran clear as a brook, here, polluted by continual vicinity to man, curdled on between rotten wharves, one murky sheet of sewerage. Fretted by the ill-built piers, awhile it crested and hissed, then shot balefully through the Erebus arches, desperate as the lost souls of the harlots, who, every night, took the same plunge. Meantime, here and there, like awaiting hearses, the coal-scows drifted along, poled broadside, pell-mell to the current.

And as that tide in the water swept all craft on, so a like tide seemed hurrying all men, all horses, all vehicles on the land. As ant-hills, the bridge arches crawled with processions of carts, coaches, drays, every sort of wheeled, rumbling thing, the noses of the horses behind touching the backs of the vehicles in advance, all bespattered with ebon mud—ebon mud that stuck like Jews' pitch. At times the mass, receiving some mysterious impulse far in the rear, away among the coiled thoroughfares out of sight, would start forward with a spasmodic surge. It seemed as if some squadron of centaurs, on the thither side of Phlegethon, with charge on charge, was driving tormented humanity, with all its chattels, across.

Whichever way the eye turned, no tree, no speck of any green thing was seen—no more than in smithies. All laborers, of whatsoever sort, were hued like the men in foundries. The black vistas of streets were as the galleries in coal mines; the flagging, as flat tomb-stones, minus the consecration of moss, and worn heavily down, by sorrowful tramping, as the vitreous rocks in the cursed Gallipagos, over which the convict tortoises crawl.

As in eclipses, the sun was hidden; the air darkened; the whole dull, dismayed aspect of things, as if some neighboring volcano, belching its premonitory smoke, were about to whelm the great town, as Herculaneum and Pompeii, or the Cities of the Plain. And as they had been upturned in terror towards the mountain, all faces were more or less snowed or spotted with soot. Nor marble, nor flesh, nor the sad spirit of man, may in this cindery City of Dis abide white.

As retired at length, midway, in a recess of the bridge, Israel surveyed them, various individual aspects all but frighted him. Knowing not who they were; never destined, it may be, to behold them again; one after the other, they drifted by, uninvoked ghosts in Hades. Some of the wayfarers wore a less serious look; some seemed hysterically merry; but the mournful faces had an earnestness not seen in the others: because man, "poor player," succeeds better in life's tragedy than comedy.

Arrived, in the end, on the Middlesex side, Israel's heart was prophetically heavy; foreknowing, that being of this race, felicity could never be his lot.

For five days he wandered and wandered. Without leaving statelier haunts unvisited, he did not overlook those broader areas—hereditary parks and manors of vice and misery. Not by constitution disposed to gloom, there was a mysteriousness in those impulses which led him at this time to rovings like these. But hereby stoic influences were at work, to fit him at a soon-coming day for enacting a part in the last extremities here seen; when by sickness, destitution, each busy ill of exile, he was destined to experience a fate, uncommon even to luckless humanity—a fate whose crowning qualities were its remoteness from relief and its depth of obscurity—London, adversity, and the sea, three Armageddons, which, at one and the same time, slay and secrete their victims.

25

Forty-Five Years

For the most part, what befell Israel during his forty years wanderings in the London deserts, surpassed the forty years in the natural wilderness of the outcast Hebrews under Moses.

In that London fog, went before him the ever-present cloud by day, but no pillar of fire by the night, except the cold column of the monument, two hundred feet beneath the mocking gilt flames on whose top, at the stone base, the shiverer, of midnight, often laid down.

But these experiences, both from their intensity and his solitude, were necessarily squalid. Best not enlarge upon them. For just as extreme suffering, without hope, is intolerable to the victim, so, to others, is its depiction without some corresponding delusive mitigation. The gloomiest and truthfulest dramatist seldom chooses for his theme the calamities, however extraordinary, of inferior and private persons; least of all, the pauper's; admonished by the fact, that to the craped palace of the king lying in state, thousands of starers shall throng; but few feel enticed to the shanty, where, like a pealed knucklebone, grins the unupholstered corpse of the beggar.

Why at one given stone in the flagging does man after man cross yonder street? What Plebeian Lear or Œdipus, what Israel Potter, cowers there by the corner they shun? From this turning point, then, we too cross over and skim events to the end; omitting the particulars of the starveling's wrangling with rats for prizes in the sewers; or his crawling into an abandoned doorless house in St. Giles', where his hosts were three dead men, one pendant; into another of an alley nigh Houndsditch, where the crazy hovel, in phosphoric rottenness, fell sparkling on him one pitchy midnight, and he received that injury, which, excluding activity for no small part of the future, was an added cause of his prolongation of exile, besides not leaving his faculties unaffected by the concussion of one of the rafters on his brain.

But these were some of the incidents not belonging to the beginning of his career. On the contrary, a sort of humble prosperity attended him for a time; insomuch that once he was not without hopes of being able to buy his homeward passage so soon as the war should end. But, as stubborn fate would have it, being run over one day at Holborn Bars, and taken into a neighboring bakery, he was there treated with such kindliness by a Kentish lass, the shop-girl, that in the end he thought his debt of gratitude could only be repaid by love. In a word, the money saved up for his ocean voyage was lavished upon a rash embarkation in wedlock.

Originally he had fled to the capital to avoid the dilemma of impressment or imprisonment. In the absence of other motives, the dread of those hardships would have fixed him there till the peace. But now, when hostilities were no more, so was his money. Some period elapsed ere the affairs of the two governments were put on such a footing as to support an American consul at London. Yet, when this came to pass, he could only embrace the facilities for a return here furnished, by deserting a wife and child, wedded and born in the enemy's land.

The peace immediately filled England, and more especially London, with hordes of disbanded soldiers; thousands of whom, rather than starve, or turn highwaymen (which no few of their comrades did, stopping coaches at times in the most public streets), would work for such a pittance as to bring down the wages of all the laboring classes. Neither was our adventurer the least among the sufferers. Driven out of his previous employ—a sort of porter in a river-side warehouse—by this sudden influx of rivals, destitute, honest men like himself, with the ingenuity of his race, he turned his hand to the village art of chair-bottoming. An itinerant, he paraded the streets with the cry of "Old chairs to mend!" furnishing a curious illustration of the contradictions of human life; that he who did little but trudge, should be giving cosy seats to all the rest of the world. Meantime, according to another well-known Malthusian enigma in human affairs, his family increased. In all, eleven children were born to him in certain sixpenny garrets in Moorfields. One after the other, ten were buried.

When chair-bottoming would fail, resort was had to match-making. That business being overdone in turn, next came the cutting of old rags, bits of paper, nails, and broken glass. Nor was this the last step. From the gutter he slid to the sewer. The slope was smooth. In poverty,

——"Facilis descensus Averni."

But many a poor soldier had sloped down there into the boggy canal of Avernus before him. Nay, he had three corporals and a sergeant for company.

But his lot was relieved by two strange things, presently to appear. In 1793 war again broke out, the great French war. This lighted London of some of its superfluous hordes, and lost Israel the subterranean society of his friends, the corporals and sergeant, with whom wandering forlorn through the black kingdoms of mud, he used to spin yarns about sea prisoners in hulks, and listen to stories of the Black Hole of Calcutta; and often would meet other pairs of poor soldiers, perfect strangers at the more public corners and intersections of sewers—the Charing-Crosses be-

212

low; one soldier having the other by his remainder button, earnestly discussing the sad prospects of a rise in bread, or the tide; while through the grating of the gutters overhead, the rusty skylights of the realm, came the hoarse rumblings of bakers' carts, with splashes of the flood whereby these unsuspected gnomes of the city lived.

Encouraged by the exodus of the lost tribes of soldiers, Israel returned to chair-bottoming. And it was in frequenting Covent-Garden market, at early morning, for the purchase of his flags, that he experienced one of the strange alleviations hinted of above. That chatting with the ruddy, aproned, hucksterwomen, on whose moist cheeks yet trickled the dew of the dawn on the meadows; that being surrounded by bales of hay, as the raker by cocks and ricks in the field; those glimpses of garden produce, the blood-beets, with the damp earth still tufting the roots; that mere handling of his flags, and bethinking him of whence they must have come, the green hedges through which the wagon that brought them had passed; that trudging home with them as a gleaner with his sheaf of wheat;—all this was inexpressibly grateful. In want and bitterness, pent in, perforce, between dingy walls, he had rural returns of his boyhood's sweeter days among them; and the hardest stones of his solitary heart (made hard by bare endurance alone) would feel the stir of tender but quenchless memories, like the grass of deserted flagging, upsprouting through its closest seams. Sometimes, when incited by some little incident, however trivial in itself, thoughts of home would—either by gradually working and working upon him, or else by an impetuous rush of recollection—overpower him for a time to a sort of hallucination.

Thus was it:—One fair half-day in the July of 1800, by good luck, he was employed, partly out of charity, by one of the keepers, to trim the sward in an oval enclosure within St. James' Park, a little green but a three-minutes' walk along the gravelled way from the brick-besmoked and grimy Old Brewery of the palace which gives its ancient name to the public resort on whose borders it stands. It was a little oval, fenced in with iron pailings, between whose bars the imprisoned verdure peered forth, as some wild captive creature of the woods from its cage. And alien Israel there—at times staring dreamily about him—seemed like some amazed runaway steer, or trespassing Pequod Indian, impounded on the shores of Narraganset Bay, long ago; and back to New England our exile was called in his soul. For still working, and thinking of home; and thinking of home, and working amid the verdant quietude of this little oasis, one rapt thought begat another, till at last his mind settled intensely, and yet half humorously, upon the image of Old Huckleberry, his mother's favorite old pillion horse; and, ere long, hearing a sudden scraping noise (some hob-shoe without, against the iron pailing), he insanely took it to be Old Huckleberry in his stall, hailing him (Israel) with his shod fore-foot clattering against the planks—his customary trick when hungry—and so, down goes Israel's hook, and with a tuft of white clover, impulsively snatched, he hurries away a few paces in obedience to the imaginary summons. But soon stopping midway, and forlornly gazing round at the enclosure, he bethought him that a far different oval, the great oval of the ocean, must be crossed ere his crazy errand could be done; and even then, Old Huckleberry would be found long surfeited with clover, since, doubtless, being dead many a summer, he must be buried beneath it. And many years after, in a far different part of the town, and in far less winsome weather too, passing with his bundle of flags through Red-Cross street, towards Barbican, in a fog so dense that the dimmed and massed blocks of houses, exaggerated by the loom, seemed shadowy ranges on ranges of midnight hills, he heard a confused pastoral sort of sounds—tramplings, lowings, halloos—and was suddenly called to by a voice to head off certain cattle, bound to Smithfield, bewildered and unruly in the fog. Next instant he saw the white face—white as an orange-blossom—of a black-bodied steer, in advance of the drove, gleaming ghost-like through the vapors; and presently, forgetting his limp, with rapid shout and gesture, he was more eager, even than the troubled farmers, their owners, in driving the riotous cattle back into Barbican. Monomaniac reminiscences were in him—"To the right, to the right!" he shouted, as, arrived at the street corner, the farmers beat the drove to the left, towards Smithfield: "To the right! you are driving them back to the pastures—to the right! that way lies the barn-yard!" "Barn-yard?" cried a voice; "you are dreaming, old man." And so, Israel, now an old man, was bewitched by the mirage of vapors; he had dreamed himself home into the mists of the Housatonic mountains; ruddy boy on the upland pastures again. But how different the flat, apathetic, dead, London fog now seemed from those agile mists which, goat-like, climbed the purple peaks, or in routed armies of phantoms, broke down, pell-mell, dispersed in flight upon the plain, leaving the cattle-boy loftily alone, clear-cut as a balloon against the sky.

In 1817 he once more endured extremity; this second peace again drifting its discharged soldiers on London, so that all kinds of labor were overstocked. Beggars, too, lighted on the walks like locusts. Timber-toed cripples stilted along, numerous as French peasants in *sabots*. And, as thirty years before, on all sides, the exile had heard the supplicatory cry, not addressed to him, "An honorable scar, your honor, received at Bunker Hill, or Saratoga, or Trenton, fighting for his most gracious Majesty, King George!" so now, in presence of the still surviving Israel, our Wandering Jew, the amended cry was anew taken up, by a succeeding generation of unfortunates, "An honorable scar, your honor, received at Corunna, or at Waterloo, or at Trafalgar!" Yet not a few of these petitioners had never been outside of the London smoke; a sort of crafty aristocracy in their way, who, without having endangered their own persons much if anything, reaped no insignificant share both of the glory and profit of the bloody battles they claimed; while some of the genuine working heroes, too brave to beg, too cut-up to work, and too poor to live, laid down quietly in corners and died. And here it may be noted, as a fact nationally characteristic, that however desperately reduced at times, even to the sewers, Israel, the American, never sunk below the mud, to actual beggary.

Though henceforth elbowed out of many a chance threepenny job by the added thousands who contended with him against starvation, nevertheless, somehow he continued to subsist, as those tough old oaks of the cliffs, which, though hacked at by hail-stones of tempests, and even wantonly maimed by the passing woodman, still, however cramped by rival trees and fettered by rocks, succeed, against all odds, in keeping the vital nerve of the tap-root alive. And even towards the end, in his dismallest December, our veteran could still at intervals feel a momentary warmth in his topmost boughs. In his Moorfields' garret, over a handful of reignited cinders (which the night before might have warmed some lord), cinders raked up from the streets, he would drive away dolor, by talking with his one only surviving, and now motherless child—the spared Benjamin of his old age—of the far Canaan beyond the sea; rehearsing to the lad those well-remembered adventures among New England hills, and painting scenes of nestling happiness and plenty, in which the lowliest shared. And here, shadowy as it was, was the second alleviation hinted of above.

To these tales of the Fortunate Isles of the Free, recounted by one who had been there, the poor enslaved boy of Moorfields listened, night after night, as to the stories of Sinbad the Sailor. When would his father take him there? "Some day to come, my boy," would be the hopeful response of an unhoping heart. And "Would God it were to-morrow!" would be the impassioned reply.

In these talks Israel unconsciously sowed the seeds of his eventual return. For with added years, the boy felt added longing to escape his entailed misery, by compassing for his father and himself a voyage to the Promised Land. By his persevering efforts he succeeded at last, against every obstacle, in gaining credit in the right quarter to his extraordinary statements. In short, charitably stretching a technical point, the American Consul finally saw father and son embarked in the Thames for Boston.

It was the year 1826; half a century since Israel, in early

manhood, had sailed a prisoner in the Tartar frigate from the same port to which he now was bound. An octogenarian as he recrossed the brine, he showed locks besnowed as its foam. White-haired old Ocean seemed as a brother.

26

Requiescat in Pace

It happened that the ship, gaining her port, was moored to the dock on a Fourth of July; and half an hour after landing, hustled by the riotous crowd near Faneuil Hall, the old man narrowly escaped being run over by a patriotic triumphal car in the procession, flying a broidered banner, inscribed with gilt letters:

"BUNKER-HILL
1 7 7 5
GLORY TO THE HEROES THAT FOUGHT!"

It was on Copps' Hill, within the city bounds, one of the enemy's positions during the fight, that our wanderer found his best repose that day. Sitting down here on a mound in the graveyard, he looked off across Charles River towards the battle-ground, whose incipient monument, at that period, was hard to see, as a struggling sprig of corn in a chilly spring. Upon those heights, fifty years before, his now feeble hands had wielded both ends of the musket. There too he had received that slit upon the chest, which afterwards, in the affair with the Serapis, being traversed by a cutlass wound, made him now the bescarred bearer of a cross.

For a long time he sat mute, gazing blankly about him. The sultry July day was waning. His son sought to cheer him a little ere rising to return to the lodging for the present assigned them by the ship-captain. "Nay," replied the old man, "I shall get no fitter rest than here by the mounds."

But from this true "Potter's Field," the boy at length drew him away; and encouraged next morning by a voluntary purse made up among the reassembled passengers, father and son started by stage for the country of the Housatonic. But the exile's presence in these old mountain townships proved less a return than a resurrection. At first, none knew him, nor could recall having heard of him. Ere long it was found, that more than thirty years previous, the last known survivor of his family in that region, a bachelor, following the example of three-fourths of his neighbors, had sold out and removed to a distant country in the west; where exactly, none could say.

He sought to get a glimpse of his father's homestead. But it had been burnt down long ago. Accompanied by his son, dim-eyed and dim-hearted, he next went to find the site. But the roads had years before been changed. The old road was now browsed over by sheep; the new one ran straight through what had formerly been orchards. But new orchards, planted from other suckers, and in time grafted, throve on sunny slopes near by, where blackberries had once been picked by the bushel. At length he came to a field waving with buckwheat. It seemed one of those fields which himself had often reaped. But it turned out, upon inquiry, that but three summers since a walnut grove had stood there. Then he vaguely remembered that his father had sometimes talked of planting such a grove, to defend the neighboring fields against the cold north wind; yet where precisely that grove was to have been, his shattered mind could not recall. But it seemed not unlikely that during his long exile, the walnut grove had

219

been planted and harvested as well as the annual crops preceding and succeeding it, on the very same soil.

Ere long, on the mountain side, he passed into an ancient natural wood, which seemed some way familiar, and midway in it, paused to contemplate a strange, mouldy pile, resting at one end against a sturdy beech. Though wherever touched by his staff, however lightly, this pile would crumble, yet here and there, even in powder, it preserved the exact look, each irregularly defined line, of what it had originally been—namely, a half-cord of stout hemlock (one of the woods least affected by exposure to the air), in a foregoing generation chopped and stacked up on the spot, against sledging-time, but, as sometimes happens in such cases, by subsequent oversight, abandoned to oblivious decay—type now, as it stood there, of forever arrested intentions, and a long life still rotting in early mishap.

"Do I dream?" mused the bewildered old man, "or what is this vision that comes to me of a cold, cloudy morning, long, long ago, and I heaving yon elbowed log against the beech, then a sapling? Nay, nay, I cannot be so old."

"Come away, father, from this dismal, damp wood," said his son, and led him forth.

Blindly ranging to and fro, they next saw a man ploughing. Advancing slowly, the wanderer met him by a little heap of ruinous burnt masonry, like a tumbled chimney, what seemed the jambs of the fire-place, now aridly stuck over here and there, with thin, clinging, round, prohibitory mosses, like executors' wafers. Just as the oxen were bid stand, the stranger's plough was hitched over sideways, by sudden contact with some sunken stone at the ruin's base.

"There, this is the twentieth year my plough has struck this old hearthstone. Ah, old man,—sultry day, this."

"Whose house stood here, friend?" said the wanderer, touching the half-buried hearth with his staff, where a fresh furrow overlapped it.

"Don't know; forgot the name; gone West, though, I believe. You know 'em?"

But the wanderer made no response; his eye was now

fixed on a curious natural bend or wave in one of the bemossed stone jambs.

"What are you looking at so, father?"

"'Father!' Here," raking with his staff, "*my* father would sit, and here, my mother, and here I, little infant, would totter between, even as now, once again, on the very same spot, but in the unroofed air, I do. The ends meet. Plough away, friend."

Best followed now is this life, by hurrying, like itself, to a close.

Few things remain.

He was repulsed in efforts after a pension by certain caprices of law. His scars proved his only medals. He dictated a little book, the record of his fortunes. But long ago it faded out of print—himself out of being—his name out of memory. He died the same day that the oldest oak on his native hills was blown down.